P9-CAR-691

ADVERSARIES

They first clashed at Entebbe.

Hashim el-Wasi, the world's most brilliant and charismatic guerrilla leader.

Colonel Avram Tal, Israel's most daring commando.

It was Tal who won at Entebbe, shattering el-Wasi's master stroke.

Now el-Wasi vowed it was his turn to triumph . . .

THE ALEPH SOLUTION

"THE SUSPENSE BUILDS, THE ACTION IS FAST-PACED AND THE CLIMAX SHOULD SATISFY THE MOST BLOODTHIRSTY READER."
—*Cleveland Plain Dealer*

"SWIFT AND SURE!"
—*Washington Post*

THE ALEPH SOLUTION

SANDOR FRANKEL & WEBSTER MEWS

BERKLEY BOOKS, NEW YORK

To our wives, children, and parents

This Berkley book contains the complete
text of the original hardcover edition.
It has been completely reset in a type face
designed for easy reading, and was printed
from new film.

THE ALEPH SOLUTION

A Berkley Book / published by arrangement with
Stein and Day

PRINTING HISTORY
Stein and Day edition published 1978
Berkley edition / February 1981

All rights reserved.
Copyright © 1978 by Sandor Frankel and Webster Mews.
This book may not be reproduced in whole or in part,
by mimeograph or any other means, without permission.
For information address: Stein and Day Publishers,
Briarcliff Manor, New York 10510.

ISBN: 0-425-04654-0

A BERKLEY BOOK® TM 757,375
Berkley Books are published by Berkley Publishing Corporation,
200 Madison Avenue, New York, New York 10016.
PRINTED IN THE UNITED STATES OF AMERICA

ℵ JULY 3, 1976 ℵ

ENTEBBE, UGANDA

Suddenly the shooting stopped, and the night retreated into its shroud of black after the redness of firing. At that first silence, the leader of the Israeli commando unit raised his walkie-talkie to his lips and said: "Transgressors eliminated. Repeat, transgressors eliminated." The Israeli paratroopers formed a double column leading from the Old Entebbe Terminal to one of the Hercules transports that had crept to within five hundred yards of the terminal. The giant plane's rear door swung open. The former hostages, most not yet fully aware that they were still alive, were hurried out of the terminal toward the aircraft, past the fallen, bloodied bodies of five Palestinian guerillas, and whisked into the large interior pit of the plane.

Inside the terminal, on the second floor, two young Israeli paratroopers held some twenty Ugandan regulars at gunpoint: No killing of the Africans unless necessary to

1

save the hostages' lives, they had been told. The two Israelis tied the Ugandans together hand-to-foot with baling wire, pulled the wires tight, and blindfolded their captives with towels. Before leaving the terminal, they threw the Africans' weapons out the window and activated a tape recorder transmitting Hebrew voices; then they tiptoed out. The Ugandan soldiers would not move until the Hercules aircraft were well on their way toward Kenyan airspace.

Hashim el-Wasi had been asleep, alone, in the new passenger lounge next door to the Old Terminal building when the clatter of Israeli uzis had broken the night's silence. The Old Terminal building had been untolerably hot, and the guerilla guards outside the terminal had seemed adequate. When the shooting began, el-Wasi's first thought was that Amin had, finally, gone mad. Then he heard the bullhorn blaring commands in Hebrew—"This is Zahal! We've come to take you home! Lie on the floor! This is Zahal!" He had opened the front door just enough to peek out, and saw the bloodied bodies of his comrades sprawled on the dirt outside the Old Terminal building where they had been standing guard. He knew at once that he could do nothing, and he watched and listened, silently, helplessly, the front door of the new passenger lounge imperceptibly ajar.

The shooting died, and el-Wasi watched the Israeli commandoes herd the hostages into the safe underbelly of the Hercules. He could have raced from his cover and sprayed enough machine-gun rounds to kill a few Jews before they could stop him, but what would that accomplish? Better to wait and taste his defeat, this failure of what he had thought would be a perfect plan to squeeze them dry and into submission.

What had been his error? To play the drama out in a backward land, depending on savages. Imagine: Amin! He cursed the name. To think that that madman would be strong enough to defend the Palestinian movement against the Israelis. Next time it would be done the right way, with proper safeguards. Next time it would be done inside the strongest nation in the world, and with the protection of that nation. Next time, the vise would be tightened irresistibly and infallibly. The next Entebbe would occur inside the United States of America.

As the last of the Hercules transports lifted off the ground and disappeared into the hot black night, el-Wasi stepped from the door and looked again at the contorted bodies of his dead comrades. Black troops began rushing toward the Old Terminal building, shooting rifles at the sky toward where the planes had left their noise. El-Wasi muttered in disgust, raced behind the new building, and disappeared into the night.

When the lead Hercules levelled out at cruising altitude after refueling in Kenya, Col. Avram Tal lay down on the floor near the forward bulkhead. It was the sweet taste of relaxation Tal occasionally indulged in after a successful mission. He tried to think of nothing. He allowed himself such quietude rarely. In a nation under perpetual siege, Tal regarded transient luxuries like the wasting of time as obscene.

The hostages who filled the plane drank toasts from bottles of wine they passed among themselves and sang to Israel and God in voices grateful for survival but heavy with the knowledge that not all had been spared. They sang to put their exhilaration to some use, to dampen the dizziness their euphoria would otherwise have caused them. Tal did not join in the singing, but the voices of the other passengers did not appear to disturb him. He crossed his arms as a pillow behind his head.

Tal thought of Jonathan Netaniahu, one of his top commandoes, dead in the sister ship behind—a crushing reminder that the mission had only been superb, not flawless. Tal cursed its imperfection, then reproved himself for the curse. In war, death was inescapable. Yet there had been an imperfection. If one detail had been altered, might Yoni still be alive? He kept working the problem in his mind, as he had been doing since the safe landing in Kenya.

"Thinking of your speech?"

Tal opened his eyes and saw a familiar figure smiling above him, dressed in the same khaki uniform all the men on the mission wore. He was one of the men under Tal's command in the elite unit of the Israeli Defense Force known only by the first letter in the Hebrew alphabet, "Aleph"—its operations so highly classified that few officials even knew that Aleph existed.

"What speech?" Tal asked.

"For the crowds that are already lining the runways at Ben-Gurion Airport."

Tal sat up. "They already know?" He sounded incredulous.

"The whole world knows."

"But it's too early for that. There were to be no announcements until we were far away from this part of Africa."

"The French released it. We've just had radio contact with Jerusalem. The prime minister, the cabinet, and most of the Knesset will be waiting at the airport. There'll be speeches and toasts, and someone has to brief the press. Since you conceived and commanded the raid, you've been picked."

"I won't," Tal said. "Let others take the glory. I have interest only in the future, and in the future there will be more attacks."

"Avram, you can hardly avoid it. We are all to go with you. That is an order from the defense minister himself."

"He'll have to change his order." Tal lowered his head again and closed his eyes. He allowed himself to slip off to sleep.

Sunlight pouring through the window awoke Tal with a start. He walked to the cockpit. Below he could see at last a sprawling expanse of copper-colored wasteland: the Sinai desert. He told the pilot to let him off at Mid-Sinai, a code name for one of Aleph's hidden bases. The pilot reminded him that their orders were to report straight for a debriefing in the Negev, then on to the airport reception. "Mid-Sinai is not on our flight plan."

"Then *put* it on our flight plan," Tal ordered. The pilot knew Tal well. He radioed to the aircraft flying in tandem that he would be making a slight detour, looked up at Tal, and shrugged. Tal slapped him on the shoulder and left the cockpit.

Twenty-one minutes later, the pilot directed his passengers to secure themselves for a landing. Anticipating comments in the cabin, he announced that this was not their final destination, so they should stay seated. He brought the plane down rapidly, pulling back hard on the wheel to level out as the hot sands rushed into view. He eased the throttle and brought the plane's wheels onto a narrow landing strip that had become visible only after he was well into his descent. The plane taxied along the runway. Without a word, Tal grabbed the small wheel on the hatch and began to spin it. Several soldiers bounded up to assist but Tal shook his head: He needed no help. It opened at the first yank.

Tal looked wordlessly at the freed hostages. Then he crouched down to jump from the plane. The drop was thirteen feet and easy for him. He landed on both feet before pitching forward onto his right knee. He braced himself with both arms to prevent his body from toppling over. As soon as Tal hit the ground the pilot gathered speed for another take-off.

Half a kilometer away, indiscernible from the air, was an opening that Israel had dynamited years ago into one of the hills of the Sinai to serve as an underground planning and operations base for Aleph. Tal began walking toward it. He had already stopped savoring Entebbe. It was time to anticipate where and what the next strike would be—and to begin devising the next Aleph solution.

א AUGUST 10 א

MID-SINAI

Word of unusual activity had reached Israeli ears from diverse sources. Particular Arab commandoes, over whom Israeli agents maintained close surveillance, had disappeared. They had not resurfaced in over a year. Equally ominous, European terrorists of the highest discipline and proficiency—sixteen of them so far—had likewise shaken the watchful Israeli eye and gone underground. And there were reports that a large-scale effort was about to unfold, but the reports were all conflicting and vague. Some informants said they had heard that huge sums of money had moved from Basle; others boasted that the kings and princes of the Arab world had finally agreed on a joint venture to rival OPEC, but this struck Israeli intelligence officers as wishful thinking on the Arabs' part. Nevertheless, the normal order was obviously being altered, and it paid to be alert to the slightest breeze.

These developments were closely monitored at the head-quarters of Aleph, whose mission is to anticipate, to inter-cept, and to repulse all Arab plans for the destruction of the State of Israel. At Mid-Sinai, Avram Tal met with his top men—all veterans of several wars and countless skir-mishes.

"Gentlemen," said Tal, "I have direct orders from Je-rusalem to explain certain occurrences. Having received these orders, I consider that we have failed to discharge our duty of ferreting out the facts before the politicians know enough to ask for them. Normally we do just that. But now something strange is happening. What can it be that is big enough to cause ordinary intelligence to pick it up and yet by some strange paradox small enough to elude us in at-tempts to discover its true and particular meaning?

"Consider these facts. Four months after our victory at Entebbe, Muhammed Raji, ranking guerilla strategist of the PLO, simply disappeared. He has not been seen since. Since then, gentlemen, not only can we not find him, we cannot find anyone to talk of him. Vanished. He is followed by at least twelve others shortly thereafter. You know them—Khadijah, al-Muqaddasi, Fu'ad, Idrisi, Hamid, Bekr, Shis-hakli, Aboud; the Europeans, Schlüssmann, Durruti, and de Boussilet, and the Japanese assassin Yushusuda. And recently still more. They are all gone. Disappeared. But they cannot have died or been sacked. They are the best. They would have been mourned by their backers or con-demned as traitors by their countries, and either way we would have heard of it. No, they have gone underground for a reason, and a stay below for this long—and for who knows how much longer?—means colossal trouble."

A man interrupted. "I wonder whether their disappear-ance might not have to do with the sudden disappearance of Hashim el-Wasi. For him to vanish from public view and even from private Arab view is amazing. His disap-pearance may be the key to the disappearance of the others."

"Perhaps," said Tal. "It is possible, but so is anything. Maybe there is a connection. But what is it? And what are they up to?"

"Avram, it is a strike—of large dimensions, you may

be sure of that. Perhaps here. And perhaps in many places. Perhaps throughout these parts or all over Europe—maybe the whole world."

"It might be," Tal said. "Why would all these guerillas have gone off into the night? One does not assemble such as these, if they are assembled, to rob a bank, to conduct a single raid, or to take a plane. Something much more must be involved. And these men seem natural material if there is a larger scheme. We shall make this, weak as it is, our working hypothesis. So, you, Ya'kov, you concentrate on these disappearances. Where have they gone? Press your men to squeeze hard until someone squeals from the pressure. And Daniel, update our information on el-Wasi particularly. When was he last seen and where? Who has heard of his doings lately? Where is he hiding and where is his money coming from? Has he left any clues about where this strike—or strikes—might take place? Yitzhak, you chart the materiel. Who's buying what? Where is it coming from and where is it going? I want reports immediately."

One of the others spoke up. "We may be missing the obvious. Until he disappeared, el-Wasi was agitating for some time to address the United Nations General Assembly in New York. The Arabs have been applying strong pressure lately, and it looks very much like permission will be granted soon. Perhaps they mean to do their devil's work while el-Wasi is in New York."

"Perhaps. But not a likely opportunity for terrorists to blow, by timing their murders during the same period. It seems more likely they'll wait some time after el-Wasi's appearance is over, see if he can succeed in pressing the world for a comprehensive settlement against Israel. And then strike when that doesn't work. But we had better be prepared before it happens."

ℵ AUGUST 25 ℵ

GRACIE MANSION,
NEW YORK CITY

"Congratulations, Mr. Mayor, it's your one-thousandth meeting since taking office. A milestone!"

Emanuel Newman, appointments secretary, kept a straight face as he burst in through the paneled door. He was wearing the rumpled gray suit that had become his trademark through more than two years of the current administration. A white shirt with a missing button rode over his considerable paunch, which he renewed each night with several beers at the White Horse Tavern. He wore a red tie decorated with white and green angels. His curly black hair, freely laced with silver, stood out in all directions. At 42, he looked a decade older. His appearance did not add to the administration's charisma but was tolerated because Newman was efficient and unflappable.

The mayor looked up. He regarded Manny, as always, with faint amusement—it was the tie, of course, and the crooked smile in Newman's very round face. "What did you say, Manny?" the mayor asked, a habit of years of association. The mayor always pretended not to hear Newman's initial comment.

"Your one-thousandth meeting," Newman repeated, completing the ritual.

The mayor removed his reading glasses and held them up to the chandelier, looking for spots. "You don't really keep count, Manny?"

"Absolutely. Everything you do, sir. Yes indeed. In fact, I have everything down on tape. The machine never stops. Every reel is stored in a plain brown paper bag. Any time you want to listen, just holler for Manny, I will fetch it, and sign out for it on a used copy of *The New York Times*."

The mayor laughed, but the woman seated on the sofa by the wall did not. Most thought Manny's puckishness refreshing in the too-frenetic hours that daily passed for work in the nation's most ungovernable city—but not Nancy Dolby, who as deputy mayor for intergovernmental relations was the highest female official in the city.

Nancy Dolby was everything that Manny Newman was not. A product of Miss Porter's, Radcliffe, and Harvard Law School before women's attendance there became fashionable, she could, at 37, be mistaken for a model. Many men still took a second look, though she affected not to notice—and perhaps really did not. Dusty blond hair worn high on her head complemented her high cheek bones. She was dressed, as usual, in a carefully tailored Bloomingdale's cotton suit, this one lime green to match her eyes. Her slim legs ended in a matching green pair of Jacques Cohen espadrilles. It was rumored that she owned more than fifty pairs. As a single woman with no apparent outside interests, whose life was her work and whose job paid her $44,950, she was, in Manny's word, "entitled."

She was not known for small talk. She did what she believed in, believed in what she did, and would not allow unnecessary conversation to get in the way of her doing it. She did not like frivolousness, and did not like Newman. She did not understand why the mayor tolerated him, but assumed this was a peculiarity of men who could not handle power without having some sophomoric release. Today, especially, she felt far from smiling.

"Manny," she said, "you're wasting time. Let's get on with it."

"Oh, Nancy, you work too hard—just a little joke."

"We don't have time for jokes today, Manny, if you're sticking to your schedule. We do still have the security meeting this morning about Hashim el-Wasi's appearance at the UN?"

"Right."

"Well, Manny?"

"Oh, yes, sir. Commissioner of police, a protocol man from the State Department, a guy from our UN staff, an FBI agent named Philip Millard, and Captain Lou de Petri of our own finest." He stopped.

"Manny, you left out the verb again," the mayor admonished.

"Right. Sorry. All those people, they are here, outside the door."

"To discuss security arrangements for el-Wasi's UN speech?"

"Right."

"On October fourth?"

"Right. Mr. Mayor, you amaze me, the things you remember about what goes on in this city."

"Manny," Nancy Dolby cut in, "show them in."

"Right."

"Mr. Mayor," said Jack Andrews, the police commissioner, when a round of greetings had concluded, "we have gone over this pretty carefully. Our job, I mean the police department's job, as I see it, is to contain the crowds and pickets that will be in place probably two days before el-Wasi shows up."

"Two days?"

"Yes, sir. That was what happened the first time the PLO spoke at the UN, in seventy-four, and we're guessing reaction will be about the same. We'll have First Avenue cordoned off from Forty-second Street to Forty-eighth.

We'll have over two thousand men out there from the afternoon he arrives until the next night, when he's due to leave."

"He's coming in one day and out the next?"

"Yes, sir," said Andrews. "That's the plan. He has no embassy. The other Arab nations don't really care to claim him, and they have their own security problems. He has no visa for the U.S. except to go to the UN. The same for his assistants who'll be with him in the UN."

"I suppose two days is better than more than two."

"Yes, sir," said the commissioner, resuming his prepared talk. "Now we think we can stop anybody who tries to crash the police line. We will have helicopters overhead, we'll have tear gas in case we have to disperse a mob that gets too unruly. And we'll have plenty of wagons."

"Wagons?"

"Paddy wagons," Captain de Petri cut in. "Anyone gets out of line, we arrest them. Also," he added, winking at the mayor, "we have plenty of clubs and guns."

Dolby, who had been writing in a yellow legal-sized note pad, looked up. "Don't club heads," she said. "Don't club at all unless you are in danger of being overpowered. And don't shoot unless you are being shot at."

"You didn't tell me the ACLU was attending this meeting," de Petri said sourly.

"Look, Captain, this city has enough problems without getting its ass sued because some trigger-happy cop decides to shoot a Polish Zionist or someone, for God's sake."

"Miss Dolby!" De Petri professed shock.

"Shut up, de Petri," said his chief.

"Captain de Petri," the mayor interceded, "you are here because your chief tells me you are a superb tactician in a crowd."

De Petri beamed.

"But you do not sound like a superb thinker. I will take your chief's judgment on your tactical abilities, and he will have me to answer to if he is wrong. But I want it understood that our aim is to keep anyone who is inclined to from tearing el-Wasi apart limb from limb, and to get el-Wasi into the UN and out of the UN, and out of the city, I might add, without incident. I certainly don't want you to be the cause of any trouble. I want you to secure the UN. That's your job. That's your *only* job. The crowd will be a little wild, no doubt. Overlook it. If worse comes to worst, you arrest, as quietly as possible. You've done it before. Can you do it again?"

"Yes, sir." The words came clipped from his mouth, as though he were executing his smartest salute.

"Don't worry, Mr. Mayor," said the commissioner, soothingly. "The captain gets a little excited at meetings. But on the streets, well, he is very cool. You have never met a better commander of his troops."

"Good. Now, what about on the UN grounds?"

"We ordinarily have no jurisdiction there. We're not free to act in the building or on the land adjacent to the building. That's international territory. Only the UN Security and Safety Service can act there. If anyone actually gets through the police lines on First Avenue and makes it to the gate—which will be closed, incidentally—and climbs over, which I can't see happening, then he's passed out of our jurisdiction. It's up to the UN guards."

"Well, suppose someone decides to go after el-Wasi on the inside?"

"That's what I was getting to," said Andrews. "We're in the process of arranging with the secretary general for him to order the UN's own security force out of the building on the day el-Wasi speaks, and for us to replace them. He can do that and said he would. And we'll be taking special precautions.

"There's a strict limit to how many of each national delegation can attend: Only the ambassador from each country and five aides—six people per country. Since el-Wasi is being given guest status as an equal for his appearance, he'll also be coming in with five aides. They will be replacing the regular PLO observer delegation. We're making sure that nobody except the six representatives of each country gets into the building, plus some representatives of the press who we'll pick. We'll have as few of those as possible.

And I don't think they're much given to violence."

"How about the UN staff, or even a waiter or a janitor, you know, anyone like that?"

"They won't cause trouble because we're not letting them in. Nobody—n-o-b-o-d-y—gets in but six men per country"—he looked at Dolby—"six *people* per country, plus some press."

The mayor asked, "Will all the delegates have passes?"

"Better than that," de Petri answered. "I'm going to be outside the delegates' door, personally. I'll have a book of photos with the faces of all delegates who're coming in. So there won't be any phony passes. Like we said, nobody will be in the building but the delegates, period. Not even me, and not even my men. Our security will be foolproof. I will be searching every goddam—sorry Mr. Mayor—every single face that enters. If I had my way I'd forget their diplomatic immunity and even search the delegates themselves so no Israeli slips in with brass knuckles and tries to level el-Wasi." De Petri smiled at his attempted joke, by himself.

"Problems like Hashim el-Wasi I don't need," the mayor said.

"Sir," said Andrews, "it's the price we pay for having the UN where it is."

"You mean it's the price *I* pay—the UN isn't in the United States, it's in New York. I have to deploy *policemen*, not the National Guard or the army. It costs this city a fortune every time we have one of these visitors. And what do we get from Washington? Prayer."

"You're doing whatever you can, Mr. Mayor. We'll have the outside completely under control. And don't worry about the inside—I mean there's nothing there to steal."

"Not even common sense," said the mayor, annoyed. Dolby wrote onto her pad: "De Petri: Dangerous."

"Seriously," the commissioner explained, "there won't be a problem because we'll be controlling all means of access to the UN grounds. We won't let anyone storm the place."

"I hope not," said the FBI agent. The paperclip he had

been twisting and untwisting snapped in half. He appeared to have been giving it all of his attention.

"Oh, Phil, not those crazy rumors of yours," the commissioner said. Phil Millard was known to believe anything that was printed out on telex machines, and the telex traffic had been heavy over the last few days.

"What rumors?" the mayor asked.

"They're only rumors, mind you, but we have been picking up a hint of trouble."

"Picking up? Where? Here?"

"Not in New York, no, thank God. If anybody was planning anything here we'd know more by now."

"Then?"

"We hear from our sources abroad that certain terrorists might be planning something if el-Wasi's speech doesn't produce results. Our sources don't know exactly when the 'something' will happen, or where, or even what it will be. In fact the whole thing is pretty much conjecture, I guess. Still, apparently there's some unusual activity in Arabia or somewhere."

"Like what?"

"All we know is some terrorists have disappeared from sight."

"That's all?"

"Yes."

"Doesn't sound like much to me. In fact, that sounds good. Anything could account for that, couldn't it?"

"I suppose so. But the Israelis have alerted us to the possibility that something might happen, so the FBI plans to keep its eyes extra open."

"You mean this is something Israeli intelligence has picked up?"

"Um hmm."

"But they don't know what?"

"Not even if."

"The Israelis don't generally panic. Do we have any plans to meet this contingency, commissioner?"

"I think our plans will cover it, sir, whatever it is. If trouble starts, we're ready."

"The President will be staying in Washington, I presume?"

"Yes, sir," said Andrews. "In view of these rumors, there's no reason to risk something even if he would otherwise be inclined to dignify el-Wasi's presence, which he's not."

"Just the same, there are degrees of dignity."

"If you say so, sir."

"I wrote him a letter about it—some time ago."

"I recall," Andrews said.

The mayor stood, to end the meeting. "I agree we must reach a settlement in the Mideast. It looks as though that may finally happen, thank God. But for that very reason I can't see letting el-Wasi speak from the UN rostrum. It's degrading."

"I agree, Mr. Mayor," said Andrews, "but there you are."

"Yes, unfortunately, here we are. Here we are."

ℵ SEPTEMBER 13 ℵ

SOUTHERN LEBANON

The enclave east of Azziye is too small to call a village. It is more a collection of wood shacks built into the hills several kilometers south of the Litani River in southern Lebanon. The area is approachable only through one dirt road most of whose length is shaded by branches of overhanging trees inhabited by birds and by camouflaged Palestinian guerillas, armed with Kalashnikovs and trained to sift approaching friends from strangers.

Inside the shack deepest into the mountain, Hashim el-Wasi stood before seventeen other men seated on the floor. They were all dark, unsmiling and armed with automatic weapons. The men on the floor were looking up at el-Wasi and listening.

"For months each of you, separately, has worked with me. I have promised each of you that the mission we are about to undertake is one which will stand alone in history, without equal, and that the world will carry you in its memory forever. Your faith in me has never wavered, your work has been unflagging, and I redeclare my pledge that our next venture will be the culmination of the many years of struggle and occasional glory that have marked your lives as Palestinian freedom fighters."

El-Wasi's forehead was already damp from the morning heat, though it was not yet eight o'clock. But he felt no discomfort; his excitement was palpable. His hands cut through the air in extravagant gestures.

"I have assembled you today in order that you may now glimpse the culmination of our efforts. Together you form a larger group. Your specialized training, your individual rehearsals, are part of a comprehensive plan. Each of you is not, as you may have been assuming, about to engage in isolated action. Rather, you are all critical parts of a vast whole.

"Each of you heads a team of three men, all dedicated to the same purpose: return to our Palestinian homeland. I have handpicked each of you here as the head of your team because of your background and your courage in past fights for redemption of our native soil."

El-Wasi paused for breath and brushed one hand through his short, curly black hair. His men sat expectantly, unstirring; their bodies sweated against brown-green paramilitary fatigues, ammunition belts thrown tight around their waists. Mosquitoes swirled in tiny clouds close to the earth on which they sat, but they were too inured to such to notice them.

El-Wasi looked directly at his men. To impress with the seriousness of intent, he knew, eye contact was essential. He made a point of it now, staring at one after another of his squatting fighters. Each met his gaze unflinchingly. Some of those in el-Wasi's private army regarded him with fear, but these men had known him from the beginning. They accorded him a great respect because he had proved his courage a dozen times over and his strategic abilities obviously outran theirs. El-Wasi sensed that an impatience was beginning to rise. He would not keep them guessing.

"In accomplishing the act for which you have trained, you and your groups will also be functioning as part of an unstoppable plan. Each of you will be leading teams that will carry out a series of acts whose sequence is known only to me. Your acts, and the overall plan of which your acts will be merely a part, will be publicized throughout the world. You will be called upon to undertake your assignment upon a signal. The signal for each of you will be your learning that another of your group has accomplished a previous assignment. In other words, the entire plan is self-triggering, and you are both the ammunition for your part and the trigger for the next. I will later advise each of you, separately, of the event which your own operation is to follow. Your own operation will take place two days after you have heard that your predecessors have succeeded. And do not fear that you will not hear of their success. The whole world will hear of it."

Pausing, he unscrewed the cap of a canteen that had lain on the ground, raised it to his lips, and drank. The water was warm, but it cooled him. He had spent the previous 53 hours in nearly unbroken consultation with various planners and operatives. Drill, anticipate, modify, and drill again. Supplies, logistics, timing, maneuvers: All were crucial, but difficult and uncertain. They had to be made certain; he had to mesh them all together.

A short man, unshaven, solemn, scrambled to his feet. He did not speak until el-Wasi arched an eyebrow. The man accepted the signal as permission. "Are we to know no more?"

"It is for the good of the movement that only I know the whole plan and its sequence of events," el-Wasi answered, "for if by any chance one of you should fail, you will possess no useful information to divulge to the enemy. You will know only what you are required to do and when, but nothing of the future after that.

"You will be aware when my portion of the mission has begun—the entire world will be aware of it. I will be visible to you at all times, and in all sections of the world. Do not now ask me how."

There would be no dissent. The men on the ground nodded their approval. The standing man resumed his seat on the dirt.

"Any questions?" El-Wasi scanned the room, wiping his forehead and flicking one hand at mosquitoes and several larger insects that buzzed his face.

His men asked him nothing. Their trust was total. They awaited his final orders.

"I leave you with this thought: Trust in Allah and Hashim el-Wasi, and you shall succeed. We have a just and righteous cause, and it cannot fail. We are about to undertake a venture that will restore Palestine to us. We are about to travel the only certain path to that land.

"The Israelis are a stubborn people, but now we shall squeeze them into destruction, and the world will be our ally."

His voice was booming, his words had overtaken him, he was addressing not only his men but all his detractors and the timid souls and nay-sayers. He held his arms wide; his fingers were curled inward, signifying that these men were his, and he would bring them to their feet, as some day—soon—he would bring the world to his feet.

"We have had previous successes and caught the world's attention, but only temporarily. Our tactical goals have been too narrow, and our implementation too naive. We shall no longer be content with the random hijacking of small groups of people. Gentlemen, you shall soon be part of the greatest capture in all history—we are about to hijack the entire world."

אOCTOBER 3א

WNET-TV STUDIO,
NEW YORK CITY

In a semidarkened room, technicians readied their equipment for the live programming that was due to begin at Kennedy Airport in five minutes. Camera crews were already positioned near the landing strip. In the studio in Manhattan, anchorman Tyler Johnson adjusted his microphone and spread out a briefing book that he had been reviewing during the past hour. His guests, a former ambassador to the United Arab Emirates, the diplomatic correspondent for *Foreign Policy Review,* and the deputy assistant secretary of state for near eastern affairs, were due in a few minutes to speculate about el-Wasi's arrival and speech. They would return the following day to hear and then discuss it.

For the next hour, Johnson would review the history of Mideast warfare and peace negotiations, terrorist and counter-terrorist activities, and show el-Wasi's arrival at

Kennedy to an audience calculated to be less than one-twentieth what it would be that evening when the reruns were played. The audience rating never perturbed Johnson. He was public television's leading newscaster, and his job was secure; several years earlier he talked a frightened would-be airplane hijacker into giving up over local television, and he had been given the national spot and a solid contract.

"Three minutes, Mr. Johnson," the assistant producer called out. Johnson looked up and saw his image in the two screens hung high up on either wall, behind the three cameras on the richly burnished red and yellow set. He straightened his tie and began giving the sound man a reading. "This is Tyler Johnson, live from New York." His standard rehearsal line.

"Pull your mike up a bit," someone called out. He did so. Someone else brought over a cup of coffee. The steam momentarily misted his glasses. He took a sip, then pushed it away. He glanced again through his notes and took out his introductory script, placing it in the center of the table. He didn't like electronic prompters; he was an old-fashioned journalist, he said, swearing he would always read from typed copy.

"Ten seconds."

He straightened his tie again, his only nervous habit. A red light in the center camera blinked on. He was ready.

JFK INTERNATIONAL AIRPORT

The Boeing 707, a special flight from Tunis, landed smoothly but did not taxi to the international arrivals terminal. Instead, it lumbered out of the landing area and onto a swatch in the middle of the field where fifteen police cars and two black limousines were waiting. A score of newsmen, photographers, and cameramen were also there. Absent was the bank of microphones that usually greets a ranking diplomat. There was no official welcoming party, not even a protocol officer. The airport was officially closed for two hours and the public could not get near the field, although there were hundreds of pickets in front of the soaring concrete International Arrivals Building. They were unaware that el-Wasi was three miles away on the other side of the airport, or that he would depart directly from there to begin the ride on an unmarked route that would take the Arab party, escorted by police, to midtown Manhattan in less than one hour.

The ground crew put a stairway in place, and the forward hatch opened. After a few seconds, a figure in a white robe peered out of the front door frame and, after hesitating an instant, began to descend the stairs. He was quickly followed by three others similarly garbed. Behind them came more robed men, the white cloth buoyed by the mild gusts of wind. The pilot and crew stayed aboard.

When they were all on the ground, six of the Arabs gathered protectively around their leader. Two men began to push their way toward the limousines, policemen guarding them in a wide circle. The leader shook his head. "I will talk to the newsmen," he said softly, in clear and barely accented English.

"Can you give us a hint what you are going to say tomorrow morning?"

"Do you think you can persuade the General Assembly to adopt your resolution condemning Israel for holding on to occupied territory?"

"Why do you condone murder?"

"What are your plans after the speech?"

"Gentlemen, please," el-Wasi said, holding up his hand almost deferentially. "Please, I will make a brief statement. I have no time for other than that. I am happy on behalf of the Palestine Liberation Organization to be given the opportunity to address the United Nations General Assembly on a matter of pressing world concern. I come in a spirit of reason. I am hopeful that we will all be equally reasonable. What I have to say will be very clear and you will hear it soon enough. I think no problem is so large that it cannot be solved if men of good faith are so inclined and have the right motivation. To that I will address myself tomorrow morning. It has been a long flight and I would like now to go. Thank you."

He clambered into the lead car, and it and the second were quickly filled. They sped away from the airfield, surrounded by police cars with blaring sirens and flashing lights.

GRACIE MANSION

"That was a pretty speech, wasn't it?" The mayor looked around the room.

"Seems like a peach of a guy. Nice, soft-spoken. Sort of like Haldeman, you know, obviously misunderstood."

"Manny, what are the road conditions?"

Newman stopped talking and reached for a phone programmed to dial numbers automatically. He pressed a button and the phone at police headquarters control began to ring. He conferred with the desk man. "Clear, Mr. Mayor, all clear. The police have cleared all traffic in the left lane, and they're coming right in. There are twenty cruisers out there and two helicopters following the procession. No sweat."

"Yeah, no sweat. Manny, turn the television on but don't bother me with it unless something happens. Christ, I wish today were the day after tomorrow."

JERUSALEM

Two people sat in a small office at the Intelligence Ministry: the chief of Israeli intelligence and Avram Tal. A television in the corner transmitted satellite pictures of the scene at JFK.

"So," said the chief. "He has come to make peace." He reached across his desk for a pipe, picked through a tobacco pouch, and drew from a desk drawer a pure silver lighter inscribed with a message of thanks from Egypt's President Sadat. It was the only trophy he allowed himself to keep. "You are silent, Avram. What are you thinking?"

"I am thinking that there were seven of them who came off the plane and got into the cars. Yet our contact at the State Department assured us there were only six visas issued, and we know that only six will be allowed into the General Assembly."

The chief puffed silently on his pipe, then reached for a phone.

Avram Tal had long ago lost count of crises. What had begun as interruptions of his life he now saw, resignedly, as its pattern.

Its first piece remained his most painful memory: at six in Belgium, wrested from his parents' grip, shipped in a stifling cattle car to Auschwitz, where he was old enough to work and hence not to be killed at once. It was late enough in the war for him to survive the bestiality of his captors, though he never again saw his parents.

For Tal, age seven and one-half, liberation meant two years in a British detention camp at Cyprus, waiting for repatriation. There he learned English. In 1947, when he was nearly ten, he finally reached the Promised Land, and was placed on a kibbutz outside Haifa. He learned to farm, to read, and added Hebrew to his stock of languages.

At 14, as was required, he joined the Gadnah, a military training unit for school children, in which he would drill weekly and serve during the summers. The following year he was sent to Yadhanah Kibbutz, on the border just across from Tulkarem, an Arab town on the West Bank 15 kilometers from the sea. There he began to learn Arabic.

In his third summer of Gadnah, he met Meir Har Tzion, one of Israel's most highly decorated soldiers, then serving in Me'ah v'Echod—the famed "101"—from which the Israeli paratroopers and other crack units derived. From Har Tzion, Tal learned of an intensity, a single-mindedness, and a life dedicated to vital action that he had not been exposed to before. A life apart could be a redeeming, meaningful life.

In 1956, at 18, Tal was drafted into the army. After basic training and three months in a regular unit, he vol-

unteered for and was accepted into Nahal, a special unit for which superior physical and mental abilities are prerequisites. In October of that year, he was mobilized during the Suez crisis, and parachuted into the Mitla Pass. For his service he received two commendations, a medal, and a six-month hospital stay, to repair wounds to his right leg and abdomen.

After serving his required three years, Tal quit the army and returned to his kibbutz, to live the life of a farmer. He had seen enough war. He would till the land now and spend his life reading and dreaming. Perhaps if the dreams were great enough he would write.

This satisfied him for only several months. During his time as an enlisted man, his immediate officers had encouraged him to take officer training, but Tal had steadfastly declined. Soon he found that the life of inaction failed to satisfy. He could not escape a restlessness within nor a rising gorge of guilt. The army readily accepted Tal for officer training.

Shortly after he was commissioned in early 1960, he was assigned an extraordinary mission. At Auschwitz, Tal had seen Adolf Eichmann, who as chief of the Gestapo's Jewish section planned and supervised the destruction of European Jewry. When Eichmann's whereabouts in Argentina was discovered, Tal was chosen as one of a six-man special abduction team to spirit Eichmann to Israel to stand trial.

As a result of his courage and skill, Tal was sent to École Militaire Français in 1962 for a three-year course. In those years the French and Israelis enjoyed good relations, and many Israeli officers received advanced training in France. On his return to Israel, Tal, now a captain, received permission to take further studies at Hebrew University. These were interrupted, briefly, by war in 1967. For his heroism in leading his men on the Golan Heights, Tal was promoted to major. He returned to the university, wrote a thesis comparing Jewish and Moslem literature, took a degree, went off on several assignments. He was instrumental, through his French contacts, in getting military boats of French manufacture, already paid for but held back by de Gaulle's antipathy to Israel, into the hands *of the Israeli navy, where they would later be usefully employed.*

His years as a career officer in the regular army ended abruptly in early October 1972, after the Arab terrorist massacre of Israeli athletes in Munich. Tal was called to Aleph—a newly formed unit for highly classified military operations—as a lieutenant colonel. To most of those with whom he had an acquaintanceship—no one knew of any close friends—Tal simply disappeared. But he was busier than he had ever been. Aleph trained and was engaged constantly. In the Yom Kippur War in 1973, Tal led the first small unit that broke through Egyptian lines and led to the encirclement of Egypt's Third Army, thus achieving Israeli's military (though not political) defeat of Egypt in that war. It was following this success that Tal began his practice of refusing medals and other forms of recognition. His wishes were considered odd but were respected as the price of military genius.

By 1974, Aleph was engaged almost exclusively in antiterrorist activity. Tal lost count of the missions. He had been fighting for 30 years. He would go on fighting, as others go on breathing, without counting the effort. As he brooded on death, so he practiced it, in half a dozen countries around his home. All around him, spilled blood and the smell of death pervaded the earth. Men he knew left real limbs and sometimes lives upon the battlefield. For what? For the sliver of land called Israel. Ha'aretz. A place where Jews could live without fear of punishment, ever, for being Jews. For that slice of land, the country paid the indescribable price of constant war. The instinct for survival overrode all other issues, and Avram Tal became a very practical man.

When in early 1976 a shell exploded a few inches away from what was then his predecessor's skull, Tal assumed command of Aleph. He was 38. His promotion to full colonel mattered little to him: He wore no insignia and his needs required little money. Aleph was his life, all hours of the day. Full-time attention must be paid. Most assuredly, closed eyes could never recapture what they had not seen. He could have been off-duty when the latest interruption *of his life—el-Wasi's arrival in New York a quarter of a world away—took place, but then some fact might have been overlooked.*

Having been seen, the fact could not be ignored. Tal realized that el-Wasi's bringing an extra, seventh Arab to America could not be accidental.

C.I.A. HEADQUARTERS, LANGLEY, VIRGINIA

The communications duty officer at the Israeli desk ripped the message from the high-speed printer. It bore an "eyes only" for the director. He folded and sealed the short paper and dashed outside the communications room to deliver it to the deputy director of operations, who was simultaneously barking into an intercom and talking on the telephone when the duty officer stuck the folded paper under his nose.

"Top priority, sir, from the Israeli desk," the duty officer said. The DDO looked up, muttered into the phone, hung up, stared at the paper, then at the duty officer, and dismissed him with a nod. The DDO drummed his fingers once on the edge of his desk, then summoned his chief executive officer and gave him instructions. Clutching the paper, he strode briskly to the elevator, and rode to the seventh floor office of the director.

"Is he back yet?" he asked the secretary in the outer office.

She shook her head.

"Can you find him for me? Super urgent."

She lifted the telephone receiver and whispered a few words, replacing it on its cradle. She began a conversation about the weather. A minute later there was a single buzz and she picked up the phone again and said, "One moment." She covered the phone with one hand and, pointing to the next room, told the man standing by her desk, "You can take it in there."

"CEO," he said after he had closed the door and heard the click of the secretary's phone being hung up. There was a pause, then the director's loud voice came on.

"Couldn't it wait?" he said, irritated at being distracted from his West Coast trip. His people couldn't seem to do anything on their own initiative. Ever since the trials a few years earlier, every damn thing was bucked up to him. No one wanted responsibility any more.

"Sorry, sir," the CEO replied. "Top priority, from Israel. Came in"—he paused to look at his watch—"exactly five minutes and twenty seconds ago."

"Very well, let's have it."

"Says 'eyes only,' sir."

"Damn it, you be my eyes."

"Yes, sir." The CEO unfolded the paper and saw the coded signature of the Israeli chief of intelligence. Then he read the message: "Seven is not six, so something is odd about the party in New York."

"Repeat that," the director said evenly, the sting now gone from his voice.

The CEO read it again.

"Okay," the director said, "sorry to grouch. I'll cut things short and be back tomorrow."

אOCTOBER 4:א
THE NEXT DAY

UN GENERAL ASSEMBLY BUILDING

The United Nations is a collection of four buildings covering sixteen acres of valuable real estate in midtown Manhattan between Forty-second and Forty-eighth streets, First Avenue to the East River. The northernmost building is the General Assembly, a four-story domed structure of white marble and limestone, bordered on its north and east by a sprawling cement patio and gardens, and on its south by a large fountain and the towering glass and marble Secretariat building. On its west is First Avenue, renamed locally United Nations Plaza. The cement wall and iron gates that ring the First Avenue side open in several places, two of which accommodate a circular driveway that leads to and from a marble canopy overhanging the delegates' entrance to the building.

A dozen entrances lead into the General Assembly building. The public entrance off the stone patio has seven large nickel-bronze doors donated by the government of Canada. Several doors open off the garden, and another door leads into it from the Secretariat.

The inside of the building is dominated by the General Assembly Hall, a cavernous arena 75 feet high that occupies most of the second, third, and fourth floors. There are several other chambers that fill out the rest of the building, but none so large or imposing as the Hall.

At midnight, more than five hundred officers of the New York City Police Department gathered at the deserted UN Plaza across the street from the General Assembly building. Captain de Petri addressed them.

"Men, do your job and do it right. I want every inch of that building searched. Look everywhere. Look in the corners, in the hallways, under the tables, in the bathrooms—and I mean don't be afraid to stick your noses into the crappers. This place has got to be secure, and I mean *secure*. If anyone tries to kill those Arabs tomorrow, they better not pull it off because of any mistake my men make, understand? Because if they do it's my ass, and if it's mine it's yours."

The men split into two groups. Half of them ringed the building, standing several yards apart, and separating the building from anyone who might pass, which, at that particular time of evening, was nobody. From now until the search was over, no one would be permitted to enter the grounds.

The rest of the police entered the building and disbanded into groups assigned to each area of the building. They crept on hands and knees in every corner, climbed ladders to inspect behind the huge tapestries that decorate the walls, poked inside the statuary. A team of technicians probed gently with metal detectors along the entire surface of the building. The job was tedious, but only through the tedium could security be assured. Two dozen trained police dogs sniffed their way throughout the building.

At 5:25 A.M. Captain de Petri placed a dime into a public telephone on the first floor of the Hall and called the commissioner of police.

"Jack," he said, "we combed this place so fine nobody

could've hid a fart from us in here. The place is safe." The commissioner thanked him, hung up, and phoned the mayor to report that the building was secure.

Captain de Petri instructed the men inside to leave and assemble across the street. When the last man had left, he removed a master key from his pocket and bolted shut the locks on every door leading into the building but one: the delegates' door on the west side of the building, at the tip of the circular driveway off First Avenue. No door but that one would again be opened, he said to himself, until this goddam circus is over.

WALDORF ASTORIA HOTEL

At 8:00 A.M., the phone rang twice in room 2017 of the Waldorf Astoria. El-Wasi reached his arm from under the floral sheet, lifted the receiver, and mumbled some words in Arabic.

"Good morning, Mr. el-Wasi, this is your wake-up call, have a lovely day," the desk clerk chirped. El-Wasi hung up. He walked over to the window, lifted a corner of the drawn shade, and peeked out.

"Zaid, it's a beautiful day for us, wake up," said el-Wasi to the man sleeping on the floor near the door. "Allah is smiling at us for doing what must be done."

Two hours later, el-Wasi and five colleagues stepped out of the hotel elevator into the lobby. The bottoms of their long billowing robes dragged along the freshly vacuumed carpeting. The robes and kaffiyehs, or headpieces, seemed oddly out of place in the milieu of suited men drifting back and forth across the floor beneath the large chandeliers.

They stepped out the front door onto Park Avenue. Two black limousines bearing flags of the PLO on both front fenders were waiting at the curb, chauffeurs at the wheels.

Several dozen of the mass of policemen who had been waiting outside for el-Wasi's exit formed a blue corridor for them to walk the few steps from the front door to the cars. Crowds had already formed behind the police. Cameras were activated from television trucks parked across the street, but the crowd of policemen was too dense for the cameras to catch more than snatches of el-Wasi's face. He entered the rear seat of the lead car, opened a window, and waved both hands at the cameras. Then he formed a peace sign with his left hand, and a fist with his right.

The driver began following the police convoy toward the UN.

GENERAL ASSEMBLY HALL

Harold Saperstein stood in the small glass booth far up on the right-hand side of the General Assembly auditorium, perched one story above the arena, looking down. He scanned the room with his minicam easily, showing the delegates milling about. This was a piece of cake. It was so simple, especially when a producer had constant access to your earphone and told you what to do.

He had been lucky. The police had notified all networks and other media that, because of security considerations, only one cameraman would be permitted into the General Assembly building and there would be no other press allowed. The press had screamed, of course, but all they managed to negotiate was that the one cameraman could have a backup cameraman, who would also have a camera, so at least the producers would have two choices to flash on the home screens. The stations had all fought among themselves for their top cameraman, but at last, when nobody budged, several flips of a coin selected Harold Saperstein, a technician few knew, and an even more anonymous assistant who introduced herself to him only as Diane, operating a back-up camera. It was agreed that Saperstein would not act as a reporter and microphones would be placed in fixed positions in the Hall so that only the delegates at the rostrum would be heard speaking.

Saperstein had been around; this was not his firt big assignment. A year in Vietnam, a hostile Republican National Convention, hardhats in New York, fires, floods, rough jostling at hundreds of press conferences, unsettling events that become routine for the men who hold open the nation's eyes. Once he had been impressed with himself, but that had been at the beginning, nearly 20 years ago. He had become so phlegmatic about his unionized hours that he rarely discussed his day's location even with his wife. It always fascinated her, when she could get him to talk, but he was wary of her own private broadcast network in the backyards of Flatbush.

Today, however, he had mentioned his destination to her.

"Arabs!" she cursed.

He shrugged. Try as he could, politics never aroused him. Technicians are rarely stirred; they are there before the makeup and see the dour faces before the fake smiles are flashed for the cameras. He scowled.

"What's the matter?" Diane asked. "Everything's working."

"Yeah," he said. He looked at her eyes, lit with excitement. He softened; he remembered his first big assignment, when he was no older than this young woman.

"Diane," he said calmly, "you know this is all a bunch of crap."

"Harold!" she said, shocked. "It's history. Doesn't anything turn you on?"

"Yeah," he answered, smiling at her ample chest.

She swiveled in a huff, looked down on the delegates below. There was a sudden stir. Every face was turning to the door on the far side of the speaker's rostrum.

"They must be coming soon," she whispered in a throaty voice, her ire forgotten. "Get that camera around."

Saperstein's arm was already in motion.

Three minutes earlier, the cameras outside had gone live as el-Wasi's limousine crept up First Avenue. They had been busy for the previous hour, but now all the delegates with their permitted entourages were already in the building, waiting only for el-Wasi.

Shortly after ten, el-Wasi stepped from his limousine at the delegates' entrance to the General Assembly, the only unlocked door leading into the building. He waved to the masses of people gathered behind police barricades on First Avenue. Several policemen were stationed under the canopy which overhung the delegates' entrance. Six television cameramen, selected as worldwide representatives of the press, had been permitted onto the grounds to record el-Wasi's entry into the building. Everyone else but delegates had been barred even from the grounds.

He smiled at the cameras, then looked back across First Avenue. The street was lined with thousands of people craning their necks for a glimpse of him. He gazed at the skyscrapers across the street. Dozens of office windows were open, with workers straining to see him. El-Wasi turned and waved at them for several seconds. Atop those buildings, he saw uniformed police sharpshooters, all armed with telescope-fitted rifles. He and his party disappeared inside.

Captain de Petri, standing outside the delegates' door, closed and locked it behind el-Wasi. He instructed the cameramen they would not have to leave the grounds, and, as they did, Captain de Petri turned to the sergeant standing beside him.

"I guess we did our job all right. No one in except the diplomats. I'll be glad when they get out already and we can all go home."

He looked at the policemen spanning First Avenue. "Thousands of men and millions of dollars for an Arab. Who'd want his ass anyway?"

El-Wasi and his group walked up to the second floor and opened a glass door. There was an immediate stirring inside the Hall.

The Hall is huge: 165 feet long, 115 feet wide, and three floors high capped by a domed ceiling. There are over two thousand seats inside. The rear of the room, which gradually slopes upward for purposes of visibility, is for the public. Today those seats were kept empty: For security reasons, the public would see it all through television. Even the translators who regularly sit inside the Hall had been reassigned to the Secretariat; the speeches would be piped in to the adjacent building and their translations into English, French, Spanish, Russian, Arabic, and Chinese would be relayed back to the delegates' earphones.

The front half of the room—the Hall's arena—is filled with seats reserved for the members of each country's delegation. The side walls are decorated with large abstract murals by Fernand Léger. Built into both side walls and facing the arena are glass-enclosed booths for interpreters and the media. Today all those booths were empty except for the one where Saperstein and Diane stood.

At the front of the arena is a large marble podium, behind which are three seats, facing the arena, reserved for the president of the General Assembly, the secretary-general, and an under-secretary general. The United Nations insignia decorates the wall behind; in front of the podium stands the speaker's rostrum.

It was ten minutes after the appointed time when el-Wasi and his five aides entered the Hall at the front of the arena. Saperstein's camera showed the delegations from all countries, present and waiting. En masse, hundreds of them stood and applauded as el-Wasi, smiling broadly, waved and led his group to the seats in the front of the Hall behind a placard marked "Palestine Liberation Organization."

The second wave of applause for el-Wasi began when the president of the General Assembly called him to the rostrum, and it continued for several minutes. He waited until the room fell quiet, and began.

"I thank you for having invited the Palestine Liberation Organization to participate in this plenary session of the General Assembly, and for introducing the question of Palestine as a separate item on the Assembly's agenda. I come here today to propose a final solution to the problem that besets us. But to understand the solution, it is necessary to see the problem in perspective. So permit me to set forth some brief history."

Most of the delegates in the Hall sat attentively. Several, especially in the back rows, paid more attention to the other delegates than to the speaker. If this was a historic moment it would be enough to say that they were present; history did not require them also to pay attention. The ambassadors from the Arab countries sat up straight in the soft, cushioned

Assembly chairs. The television cameras were on, and it was important for them to nod and smile and frown at just the right phrases.

From the podium, el-Wasi launched into his standard speech on the ideological nature of Zionism.

"The roots of the Palestinian question reach back into the closing years of the nineteenth century, to that period which today we call the era of colonialism. This is when Zionism as a scheme was born.

"Zionism is an ideology that is imperialist, colonialist, racist. It is profoundly reactionary and discriminatory. Zionism's core proposal is that the only solution for the Jewish problem is for Jews to alienate themselves from communities or nations of which they have historically been a part. When it is proposed that Jews solve the Jewish problem by emigrating to and forcibly settling the land being peacefully inhabited by another people, exactly the same position is being advocated by Jews as the one urged by anti-Semites against Jews."

Thirteen rows from the podium, the Israeli ambassador wrote furiously with a thick black pen.

"The Jewish invasion of Palestine began in 1881," el-Wasi continued, slowing his cadence. "Before Jews began flooding the land, Palestine was a verdant country, inhabited mainly by an Arab people energetically enriching its Arab culture. For the next thirty or forty years, the Zionist movement began settling tens of thousands of European Jews in our homeland, resorting to trickery and deceit in order to implant them in our midst. In the wake of the Balfour Declaration in 1917 and over the next thirty years, the Zionist movement succeeded, in collaboration with its imperialist allies, in settling hundreds of thousands more European Jews on the land, usurping the property of Palestinian Arabs."

El-Wasi's usually sweeping gestures seemed curiously restrained. He held his torso nearly rigid.

"By 1947, early in its history, this General Assembly, in collusion with the Zionist movement and its imperialist friends, approved a recommendation to partition what it had no moral right to divide—an indivisible Palestine, my homeland. When for all time we rejected that decision, our position corresponded to that of the natural mother who prohibited King Solomon from carrying out his judgment."

The Moroccan ambassador winked across the aisle at one of his few close friends in the Assembly, the ambassador from Algeria. "Fascinating," he mouthed. Catching the sarcasm, the Algerian ambassador grinned and nodded, then remembered to freeze his face into an expression of studied interest.

"Furthermore, even though the partition resolution granted the Zionist settlers most of the land of Palestine, they were not satisfied. No, they commenced to wage a war of terror against the civilian Arab population. They destroyed and obliterated Arab towns and villages and built their own settlements on the ruins of our farms and our groves.

"With support from imperialist and colonialist members, the Zionists managed to worm themselves into the United Nations. They succeeded in deceiving world opinion by presenting our cause as a mere problem of refugees in need of charity."

El-Wasi gripped the podium with both hands and leaned his body forward slightly, as if his back ached. His words grew clipped together in measured concealment of his anger.

"Not satisfied with this, the invaders launched two large-scale wars, in 1956 and 1967, thus endangering world peace and security. The situation has been rendered more serious by the enemy's persistence in maintaining and consolidating its occupation, thus establishing a beachhead for world imperialism in the Mideast. All Security Council resolutions and appeals by world public opinion for Zionist withdrawal have been ignored. Even in the perfidious discussions with Cairo, the invaders expressly disclaim any intent to return the Palestinians' land."

Sitting in a single row, el-Wasi's five robed companions no longer watched their leader. Now, they scanned the great Hall. They were silent and unobtrusive.

"All this must now be remedied," el-Wasi said. He spoke the line quietly, enunciating each word deliberately. Several delegates who had been staring off at the high windows or inspecting the tracery around the dome refocused their attention to the rostrum. His men looked back at him.

"On many occasions in the past I have warned the Zionist government, and have advised this august tribunal, that although one of my hands holds an olive branch, my other hand holds a gun. I have given the world the choice of which hand shall be used. I have waited patiently for the world to make that choice, as my people have waited and suffered outside their homeland for more than thirty years. Our waiting can go on no longer. By failing to act, the world has forfeited its chance to choose. With the greatest reluctance I am at last choosing for the world. And thus I now tell you that I must permit the olive branch to fall."

At those words, Nachman Ben-Eshai, Israel's UN ambassador, and the other members of the Israeli delegation rose from their seats near the front of the arena. Heads turned in their direction as they walked toward the aisle leading to the main door.

El-Wasi nodded without a word in the direction of the PLO table. Immediately, his five assistants leaped from their seats and began to dash: one to the rear of the Hall, one to each of the sides, and two to the door where the Israeli delegation was headed. The Israelis continued toward the door.

The Hall was in an uproar. "What in bloody hell is going on?" one of the British delegates muttered to himself. No one was looking any longer at el-Wasi; the center of action had shifted to his men, racing through the Hall, and to the Israeli delegates walking, expressionless, in a slow stride toward the exit.

"My friends," el-Wasi shouted into the microphone, trying to quiet the buzzing of the delegates' voices. "My friends," he repeated, "please be calm. We mean no one any harm."

As he spoke, el-Wasi grasped the center of his white robe and pulled it apart at a fold. Those who turned to watch at the sound of his voice saw a blunt object taped to his chest. El-Wasi wrapped both hands under it and pulled; the microphone caught the swishing noise of surgical tape being scraped away from the skin. El-Wasi winced, but in the same motion he swung the object out from his robe and waved it firmly in his right hand. Unmistakably, it was a squat submachine gun—a .45 caliber Ingram model 10, only ten and one-half inches long; American designed, it was licensed in Chile and Yugoslavia. His finger was already on the trigger.

"My friends," he said, his mouth pressed next to the microphone, so that his words came out thick and harsh, "it is with the greatest reluctance that I am forced to announce that nobody in this Hall is free any longer to leave."

Delegates jumped to their feet. Angry cries, from Arabs no less than from neutrals, rang out across the room. Now the Israelis were joined by several ambassadors hurrying toward the exit. Others began to push; two ambassadors fell to the floor. Most of the delegates remained seated, paralyzed into inaction by the general mood of fear and the air of chaos.

El-Wasi inclined the gun toward the ceiling, and squeezed the trigger, firing several rounds into the dome. The rapid succession of shots, picked up by the microphone, echoed loudly throughout the Hall, and splinters of glass from the skylight rained to the floor. Everyone stopped moving. Not waiting for further distraction, el-Wasi took the microphone again.

"Please, my friends, stay seated, stay calm," he said, smacking the T-shaped gun hard on the lectern.

"I will now address not only you, but the world outside that is viewing us through the eyes of the television cameras in here with us."

The Israelis stood in place. Most of the delegates who had risen moved quickly back to their seats. A few stood uncertainly, looking to the seats and the doors, then finally to el-Wasi at the podium.

"The Palestinian movement has just begun an operation that no one is capable of stopping. As I speak with you, my brothers here with me are lining this Hall with sticks of extremely powerful explosives which we brought in with us. If any door opens, everyone in this room will be instantaneously annihilated. We are fully armed. Each of us has this"—he held up the submachine gun in his right hand—"and enough rounds of ammunition to kill everyone in this room ten times. Do not try to storm us from outside, or you will die and everyone inside will die, if not from our bullets then from the explosives which are now being put in place."

Across the room two Arabs were playing out a wire that had been coiled inside a large black attache case. At their sides, within a half-second's grip, lay two more Ingram 10s. As they strung out the wire, they shuffled forward, half on their knees, and with their empty hands brought the guns along. Two others repeated this process at the opposite wall. A fifth Arab stood watch from the back, his gun firm in both hands.

"I hope, I know, that you on the outside are wise enough to know that my brothers and I are not afraid to die for our cause. I pray that you will have the good judgment to listen to what I have said. Unless you do, no one in this Hall will survive."

One of the Arabs left his wiring and slipped out of the Hall, gun in hand, through a rear door before it was wired. He quickly found the staircase and raced up, taking the steps three and four at a time, pulling hard on the banister. On the next landing, he began pulling at each door, looking for the one that would open.

Inside, el-Wasi was still speaking. "We are calling for the dismantling, now, of the Zionist state that occupies Palestine. The form in which this dismantling shall occur is a matter that we all may discuss in a democratic manner, but the fact of the end of Israel will, I repeat, will be accomplished before we leave this room. You inside this room are the world's representatives and are thus in a figurative sense the world itself. We hold no hatred toward any of you personally, but it is only through holding the world hostage that our just goal will finally be accomplished."

A member of the Italian delegation, still standing near the Israeli group, saw that el-Wasi was looking out toward the middle of the assembly. He took a hesitant step toward the side door. The Arabs on the floor were working far down the wall and were preoccupied with the wiring. He began to walk a little more swiftly. His face was flushed. He focused on the door handle, when a burst of gunfire whizzed past him from the back, slamming holes into the door twenty feet in front. He sank to his knees, untouched, covering his head with his arms.

El-Wasi stopped at the noise. He signalled to the Arab at the rear to hold his fire, then said to the audience: "I mean what I say. You are our hostages, and I plead with each of you to stay in your seats and not to move. You, on the floor, if you are not hurt, stand up now and take your seat."

Shaking, the Italian rose and staggered eighteen rows down the center aisle to an empty chair.

El-Wasi waited until the man sat down and then resumed.

"I must inform those of you outside this Hall that the world is now also our hostage, not only figuratively but literally. For as long as it takes this Assembly to establish by its vote a Palestinian government in the territory now occupied by what is called the government of Israel, then for that long the world will be subjected to a scourge of reprisals such as it has never felt."

The Moroccan ambassador could not sit still. He shifted back and forth in his seat, moving his legs nervously, shuffling his feet along the floor. "Try to relax," his deputy whispered. The ambassador gave him a pained look. He folded and unfolded his arms across his chest.

"The Palestine Liberation Organization has designed, and has ready, a coordinated series of action projects, worldwide. They will occur, at fixed intervals, one after the other. They will become increasingly severe. Do not suppose you will be able to anticipate or stop them. You will not know where the next of our actions will occur, nor in what form. You will not even know on which of the six continents to anticipate any of them. But you will know, after they have occurred, that they are actions of our movement. Our brothers are already in the field, ready and equipped to carry out their missions. This series of actions will cease only when you in this Hall vote to dismantle the Zionist imperialist regime now holding Palestine, and when you install as rulers in their place the representatives of the Palestinian national movement.

"Shortly, I will submit to this General Assembly a formal resolution calling for the end of the State of Israel. Pass it, and expeditiously implement it, and you will be free to go. You, the delegates of the countries of this planet, and the world community outside, have the keys to your own freedom. You must use them."

At the glass door at the right of the Hall, Zaid ibn Haritha beckoned with his submachine gun to the six members of the Israeli delegation to sit on the floor, where they were standing. They sat.

On the next flight up, one of the doors finally gave and the Arab bolted in. Saperstein and Diane were so intent on the Hall below that they did not hear the sound. Diane was behind the heavy camera, sitting in its wheel mount; the camera was focused on the podium. Saperstein held the portable camera, and was panning across the audience. He had spotted the Moroccan ambassador fidgeting and had shown the entire sequence to a television audience that was worldwide. Only when he felt the muzzle of a gun flash against the side of his head did he realize that he was no longer merely recording the story below. He instinctively raised his hands above his head, dropping his camera in the same motion. Diane heard his camera hit the floor and saw the Arab swing his gun around to her breasts. She quickly got off the wheel mount, and in doing so knocked the standing camera askew so that it was now turned toward the rear wall of the booth.

When Saperstein's camera fell from his hands, studio technicians cut to the stationary camera. When it showed nothing but a bare wall, they cut back to the portable. For the next minute, millions of people watching television saw only the ceiling of the small glass booth. The Arab ordered Saperstein to pick up his camera. Then millions of TVs showed in quick jerky movements the floor and door of the booth, then the hallway on the third floor, then the stairway leading down. Then the picture showed only floor again and a closed door. The door opened and the camera swept upward from the door sill, and the world again saw el-Wasi. He ordered Saperstein to keep the camera going in the Hall.

Saperstein told the Arab guarding him that if this was going to last more than an hour the portable camera would be too heavy. The Arab called over one of his colleagues. In Arabic, he said that he would be taking Saperstein back up to bring down the larger camera. He ordered Saperstein to hand the portable one to Diane.

"Watch her," he said in English to his comrade. "If she tries anything, kill her."

CITY HALL

"Maybe they're auditioning for Candid Camera," said Manny, breaking the silence of the shock. "Or Kojak."

The mayor answered: "Manny, this is not a joke, for once keep quiet. We have just seen maybe the beginning of the end of the world. Why in hell is man such a dumbfool creature that he stands on protocol? Why didn't I just order those bastards searched?"

"Mr. Mayor, it's not your fault—"

"Myra," to the secretary, "get me police headquarters. Manny, keep your eyes glued to the TV. Nancy, get the borough president and the deputy mayor over here. We have a goddamned crisis."

The police commissioner was first to arrive. No, there was no panic on the street, but the news hadn't really reached outside completely. Police were being pulled in from all around Manhattan. Yes, he agreed that people had to be stopped at all costs from storming the UN. The men had bullhorns; they were warning the crowds now.

"Are the Arabs all inside?"

"As far as we know, yes, sir."

"What can we do? Can we rush them?"

"Absolutely not. No, sir. We don't know what kind of weapons they've got, other than what we can see on camera. They apparently have five men in there aside from el-Wasi; all appear to be armed with submachine guns and maybe more. But I can only see four of them right now—" The mayor swiveled to look at the TV screen. "The other must be laying the explosives, I suppose. I don't know. Can't tell. We're trying to get through to the TV people to train the spare camera on the rest of the chamber so we can get a looksee at the studio as to what else is going on. But for some reason we can't connect with the chamber. It seems to be out of voice contact. Until we do know what's going on, we can't risk anybody trying to get in there. We don't know what will go off."

"Or who."

"Or who. Right."

"I suppose the police outside understand the problem?" the mayor asked.

The commissioner nodded. "Yes, sir, they aren't making a move until the situation is clarified." He drew a sketch of the UN grounds from his briefcase. "We've posted guards around all entrances." He made small Xs on the paper with a red pencil he picked up from the mayor's desk. "Here, and here, and here." He fell silent as he marked them off. "No one's going to get in."

"Can we talk to anyone in there? Is there any way to get through to the American delegates or anyone else on the floor?"

"Apparently not. The floor microphones have been killed. You can hear that only the studio announcer, what's his name, you know, Tyler Johnson, is talking. There's no sound at all being broadcast from the UN. I don't know what happened. Maybe they cut the cable."

Captain de Petri was standing directly outside the main entrance when the call came for him over the squad car radio. "We have a ten thirty-three, for de Petri, headquarters emergency. Please respond." De Petri rushed to the car, grabbed the microphone, and, breathing heavily, said "This is de Petri, go ahead."

"De Petri," said the commissioner, "we got a Class A Number One emergency on our hands. Now listen. The Arabs have taken over the place."

"What place, sir?"

"They have hijacked the damn building you've been guarding. They are holding hundreds of people hostage inside. Everybody in that room. It's sealed. And we intend to keep it sealed—from the outside—for now. The news is just going out now. When your friendly fans hear that they may go berserk. But you keep them under control at all costs, do you understand? At all costs. I don't intend to have World War III blamed on me because I couldn't get my captain to understand a simple order. Do you read me? Are you there?"

De Petri slumped against the car, his eyes closing momentarily. The color drained from his face. "Captain, are you all right?" yelled a nearby lieutenant, noticing the solitary figure. De Petri pulled himself up.

"I'm here, I read you, I understand. No one gets across the line. You may depend on that, sir."

"Yeah, well don't panic them and don't stampede them with any unnecessary announcements. Use those bullhorns only if you need to."

"Yes sir. Out."

De Petri threw the microphone onto the seat of the car. He waved his principal deputy over. "Grogan, we got the world's biggest trouble." He filled Grogan in, directing him to alert the other officers of what might hit within minutes. Reinforcements were being called. Squad cars screeched onto First Avenue. Riflemen were posted behind each car. Bullhorns were readied, in case anyone decided to rush.

The picketers stopped at the sight. "They're getting ready to shoot us, oh my God," someone yelled out. No one moved. Slowly the meaning became apparent, as radios spread the news to the crowds. A few people pushed against the police line, but not very vigorously, and the line held. One irate citizen rushed through a hole, only to find himself alone in the middle of a vast empty promenade menaced by dozens of gunmen who trained their weapons on him. "Go back, get back," a bullhorn blared. Confused, the man whirled in a slow circle, looking for cover, then slunk back into the crowd. A soft wave of nervous laughter reached

Captain de Petri. He watched quietly for two minutes, then took the microphone and called in a message: "Secured—for now."

"I have the word from de Petri that things are under control outside," the commissioner told the mayor. "But now we've got six television crews and about fifteen-odd radio stations that want to set up alongside. I told the men to hold them off for a while, but they're really screaming to get through."

"I know," the mayor said. "Their bosses are jamming my telephones. Look, we can use some eyes and ears down there. We'll clear one each; they can operate a pool. Let them work it out among themselves, but position them on the west side of the street. Don't let them get near the building."

"Yes, sir."

"Oh, and chief?"

"Yes, sir?"

"Good work."

"Thank you, sir, but nothing actually happened, sir, outside, that is."

"That's what I mean."

At that moment, the networks took the morning quiz programs off the air. The picture that the national audience, soon to grow rapidly, could see was a small knot of men huddled in a conference around the rostrum; the camera was focused on el-Wasi, who could be seen whispering to the president of the General Assembly.

"We have no sound from the floor of the General Assembly," Tyler Johnson was saying. "And we have been unable to reestablish voice contact with our cameraman. It looks like the microphones have simply been unplugged, presumably to prevent us from hearing what they are saying. From what we can see, they appear to be tacking something down. We are going to cut to our second camera to show you the scene from the far end."

There suddenly appeared a vast sea of delegates, most rooted to their seats, a few standing. Beyond them were two white-robed men, unwinding a cable against the arcing glass doors. "We can't tell for sure, but I gather that some sort of explosive charge is being laid," Johnson said.

Just then an electronic squeal interrupted Johnson's commentary. There was an audible click, and the sound of an overamplified microphone came on with a surge. Loud voices talking a distinctly foreign language. Some sort of argument. One of el-Wasi's men came running up, pointing, or so it seemed, directly at the camera. He was a long way off. The camera zoomed in. The Arab was pointing straight at the audience and appeared to be yelling. Then el-Wasi gained the microphone and speaking again in fluent English directed Saperstein to kill the second camera and to refocus on the rostrum. This Saperstein did. "I want only one camera on, and I want it to stay fixed on this spot," el-Wasi said calmly. As if an afterthought, he added: "I am sending one of my brothers to you. Do not be alarmed. I do not wish to have to contemplate the possibility of the red light on the other camera reawakening. It will be put to sleep permanently."

The sound of Saperstein's voice was suddenly piped through the national audio hookup. "Jesus, I think they're going to shoot the camera!" The main camera continued to focus on the oncoming terrorist, who raised his gun at an angle two feet away. A shot and then a splatter of glass. Across the river, among a company of ladies having morning coffee, Mrs. Saperstein fainted.

El-Wasi's voice boomed over the microphone. "You will now return your camera's focus to the rostrum and await further instructions."

"They mean to control it all," the mayor said. "We are to see only what they want us to see, and evidently it isn't going to be much."

"So what do we do now?" Nancy Dolby asked.

"What do you recommend?"

Before anyone could respond, the picture on the screen changed abruptly. "This is the scene from First Avenue. Police estimate the crowd at around four thousand but there are unconfirmed reports that people are streaming to the site. According to one police radio call that a reporter overheard, upwards of ten thousand people may arrive within the hour. Police are urging everyone at the UN to disperse, and requesting all others to stay away. This is not the World Series, ladies and gentlemen. This is a potential cataclysm. So please stay away. There is nothing to be learned by lining up, and you will only interfere with the police." The crowd was still respecting the police lines, but it was chanting something that the outdoor mikes could not pick up. The image of the General Assembly rostrum returned.

"If ten thousand people are coming, it'll be beyond the capacity of the police," Dolby at length replied. "I think we need the Guard or even the army."

"I doubt we will get either, under the circumstances."

"Probably not, but can't we say we tried?"

"Myra, get me the governor. And after that, the White House. Nancy," he said, turning to her, "have you ever been to Washington?"

Startled, Dolby stopped writing. She uncrossed her legs and brushed her hair with a sweep over an ear. "Sure, but a long time ago."

"Did you ever take a tour of the White House?" he persisted, standing close and looking down at her. She unconsciously drew her legs tighter together.

"Not inside, but I've driven by. Why do you ask?"

"Because I think it's time you took a tour."

"Now?"

"Soon, I think. Go pack a bag. A big one. You may be staying for a while."

"What for? Are you pulling my leg, sir?"

The mayor fixed her with a steady glance. "I have never been more serious. There is nothing we can do; that is obvious. Any serious planning will have to be done in Washington, at the White House. All we can do is hold things in check here. But I need someone, this city needs someone, involved in that planning. You're that person. So go get ready. Myra, have a car ready for Nancy."

"A car? Well my goodness, Mr. Mayor. First class to Washington!"

"The car is to take you home and then to the airport. And you don't travel first class, you travel coach. You know the rules. Of course, you'll get your expenses, but you will probably not need to spend much. And Nancy."

"Yes?"

"If someone wants to buy you dinner, that's okay. The honor of New York is not at stake, not that way."

"Mr. Mayor, you are picking up bad habits from Manny."

"Maybe, Nancy, but remember, I know that crowd. They can be rough. Resist the temptation to prove yourself. I know you're better than they are. That's why I have you working for me. But sometimes you have to bend a little. Allow them their prejudices, okay? Remember, they're not as progressive down there as we are up here."

The intercom buzzed. "The governor is on the line." Dolby jumped up, waved, and walked out the door. On television, Johnson was hoping to have a comment from the White House any minute.

THE WHITE HOUSE

Thirty-two minutes after el-Wasi announced to the world that he had captured the United Nations, the president of the United States summoned to his office certain individuals who would constitute the nucleus of what would shortly become the Emergency Group. That would not be its formal name. A detailer at the Pentagon, assigned the following day to speed personnel to the top-level executive group formed to deal with the crisis, dubbed it the Ad Hoc United Nations Executive Strategy Group. It would be referred to in Defense Department memoranda by its Germanic-sounding initials, AHUNESG. This name was duly noted in the military orders and in the memory banks of certain Pentagon computers, thence to CIA computers, and eventually into files maintained in Moscow, London, Paris, Peking, and the *New York Times* and *Washington Post*. But none of the members of the group itself ever used the name; on the few occasions when they had time for introspection, they thought of themselves simply as the Emergency Group.

The president himself needed no briefing. Together with his national security adviser and the vice-president, he had watched the takeover on television. Within a minute of el-Wasi's announcement, the press secretary joined them from his office where he had been chatting before the telecast with a senior journalist from Los Angeles who wanted a half-hour with the president. And before the talk was finished, the president placed calls to the chairman of the Joint Chiefs of Staff, the director of the Central Intelligence Agency, the director of the Federal Bureau of Investigation, the attorney general, the governor of New York, and the mayor of New York City. The attorney general came by taxi a few minutes later. The director of the CIA was in San Francisco and would not arrive for several hours. A splendidly beribboned general alighted from a large helicopter on the White House grounds and strode directly to the Oval Office.

A meeting was already in progress when General Cavanaugh rushed through the side door, nearly colliding with the appointments secretary, who was hurrying out to placate a civic group whose picture-taking session with the president would have to be delayed. The president waved Cavanaugh in but continued talking animatedly on the telephone while crouched over his desk.

"No army troops yet," he said.

"Mr President, the mayor is holding," said a voice on the intercom.

"Mr. President—," General Cavanaughaugh began. The president pointed to the sofa on the side. Cavanaugh walked across and, shaking the others' hands, sat down. "How did they get in there with guns? What in the hell is wrong with security?"

"The 1974 precedent," the security adviser said dryly. "They carried guns in then, too. Security should have known better."

"But didn't."

"What do you suggest?"

Cavanaugh shook his head.

"Look," the president was saying into the telephone, "I can't tell you how to deploy your police, but for now just make sure they don't make any more mistakes. No. I will not. For Christ sake, it only happened half an hour ago. We're meeting now. All right, send someone down. What? Let me get that name." The President scribbled a name on the yellow pad that sat on his otherwise clean desk. "Yeah, we'll be here." He hung up the phone.

The four men stopped talking and looked at him. "The mayor wants the National Guard, and the governor won't give it. The governor wants the army, and I won't give it. What do I want?"

"And who won't give it to you?" the vice-president said softly.

"Christ, they're giving it to me, all right, to us. Hank, what is the situation?"

General Cavanaugh summed it up, his information being somewhat staler than what the group already knew from the television set that continued to bleat from its corner.

"All right, Hank, in other words, we don't know anything, do we?" the president said, his eyes level with Cavanaugh's. "What do you propose?"

"Mr. President, we have contingency plans. Let me—"

"Mr. President," the security adviser interjected, "I doubt that any plan could have been prepared for a contingency like this. I think we will have to assemble a team and formulate our own plan, right from here."

"A team consisting of whom?"

"We'll have to feel our way. But those of us in this room for starters. Probably the director. The top Arab specialist at State. A psychological consultant on terrorists. I suppose a State Department legal adviser. Maybe others. I don't know; I want to consult the books and see who was put together for the Cuban missile crisis."

"Very well," said the president. Holding a scrap of paper in his hand, he stood up and turned to the vice-president, "You chair this team. I want it ready to meet by the time the director arrives. Oh, and take this—you might want to invite the mayor's liaison."

"Yes, sir," the vice-president said. "The director is due at four. Shall we meet here at four-thirty?"

The president nodded.

A secretary knocked, entered. "Mr. President, the Rotary delegation is here."

GENERAL ASSEMBLY HALL

Shortly after the takeover, el-Wasi announced on television the rules that would govern his household in the Hall.

Because 899 hostages were too unwieldy for six men to control, el-Wasi directed that each country's ambassador to the UN would remain as solitary hostages. The five associate delegates of each country—except Israel's—and the Assembly's three presiding officers, were directed to leave, in el-Wasi's own way.

First, he ordered the United States, or New York City, or whoever was in charge outside, to bring two portable television sets to the delegates' door outside the General Assembly building, and to leave them on the ground, with nobody nearby. He warned that if anyone tried to harm his comrade who would bring in the TVs, everyone in the Hall would be destroyed. El-Wasi gave one hour for the television delivery to be accomplished.

Precisely an hour later, the door at the delegates' entrance opened slowly, and a white-robed figure reached outside and pulled two televisions into the building. It had not been an easy delivery. A local special agent of the FBI had called a contact at Sears Roebuck on an emergency basis, who had immediately dispatched a delivery man with two televisions to the gate on First Avenue at 45th Street. But on arrival the deliverer had insisted on payment COD, failing which, he maintained, the sets would not be turned over. Two burly sergeants of the NYPD physically separated the sets from his hands.

El-Wasi and his men placed the two TVs on the rostrum. He switched one on and turned from channel to channel. They all carried the same picture: that of el-Wasi switching channels. He looked in Harold Saperstein's direction, and saw the camera facing him. Then he spoke.

"I know that here in America you have what is called a 'free press.' I hope you will not consider the following request to be an intrusion on that principle. I assume that all networks have cameramen stationed on the avenue outside this building. From now on, the cameras of one of those networks must focus on the front entrance, where the delegates entered, where I entered." He looked down at the tuner on one of the television sets. "Channel 7 will be good enough. Channel 7, I trust you will forgive this preemption. You are to have a camera focused permanently on that doorway out front, and on the walkway leading to that doorway. That picture is to continue until further orders— 'orders', that is a poor term—until further request. No other picture, and no 'commercial interruption.' As I shall shortly explain, we will be making certain uses periodically of that door, and I want to be able to see it whenever I want, just by switching to Channel 7.

"Please take your time deciding whether to comply with this request. You have three minutes."

El-Wasi looked at his wristwatch and left the podium. Three minutes later he was back at the podium, and looked down at the television turned to Channel 7. The picture was of the delegates' entrance to the General Assembly building, and the walkway to that entrance, shot from just outside the gate on First Avenue.

"Thank you. Let me assure you, the assembled delegates are grateful for your compliance."

In a room high up in ABC's headquarters overlooking Avenue of the Americas at 54th Street, a news executive swore. "Barbara Walters is going to be pretty pissed off," he said to his companion.

"Yeah, I guess so, but it's one way to dissuade her from trying to get in the UN personally. Besides," the other said as if an afterthought, "it's only in New York. I don't sup-

pose el-Wasi cares if we don't show that door anywhere
else. Tell Barbara she can still play west of the Hudson."

El-Wasi then announced that each of the associate delegates would be led, singly and blindfolded, from the Hall
to the delegates' entrance; each was then to walk quickly
from the UN grounds past the gate, onto First Avenue. As
the television showed each man leaving the UN grounds,
another would be permitted to leave. The entire Israeli delegation would remain inside the Hall.

Nearly eight hours later, 743 hostages had been released,
and 156 remained—the UN ambassadors, the entire Israeli
delegation, and the two TV technicians.

El-Wasi directed that quantities of food be delivered
three times a day, at eight-hour intervals, to be deposited
beneath the marble awning in front of the delegates' entrance to the building. The food would be placed on a multi-
tiered wheeled tray such as airlines use, but extra large,
because only one cart would be permitted in per meal. One
of el-Wasi's aides would leave the Hall, through one door
that would be temporarily unwired—that door would be
known only to those inside the Hall—walk out of the building through the delegates' entrance, and wheel in the food.
The Palestinians and the delegates would all eat from the
same delivery, but the Palestinians would not taste the food
until some time after the delegates had finished. A mobile
bathroom was also to be delivered, the same way. With the
exception of those deliveries, nobody and nothing was to
enter the building.

All of these deliveries would be taken into the building
and the Hall by a single Palestinian. If he did not return
within a reasonably short time after leaving the Hall, el-
Wasi would assume he had been harmed, and would detonate the explosives. El-Wasi had considered all the possibilities. If something were to happen that should not, or
if something were not to happen that should, the Hall, and
everyone in it, would return to ashes.

MOSCOW

Separated from New York by seven time zones, it was nearly 6:30 in the evening Moscow time when el-Wasi's plan became clear to certain men sitting in a room with high ceilings and elaborate paneling in the Kremlin. Gletuzshneyev, who was responsible for Arab intelligence, had unaccountably departed for his apartment across the city and a car had to be sent to overtake him and summon him back. On his return, vodka was brought in on a tray and the men sat back in thickly upholstered chairs to assess this turn of events. It had evidently caught them all, even Gletuzshneyev, unaware: He had gone home earlier in the confidence, bolstered by the assurances of his operatives, that nothing untoward would happen. "No surprises?" he had cabled the day before. "No surprises," had been the response that morning. Now there was muttering.

"Is this our operation?" one of them demanded of Gletuzshneyev.

He shook his head.

"Do we have anyone in it?"

He shook his head again.

"Our money?"

Gletuzshneyev nodded for the first time. "Yes. We have been supplying el-Wasi, at his request, with certain funds on which he could draw without knowledge of the pan-Arab community. Maximum secrecy was what he required."

"Even from us?"

"Naturally. He was especially anxious that we not appear to be involved. I agreed not to ask questions. It is better that he act on his own. His victory is ours, his failure is not. Our honest ignorance helps. Otherwise American resistance would be stiffer."

"It will be stiff enough."

"Perhaps."

"So. You are holding back something from us. Come, Gletuzshneyev, you are uncommonly cheerful."

The large man lowered his head modestly.

"What is his budget?"

"I know only the amounts I have supplied."

"And that is—"

"That is two point three million American dollars, more than a million pounds sterling, two million French francs, and forty million yen."

The man opposite him whistled. "That is a fancy sum."

Gletuzshneyev agreed. "It is a goodly price, but we are investing in an important operation: control of the Mideast."

"But that much money with no strings?"

"One does not instruct el-Wasi. I did venture the suggestion to him that whatever he planned to purchase with the Soviet largesse he not allow to sit and rust. We only pay for working equipment. He told me not to have such fears."

"And do we fear for our comrade, the ambassador to the United Nations?"

Gletuzshneyev shook his head vehemently.

"But do we not protest such treatment of a Soviet official?" his inquisitor persisted.

"Oh, protest, of course. Everyone will expect that. But we must not do more than protest. We do not bait Washington over this affair."

A florid-faced man toyed with his vodka glass, frowning. "And el-Wasi, he expects more help from us?"

"He expects nothing—and suspects nothing, either. We must let el-Wasi play out his scheme. He may succeed. If he does we will congratulate him, offer political assistance, and move in later. For now, gentlemen, we need only sit back and watch. We are not involved." He reached for the vodka and filled five glasses. Nodding to each of the men, he lifted his drink and downed it in one swallow.

THE WHITE HOUSE

At 4:30, the vice-president called the Emergency Group to order for the first time. There were present six men and a woman, not counting the vice-president himself. They sat in a large conference room in the basement of the West Wing, a few feet away from the silent bank of computers that served the security adviser and the president directly. The room was electronically secure and was physically guarded by a Marine detachment. No one could enter without special credentials. In one corner were three large televisions; across the room was a sofa, on either side of which sat a white telephone.

"I don't suppose we will want to begin with formalities or stand on them," the vice-president began. "You know why we are here. The president has charged us with laying out for him the options that are open. What can the president do and when should he do it? If these options include a complete solution to this 'hijacking of the world,' as everyone seems to be calling it, so much the better. But we'll also take a temporary solution too, if we can find one. The solution has to be a fast one or it is no solution, but it can't be so fast that it makes things worse. It has to work—and by 'work' I mean it has to result in the capture of the terrorists, the release of all UN delegates unharmed, and maintenance of the present state of affairs in the Mideast. There can of course be no 'dismantling' of Israel.

"We are almost all here. Dr. Kowalski, the security adviser, has been detained on a special assignment. The director, I'm informed, has landed in Washington and will be here momentarily. This group is charged with staying together until the siege has ended. We are a working group. You have all met each other, I assume, and it ought to be apparent why each of you is here. So let's get going. Let me put the first question, which I gather you've all been talking about anyway, to Will Watkins. Since you're the ranking Arab specialist, tell us what you think. Can they do these crazy things they claim? Will they do them if they can? Or is it all a bluff?"

"I just can't say. We're really all shooting in the dark at this point, sir. If they have enough money and if they have trained well enough and secretly enough and if they have used their best men, then maybe they can and maybe they will."

"Oh, Christ," said the one man in uniform, Lt. Gen. Grant W. "Whiskers" Sykes, chief of the army's Office of Strategic Plans and General Cavanaugh's deputy for the Joint Chiefs. Sykes, an expert in guerilla tactics, as famous for his impatience as for his taciturn mien, said: "Too many ifs. Of course they can, man. The question is *what. What* will they do? I can think of a hundred things, offhand."

"For example?" the vice-president asked.

"They can execute a few ambassadors. They can blow up bridges, dams, ships. They can hijack airplanes, blow them up, too. They can firebomb movie theaters and drug stores and restaurants. They've done all these things before. They can easily enough do them again." He slumped back in his chair.

"Do you think they will?"

"Probably." This from Dr. Newton Moore Jones, chief of psychiatry at Veterans Memorial Hospital in Washington, and an expert in the psychology of terrorists. "This is not an elaborate joke. These are rational people." He drew on his pipe.

"Highly irrational, I'd say," the vice-president responded.

"Not so. You see—" Jones was interrupted by a knock at the large oak door in the far corner of the room. Everyone looked around. The door opened, and the uniformed arm of a Marine sergeant was visible. The director of the Central Intelligence Agency, Corbin Williston, walked in.

"Mr. Vice-President," he said, "I am sorry to be late. Traffic seems to be unaccountably heavy for a Wednesday afternoon." He strode to the empty chair on the vice-president's right hand.

"We understand, Corbin, and I hope you don't mind that we have begun. Not, I think, that we have gotten very far, except to confirm our own ignorance."

Williston surveyed the room, spotting Nancy Dolby and the yellow lined pad in front of her. "Mr. Vice-President, before we go on, I thought I had explained my request that this group operate in strict secrecy and that no stenographer be present."

Dolby returned his glare. "I'm not a—"

"Corbin," the vice-president interrupted, amid a few nervous chuckles, "Miss Dolby's whammy is worse than yours, especially when riled. May I introduce the deputy mayor of New York."

Dolby stood up and extended her arm to Williston. "I'm pleased to meet you, Mr. Williston. I think you'll find, in addition to everything else, that I even know how to take notes." She smiled stiffly and sat back down.

"Delighted," said Williston, unconvinced. Jones looked at her jot onto the note pad: "Williston: chauvinist."

"Now Corbin, here's Art Doolittle, chief of cryptanalysis at the Defense Intelligence Institutes."

"Yes, I know of your work."

"I'm honored, sir."

"And Will Watkins, specialist in Arab affairs at State." Watkins leaned across the table to shake hands.

"Dr. Newton Jones, chief of psychiatry at Veterans and special consultant to the Defense Department." They nodded gravely.

"And Jennings Pinckney, legal adviser to the secretary of state."

"Hi," said Pinckney, instantly regretting the foolishness of the sound.

"And that's the lot of us, at least for now, except of course for Dr. Kowalski. Please take a seat, Corbin."

"I think it is just as well to confine it to this group," Williston said. "If it gets any larger we'll just be getting in each other's way."

"The president wants this group to come up with a plan of action," the vice-president said. "That doesn't preclude him from asking others to do so as well, and he intends to feel free to consult with any of us individually, as he sees fit."

"I understand," Williston said. "And I might suggest, for the benefit of all of us, that we agree on one or two ground rules at the start."

"What do you have in mind?"

Williston leaned forward, looking slowly at each person around the table. "These proceedings have to be absolutely confidential. It is the nature of intelligence that any scrap of information can be useful, no matter how trivial it may seem, to one who is trained to fit it together with other scraps. So for starters," he looked at Dolby, "no one should carry any notes out of this room. If necessary, and I suppose it will be, we may all consult our staffs to follow up suggestions or plans this group may come up with, but no talking except by secure phone or in person in a secure place. No conversations about any of this otherwise. You would be astonished at what those who want to can pluck right from thin air."

Dolby, who had begun drawing lines on her scratch pad when Williston started talking, now doodled the word "anal."

"I see no objection in principle," the vice-president said. "I assume I'm speaking for the group. O.K.? Good. Now then, we were talking about what el-Wasi might have in mind. Corbin, have you had a chance to review your files?"

"Yes, sir."

"And?"

"We know as little—"

Sykes snorted.

"—as the military does. But what we do know, I have here." He pulled a file from his briefcase, and removed eight copies of a small report which he distributed. "This is a summary of what we know about el-Wasi. I suggest everyone take a couple of minutes and read it."

DOSSIER: HASHIM EL-WASI

Hashim el-Wasi was born in 1936 to a religious family in Jerusalem, in what was then British-Mandate Palestine, and has carried a deep sense of his Moslem identity throughout his life.

El-Wasi's father was active in counterinsurgency operations directed against the Jewish underground. In 1948, when the State of Israel came into existence, el-Wasi's father remained within Israel to participate covertly in the war. Two days after it began, el-Wasi was awakened by gunfire in his home, and saw Israeli machinegunners kill his father.

El-Wasi fled with his mother and sister to the Gaza Strip and joined several hundred thousand refugees encamped in squalor: shacks without running water, cramped, inadequate, and nearly devoid of health or hygiene care, and barren of any cultural, educational, or economic life. During the first year in Gaza, el-Wasi saw both his sister and mother raped, by masked and unknown men, while others held him at knife-point.

He was educated early in revolutionary tactics by many of the cells that developed in Gaza. Available information suggests experience in constructing and placing demolition charges in sensitive areas during clandestine forays into Israel: exploding homes, warehouses, pumping stations.

With financial and other assistance from Libyan activists enrolled in Egyptian schools, el-Wasi began formal education. In the mid-fifties he studied at the university in Alexandria, where he showed particular interest in religion and political science. With financial assistance from President Nasser, he and several friends created the General Union of Palestinian Students, which still exists. Members of this group, including el-Wasi, received training from Egyptian military personnel and conducted occasional raids into Israel.

After taking his degree, he won a scholarship to study law in the United States at the University of Chicago. He attended there for nearly three years but returned to Egypt before receiving his degree.

In the early sixties he traveled extensively throughout Egypt, Jordan, Syria, and Lebanon. His activities appear to have been organizational and political, rather than military. He also visited Libya, where his activities appeared to be financial.

El-Wasi appeared greatly concerned during this period at the absence of a centrally recognized and coordinated Palestinian organization. In May 1964, he convened leaders of various Palestinian military factions and organized them into a Palestinian Constituent Congress. This group hosted a series of national councils, which evolved into an umbrella organization called the Palestine Liberation Or-

*ganization. From its earliest days el-Wasi was a member
of the PLO's Executive Committee, and later became head
of the movement.*

*At its inception, el-Wasi drafted the PLO charter, which
the Executive Committee unanimously approved. El-Wasi's
political motivations can best be understood by reference
to several of that charter's points:*

- *Palestine is the homeland of the Arab Palestinian people.*
- *The Zionist occupation and the dispersal of the Palestinian Arab people do not make them lose their Palestinian identity or their right to live in their homeland.*
- *The Palestinian masses constitute one national front
working for the retrieval of Palestine through armed
struggle.*
- *The 1947 UN Partition Resolution, and the establishment of the state of Israel, are illegal.*
- *The PLO is the representative of the Palestinian revolutionary forces.*
- *Commando action constitutes the nucleus of the Palestinian popular liberation war.*

*In December 1968, el-Wasi achieved his first notable
accomplishment as a military tactician when several of his
soldiers attacked an El Al plane at Athens airport, killing
an Israeli passenger and wounding a stewardess. Several
months later he organized a similar gunfire attack on an
El Al plane in Zurich airport, killing the copilot and wounding the pilot. He reportedly was behind several other partially successful terrorist attacks on civilians during the
next several years. It is significant that el-Wasi's powers
as a spokesman permitted him to convey his religious fervor
so effectively that the fighters who did his bidding acted
basically as kamikazes, with only a minuscule chance of
survival for themselves.*

*By the early seventies el-Wasi's activities had escalated.
In February 1970, he personally planted explosives in the
wings of a Swissair plane which blew up in midair, killing
47 passengers and crew members, including 15 Israelis.*

By the end of the year he had demonstrated an effective capacity for coordinated international activity: His men hijacked three planes en route from Amsterdam, Zurich, and Frankfurt to New York, with over four hundred passengers among them, forced them to land in Egypt and Jordan, and blew up the planes there.

El-Wasi's activities were sufficiently successful that the king of Jordan, where el-Wasi had conducted many of his training sessions, apparently feared that his skills might be turned toward the throne, and he was expelled that September. Thereafter el-Wasi's major outposts were in various villages in southern Lebanon. To protect himself from a growing list of enemies, including jealous leaders of several rival Palestinian factions, he built up a cadre of extremely loyal lieutenants, who led units that killed numerous civilians over the next several years.

Shortly after the separation of powers following the 1973 Mideast war, el-Wasi concluded that the world did not recognize his movement as a valid and institutional antagonist of Israel. In successive months during the spring of 1974, therefore, el-Wasi's suicide squads struck twice inside northern Israel, killing Israeli children inside the settlements of Qiryat Shemona and Ma'alot. Half a year later el-Wasi received his first invitation to address the General Assembly of the United Nations, which he regarded as the first formal international recognition of himself as leader of the Palestinian movement.

In 1975, el-Wasi suffered what he considered a profound military defeat. He equipped one of his teams with grenades and bazookas for an attack on a departing El Al jet at Orly Airport in Paris. His apparent objective was to demonstrate the PLO's abilities with weaponry far heavier than had been generally imagined. The attack failed, and his men were forced to barricade themselves inside the airport bathroom. Although they were eventually released safely following negotiations, el-Wasi feared that this defeat would seriously undermine his prestige throughout the Arab world.

He therefore considered it imperative that his next operation be both spectacular and successful, so he set in motion the hijacking of an Air France jet in June 1976. He travelled clandestinely to the Entebbe Airport in Uganda to negotiate personally for the release of imprisoned terrorists in return for the lives of the passengers.

Notwithstanding his escape following the Israeli rescue operation, the debacle at Entebbe was a deep professional humiliation. El-Wasi's personal participation in the project soon became known within the Palestinian movement, and he feared serious damage to his position as leader of the movement. He appears to have gone underground for months at a time. It was at this juncture that he turned his efforts once more toward diplomacy rather than military strategy. His bid for an invitation to address the UN General Assembly was an effort to reassert his supremacy at the apex of the Palestinian hierarchy.

El-Wasi's accomplishments stamp him as a man of substantial intellectual, organizational, and military abilities. He is functionally rational in all respects, though many of his actions appear to have deeply rooted religious motivations. His leadership of the Palestinian movement obviously requires great personal skill and perseverance. His extraordinary perception of human psychology means that he cannot be approached by simple appeals to his ego or flair for the dramatic. El-Wasi is politically sensitive, as well as being militarily bold and skilled. He is, in short, a very difficult adversary.

While the Emergency Group read there was a knock at the door and the guard delivered a note to the vice-president. He handed it to Williston, who read it quickly and tucked it into his pocket. The vice-president looked at him. He nodded slightly.

"This is all very odd," Watkins muttered.

"How so?"

"Well, aside from what we know about him, there is so much we don't know. He is apparently an able theoretician, but there don't seem to be any writings. To whom does he theorize? And about what, exactly?"

"Dr. Jones?"

"I share Mr. Watkins' unease. We know too little about him to formulate a plan. We need more."

There was a silence. "Do we need so much for a plan of rescue?" Dolby asked.

"Absolutely," Jones said. "It's essential. We must try to anticipate how he will react to whatever we propose. You can't storm a place like the UN, if that's what you have in mind. We have to try to talk him out."

"Unlikely," said Sykes.

"How are we going to get this information?" Dolby asked.

"That, my dear Miss Dolby, is a good question," Williston answered. "We're working on it."

She underlined the word "chauvinist" on her pad. "I think we should consider recommending that the President order the army to storm the place."

"Our agents abroad are making inquiries as we speak," said Williston, ignoring her suggestion. "I expect that we will know more by morning."

"But in the meantime shouldn't we be planning how to break in there?" Watkins asked. "I mean real plans. It's very tense in New York. How can we wait for some agents to tell us about el-Wasi's mother or whatever?"

"I don't like this waiting any more than you. I want action, too," Sykes interjected. "But Williston is right on this. We don't know enough. We don't know if it's bluff, whether el-Wasi will deal, whether he really wants what he says, whether it isn't just some publicity stunt."

"I doubt that it's a stunt or a bluff," Williston said. "From what we do know—there have been rumors of activity in Iraq, Syria, and South Yemen—something big has been afoot for a while. I will not be surprised to learn that whatever it is, it's exactly what el-Wasi referred to. In fact we have information that suggests Arab agents are already in the States. The FBI is looking for them right now."

"In New York, I presume, for a seventh Arab in a white robe?" Dolby asked.

Williston had requested the FBI and Secret Service to leak no information to anyone, particularly New York City officials. He exchanged a glance with Sykes, then turned back to Dolby. "Who told you about the seventh Arab that got off the plane?"

"Nobody," she answered. "I saw it on television. I counted them."

"I see." The others smiled.

"Who told you, Mr. Williston?"

"That, I'm afraid, I am not at liberty to say, Miss Dolby." It sounded limp. Dolby was about to speak again, but remembering the mayor's instructions, stopped short. She toyed with the top button of her blouse as Williston sat back in his chair.

"Then I take it there is nothing more we can do today?" the vice-president asked. He looked around the table. No one spoke. "Okay, we stand adjourned until, say, eight-thirty tomorrow morning—or sooner if necessary. For those of you who do not already have them, direct lines to the White House will be installed in your home or hotel room by this evening." He started to rise.

"Mr. Vice-President, before we leave, one note of cheer, with your permission," Williston said. "I received a note a few minutes ago confirming an addition to our group. A foreign addition. One of the most highly placed and secret operatives in Israeli intelligence. The name would mean nothing to you, but he will be joining us tomorrow. The Israeli government's decision to cooperate was crucial and we have Dr. Kowalski to thank for it. That is where he has been this afternoon, arranging for our tenth member."

Now the vice-president stood and as the group dispersed, he signaled to Williston to stay back.

"Can I offer you a lift?" Sykes called out. "The chopper is ready."

"Thanks, in a moment," Williston said, then turning to a somber vice-president.

"What can you tell the president at this point? We seem to be no better off than this morning."

"We're not, unfortunately. I'll just have to tell him to keep a tight ass."

FORT BRAGG, NORTH CAROLINA

It had disturbed his first morning cup of coffee. Col. Arthur McDougal crumpled the top-secret message he had just received from the Pentagon and tossed it into his shredder. He stared out the window morosely. The message contained but a single word: "Prepare." It was the prearranged signal that meant his squad had been tapped for the dirtiest job in the world at the moment: the liberation of the United Nations.

Colonel McDougal commanded the K Detachment of the U.S. Army Special Forces. This detachment, like its predecessors D through J, had undergone antiterrorist training at Fort Bragg, and it was now supposed to be an elite unit of commandoes capable of striking back anywhere within the continental United States. But Colonel McDougal knew better than anyone that his 193 handpicked volunteers from all four uniformed services were not yet competent to do the job.

To begin with they had rehearsed mainly on Boeing 707s, and the only building they had ever swarmed into had been a deserted two-story barracks that was not ringed with explosives and armed gunmen inside. This was certainly not the training of the German antiterrorist commandoes of GSG 9 who had performed with surgical proficiency at Mogadishu airport in Somalia in October 1977. McDougal had pleaded with Washington for a larger budget, more training time, and a broader array of targets on which to practice. But the operational authority was confused, with more than twenty-five separate government agencies represented on a Working Group on Terrorism that spent most of their time fighting among themselves. None claimed exclusive jurisdiction and none ceded it to others. Not until 1978, in fact, had it become clear that the army, not the FBI, would have primary responsibility for domestic operations of the sort now required in New York. And K

Detachment's planning operations were kept so secret that they remained unknown to any member of the Emergency Group but Dr. Kowalski.

McDougal kneaded his knuckles on both temples, brushing his closely cropped gray hair up and down. It was the only way he could think clearly through panic. There was still a chance—if he had time to prepare a tailored attack and if he did not have to accept a canned scenario from some "crisis manager" who dictated impossible schemes from the safety of an office that never saw the light of day in the "B" ring of the Pentagon. But how much time could he buy?

He picked up the telephone, his mind made up. Relentless rehearsal would begin immediately. His staff officer came on the line. "Purple alert," McDougal barked, and there was no mistaking his tone.

"Yes, sir!" the major said in a voice full of enthusiasm. McDougal winced at the eagerness. He too had had it once. That was before the experience of battle had convinced him he had chosen a foolish career. McDougal learned to detest heroics, and now he would be demanding it of all his men. This whole operation would be brutal.

He needed help, someone outside his chain of command, someone knowledgeable, someone he could trust. He knew only one such person, a man he had served under years before in Vietnam, "Whiskers" Sykes. Pray that he was not on leave in Katmandu. It was risky to breach security like this but he considered it essential. McDougal put through a call to Washington.

MID-SINAI

Dressed in flight gear, Avram Tal faced several dozen Israeli agents inside one of the hills that served as a briefing room. They wore plain khaki uniforms, devoid of any insignia, not even military rank. To outward appearances they were unarmed. They were the Aleph commandoes. There was a chill in the air and the muffled drone of aircraft a distance away.

"Now we know the meaning of those whispers we have heard for so many months. Our enemy has chosen a bold course. Now their plan, if not the means of implementation, is in the open. And what is known even a little, can be known, to us, completely, in time. I assume el-Wasi's colleagues will be operating in watertight units of three or four and that they are already dispersed. My part, unfortunately, is to be played in Washington, where I have now been ordered to go. But we will still be working together.

"Mordecai." Tal looked at a man directly in front of him—Mordecai Ofir, his chief of staff. Ofir, a tall man with closely cropped brown hair and dark, piercing eyes, had had private discussions with Tal that morning. "I'm leaving you in command here in Israel while I am away. In time you may be following me with a group of the other men."

Neither Tal nor his men were given to displays of emotion. He held himself erect and cocked his head slightly to one side. "Shalom," he said. Then he waved to them and walked out into the night and a waiting plane.

אOCTOBER 5:א
THE NEXT DAY

CHICAGO

At 1000 East Ohio Street, on the west shore of Lake Michigan, sits the James W. Jardine Water Purification Plant, the largest of its type in the world. The 1.7 billion gallons of water it filters each day are delivered to more than three million people in Chicago and fifty-four suburban communities by means of seven pumping stations located throughout the city.

Shortly after 2 A.M., an eighteen-wheel trailer-truck pulled up to the south doors of an old armory two blocks from the Chicago Avenue pumping station, which delivers water to more than 180,000 people in central Chicago along the posh residential area known as the Gold Coast. The man in the passenger seat jumped to the ground and went to the large doors. He turned the dial on the combination lock several times, then swung them open. The driver flashed on his headlights and drove into the dark cavernous building. The other man closed the doors behind.

The driver left the truck, taking with him a 40-watt battery-operated floodlight, which he placed near the far wall. In the dim light they could see that the armory was empty. The other man walked to the rear of the truck and opened the back door. "Let's get to work," he said, and a third man climbed down from inside the trailer onto the concrete floor.

The emptiness of the armory made it appear even bigger. It was windowless but for one wall, and the ceiling was over thirty feet high. In a corner on the back wall was a thicket of pipes that came up through the floor and extended to the ceiling. The driver walked to the back of the truck and signaled to the others. They opened the back door. Inside were dozens upon dozens of gleaming barrels stacked along the sides and lashed together with rope. In the center was a large electric water pump. The three slid the pump down off the truck, and two continued to shove it close to the tangle of pipes. The third man untied the ropes and began to roll the barrels down the slide toward the pump.

Thirty minutes later, one of them, a plumber by training, succeeded in tapping the discharge end of the pump into a large pipe connected to the water main. After the last bit of tightening, he let his wrench clatter to the ground. He turned a valve on, and water began to flow backward from the large pipe into the pump. He emitted a satisfied grunt and shut the valve again. The other two, meanwhile, had been splitting open the barrels and pouring their contents, a fine red powder, into a large funnel that emptied into a conveyor belt, which in turn ran to a bowl-shaped metal drum, open from above. The plumber connected a pipe from a spigot on the side of the drum into another water pipe on the side of the wall. He then opened the valve at both ends and water began to fill up the drum, which would serve as the pump intake. The drum was large: It would hold 500 gallons of water, and the rate of flow from the pipe on the wall meant that it would be 40 minutes before it was full. The other two continued to pour the red powder into the funnel.

At 3:15, when the drum was filled about halfway up, one of the men flicked a switch and the conveyor belt began to turn. It squeaked a bit, but ran smoothly enough. After the black rubber belt finished a full cycle, the same man pulled a lever on the funnel overhead and the powder began to spill down onto the belt, making a long lumpy tail that lurched forward and fell off into the drum ten seconds later. After two or three minutes, the water in the drum turned a deep claret-red.

At 3:30 only three feet of air remained at the top of the drum. The plumber climbed up a ladder propped against the side and peered in. He made a motion as if to drink it and looked at the others. He grinned.

"Ready?" the short one asked.

"Ready," said the plumber, clambering down the ladder. The third man ran to the wall. On a signal he opened the valve on the pipe on the wall. Water began to run into the pump's discharge end. Simultaneously, the plumber started up the 75-horsepower motor. Clanking and sloshing noises now filled the room, echoing off the high ceiling. The incoming rush of water was stopped within seconds, and the flow reversed, the pump sending the murky red water from the drum back up into the water main. The plumber scurried around his machine, checking. The seals did not leak. Water continued to flow evenly into the drum, met by the continual spray of the conveyor belt's cargo.

"How long?" the short one asked.

"About forty minutes. If we had not found a building like this so close to the pumping station, much longer. But the water has very little distance to travel. We could not have ordered a better location."

"Unguarded."

"Of course. Americans have not yet learned to guard everything. Perhaps after tonight they will."

They fell silent. At 3:55 the short one went to the cabin of the truck. From the seat he took a small box and carried it to the belt. He untied the brown twine and tore off the paper in which it was wrapped. "Now?" he asked. The others nodded. "Now, I think," he said faintly. He opened the box, tilted it sideways, and began to sprinkle a fine white powder over the belt as he walked down its length. He emptied the entire contents, 3 kilograms, then threw the box on the ground. Within ten seconds the white powder disappeared over the side of the drum.

The three stood and watched in silence. "When," the plumber asked at last, "do we get paid?"

The driver stared at him. "You will be paid when the entire job is successfully completed."

At 4:10 the supply of red powder was exhausted. "Finished," said the short man. The plumber pulled down a lever, shutting off the pump. Then he quickly turned the two valves on the pipes on the wall. All water ceased flowing.

"Quickly," said the short man, "you know what to do. We have only five minutes." They ran to the truck. From the cabin, the man who had driven the truck extracted a small suitcase and ran to the west wall, placing the suitcase near a door. The other two each took what appeared to be fire extinguishers and began to spray the room, beginning near the pump and pipes and working their way backward toward the door. When they were about fifteen feet away from the door, the man standing there opened the suitcase and removed a small gun coupled with a silencer. "May Allah be merciful," he murmured. Then he stood in the doorway. The backs of the two men were silhouetted against the floodlight. He fired twice. The two bodies crumpled to the ground.

Grabbing one of the extinguishers, he sprayed their bodies and continued to spray as he backed up to the door. He put the extinguisher down when he came abreast of the wall and began to undress. From the suitcase he took a neatly pressed business suit, a shirt, tie, and a pair of spit-polished Gucci loafers. He dressed quickly, more from the cold than from his timetable. He was on schedule. He knotted the tie and felt underneath the other two suits for an envelope. From it he took a small penlight and examined the three passports inside. He put one inside his jacket pocket. He then scooped up the suitcase, the discarded clothes, the other suits and shoes, and the remaining passports and carried them to the bodies. He dropped them on top. He took the fire extinguisher again and soaked them thoroughly.

Then for the last time he went to the truck and removed a steel five-gallon can of gasoline. He picked it up, his fingers almost slipping as he lowered it to the ground. He held his arms far out; he did not wish to soil his suit. The can made a sharp retort when it hit the ground; he could not hold it the last six inches. He swore out loud now, as he pried the lid off the can. Then he walked to the rear of the truck and removed the gas tank cap.

He did not pause to look around. He walked straight to the door, stopping only to pick up the other fire extinguisher. He sprayed out a line on the floor from the bodies to the door. He tossed the can inside the room and felt in his pocket for a pack of matches. His hands were trembling slightly as he lit the first. He tossed it to the ground, but the flame went out before it hit the floor. He stooped over, and quickly lit three matches, touching them to the spot where he had sprayed. The flame of the third match caught, and a streak of fire sped down toward the bodies. These burst into flame. He waited a few seconds, until he was sure that the clothes and bodies would be consumed and that the fire would continue on toward the waiting pools of gasoline. The fire fanned out along the floor. He had three minutes, at most.

He walked out the door, leaving behind the musty air of the armory, and turned right. At the corner he turned left and walked a block to the Ritz-Carlton Hotel, where taxis are always waiting. "O'Hare," he said, slamming the door.

"Right," the cabbie answered, without turning around. The car pulled away from the curb.

"How long to the airport?"

"Twenty, twenty-five minutes," the driver responded. "You in a hurry?"

"No, no hurry. Take your time." He closed his eyes and leaned his head back. As they rounded the corner and began up North Michigan Avenue, they heard the explosion. The taxi did not slow.

The man got out at the O'Hare Hilton. He registered under an unremarkable name, then found a pay phone in the lobby. He dialed a police precinct.

"Sergeant Bevins," a voice answered.

The caller spoke several sentences in rapid Arabic. Bevins looked at the receiver.

The caller heard someone in the background call out to

Bevins: "What is it, Charlie?"

"A wino," Bevins replied, "talkin' drunken Spanish."

"Hang up on him."

Bevins spoke again into the receiver. "Talk English or I'll hang up."

"Very well," the voice answered. "Listen closely because you'll only get it once. The lives of two hundred thousand people in Chicago depend on your listening and remembering what I have to say."

"Say, what is—"

"Just shut up, Bevins, and listen. The Chicago water supply has been contaminated. Do not drink the water. Do not let anyone drink the water."

"Yeah? How do I know that? And who are you? Why are you telling me this? What do you want?"

"I am calling to warn you. If you do not take action, officer, I shall let your chief and the mayor know that it was you who failed to prevent a catastrophe."

"Is that so? Hey, Mike, something's wrong. Fellow says the water's contaminated. Go turn on the water, will you? Tell me if you see anything funny."

The conversation stopped. The Arab heard a muffled cry; "Oh, sweet mother of Jesus."

"What is it Mike?"

"It's fucking red as a monkey's ass."

"I repeat, Mr. Bevins," the man said from the pay phone, "that water is deadly. Do not drink it. And you had better sound the alarm."

"Hey! Who the hell is this?"

"A friend." He hung up the phone. He looked at his watch. 4:58. He took the elevator to his room and stretched out on the bed. He fell asleep at once. All that remained was to wake in time for an afternoon flight to London, and on to Cairo. From there it was an easy journey to his next assignment.

At 5:05, as the Arab fell asleep, a man several miles south stumbled out of bed with a terrible thirst. Careful not to wake his wife, he felt his way in the darkness for the bathroom. He found the faucet with his hand and reached for the plastic bathroom cup. Unable to see the water's color, he filled the cup and drank. His stomach seemed to explode and he sank to the floor. His wife would discover him two hours later, dead.

Miraculously, he was one of only 89 unlucky ones. Within ten minutes of the Arab's call, sound trucks were beginning to patrol the streets with warnings. The radio stations had been alerted. Those who turned on their lights before drinking could see the thick wine-colored liquid, and hesitated. Most of Chicago awoke to a message repeated over and over: "Do not drink the water."

In the meantime, firemen sought to subdue the armory blaze with gushing red water. Twelve hooks and ladders answered the call. But there was little to save. When they finally extinguished the fire, little inside was left to be identified but two skeletons, some lumps of metal, and an 18-wheel truck.

GENERAL ASSEMBLY HALL

The ambiance of the Hall had changed. Wires tied to explosive charges traced the walls and every door. The Palestinians stood guard at each of the four walls, their guns always within reach. The delegates had been ordered not to leave their seats without permission.

At four-hour intervals, those occupying different sections of seats were permitted to stretch by walking for several minutes up and down a designated aisle. Any delegate wishing to use the lavatory could, by raising his hand, do so. It had been placed in the rear section of the Hall, too far from any of the doors to try to outrun the guns.

El-Wasi sat in one of the chairs on the podium. The other two chairs were empty. On the podium were his two television sets. El-Wasi ignored the one showing the deserted delegates' entrance to the building; the picture never varied, and it showed life only when, three times a day, the police rolled up the large multi-tiered food cart and one of the Arabs emerged briefly to roll it in. El-Wasi smiled as the newscaster on the other set concluded a description of the poisoned Chicago water supply. Then he saw his own face on the screen, watching the television. He switched it off, walked off the podium to the rostrum, and began.

"We appeal to you to enable our people to establish national independent sovereignty over our own land. Though our appeal is now no longer passive, bear in mind that we are still a peaceful people. Be grateful that it is we, rather than our less moderate brethren, who now confront you. We have today given you a sign both of our benevolence and our power. You in this Hall are probably the only people in the world who have not yet heard that we have successfully poisoned the water system of Chicago."

A stir spread across the Hall. El-Wasi paused, to let his casual announcement sink in and be appreciated.

"Yet we are not people of death, but of life, and so we gave the people of that city a warning—we turned the water red so they would know not to drink. Next time, we shall not be so considerate. There will be no more warnings. And the red next time will be blood."

El-Wasi was pleased. This time the delegates were paying him respectful attention. He could afford a generous statement, a message of hope. He held his right hand up high, as though he were pronouncing a benediction.

"But there need not be a next time, as you know. You should not look at yourselves as the jailed but as the jailers—your freedom is your own choice.

"Enough of generalities, enough of talk. We have had too much of that for too many years. We must now be practical and turn to the business side. The PLO has drafted a proposed resolution which, in accordance with the duly promulgated rules of this Assembly, we hereby move this body to vote upon and accept. I will read it now. Upon its acceptance and implementation by immediate action of the major powers, this siege will end.

> The General Assembly, having met in special session at the request of the Palestine Liberation Organization to consider the question of the future of the land of Palestine, and having concluded that the present situation in Palestine is one which is likely to impair the general welfare and friendly relations

among nations, does hereby affirm, resolve, find, and decree as follows:"

The ambassadors of several countries were taking notes. Many had found the pain of confinement tolerable by seeking pretexts for attention on something other than their own situations. A proposed resolution was just the thing to occupy them. El-Wasi continued.

"1.   The resolution of the General Assembly of November 29, 1947, heretofore regarded as legitimatizing the present State of Israel is hereby revoked and declared null, void, and of no legal force or effect;

2.   All armaments of any nature presently in the possession, custody, or control of the Government of Israel or any citizen of Israel shall be forthwith delivered to depositories to be promptly established by the General Assembly, and to be delivered to such agencies as the succeeding Government shall decree;

3.   The existence of the State of Israel is hereby terminated, effective immediately;

4.   All territories appropriated by the State of Israel subsequent to June 5, 1967, shall be restored forthwith to the countries from which those territories were appropriated;

5.   The territory, previously Israel, remaining after the return of the lands set forth in the preceding paragraph shall be hereafter known as Palestine; and

6.   The Palestine Liberation Organization is hereby recognized as the lawful Government of Palestine."

El-Wasi looked up from his papers. "Fellow delegates," he said, "we now vote."

The podium in the Hall is flanked on both sides by two prominent panels on which are printed the names of all member states of the General Assembly. Beside each name are three bulbs, each a different color. Each member country records its vote by pressing one of three buttons at its table, which activates a corresponding bulb beside its name on the panels in the front. A green light reflects a "yes" vote, a red "no," and a yellow "abstain."

"I call on the ambassador of Afghanistan," el-Wasi said.

WASHINGTON, D.C.

The first news that the Chicago water supply had been poisoned reached the CIA communications center over the AP wire service at 5:27 A.M. The duty officer did not at first connect it with the director's request to be awakened at any time that any news seeming to relate to the UN hijacking came in. His instruction was: "Bombings, hijackings, explosions, major kidnappings, political assassinations, any bizarre killings other than random individual ghetto murders, and anything else that might be part of the UN terrorists' threats." It took a few minutes to realize that the poisoning of a city water system could fit the scheme and was included in the instructions. The duty officer made the connection when an AP amplification at 5:35 stated that an anonymous caller speaking a foreign language had warned the police without making any demands.

At 5:36 the telephone rang in Corbin Williston's McLean bedroom. "Sir, Duty Officer. Sorry to wake you but I think they've struck." Williston pushed the conference call button on his telephone and the duty officer's voice filled the room. Williston began dressing as they talked. "No, don't wake the president. There's nothing he can do at this point. He'll find out in an hour anyway, and we should know more then. But call the vice-president now and tell him I suggest we meet at 7:30 at the White House with the Emergency Group. And send the car out immediately. I'll stop by my office first."

The White House switchboard never sleeps. By 6:15, every member of the Emergency Group had been called at the request of the vice-president and summoned to the early morning meeting. General Sykes was already dressed and in the midst of preparing breakfast; the others were soundly asleep. Nancy Dolby walked groggily down to her hotel lobby and saw a stack of newspapers tied in a bundle on the front desk. The headlines were huge. "Can I buy a paper?" she asked.

"Your room number, Madam?" She gave it. "I'll just

scratch your room off the list and you can have one now," said the clerk. She was staying in one of those hotels that believes it can afford to throw in a 20-cent newspaper for a $40-a-night room. Nancy Dolby, who never stayed in hotels, thought it gracious.

"ARABS HIJACK UN, HOLD 156 HOSTAGES," the headline screamed. A large center picture, obviously taken from a TV screen, showed el-Wasi standing at the General Assembly podium holding a gun. This was all terribly old news, Dolby thought. Nothing about any new emergency. Then it dawned on her: all this had happened less than twenty-four hours before; this was the first morning edition to hit the streets with news about any of it. Probably nothing that happened past 10 or 11 o'clock last night could be printed. Whatever she read in the papers was likely to be very old to her from now on.

It would be a crime to pay five dollars for breakfast in the hotel. New York could treat her when she really needed it. She went outside and found a coffee shop.

The place was empty, except for a counterman whose back was turned as she entered. He was fussing with several large coffee urns, preparing for the morning rush. The radio reported sketchily on the disaster in Chicago. She listened silently and, when it was over, cleared her throat. The counterman turned around and stared. Women with an air of such self-assurance and expensive tastes did not sit at his counter very often. She returned the stare coolly, without averting her eyes.

"Morning," he finally said. "Coffee?"

She nodded, said, "and buttered toast," then looked down at her paper and ignored him.

"How do you suppose they could poison the whole water supply like that?" the man asked her. She shook her head. He slid a mug of steaming black coffee along the counter. "They must have a bunch of confederates, if you ask me. Next thing you know we'll have to boil all our water. Not that anybody'd drink red water, no matter how goddamn clean it is."

She looked up at him.

"Oh, excuse me, Madam."

She smiled. "Doesn't bother me. I'm from New York."

"Well, you picked a good time to be out of that city, that's for sure. Although they've already struck there, so the people there are probably safe." He lowered his voice. "I have a theory about what they're going to do, actually."

"What's that?"

He paused to pull two slices from the toaster. As he served them to her, he looked around as if checking for eavesdroppers. No one else was in the place.

"I think they're going to hit every major city one at a time. Different trick in each place, you know. See, these guys in Chicago take off and fly down here and blow up the Washington Monument and go to Miami and set it on fire. You know, stuff like that."

"You think they can do that?"

"Well look what they done to Chicago. Why not? Probably can do anything."

"That's pretty expensive to do an operation like that."

"Nah. Besides, they've got all that oil money. Everytime you get in a car, you're settin' up another city."

"Setting up?"

"For poisoned water, you know, or bombs or whatnot. Yeah, they've got us now. The president, he'll say we won't give in, but then he'll just make a coupla phone calls and give it all away. He's probably rigged this thing with the Arabs so's they can make a deal under the table and get this Israel thing off his back once and for all. Probably has some committee workin' away on how to whip the pants off those guys in New York and all the while he's talkin' on the phone to Egypt. Only question is how many cities he'll let them blow up first."

Dolby fumbled in her purse for money. She stood up and put a dollar-bill on the table. He saw the distress on her face. The corners of her mouth pulled down in a tiny frown and her look was definitely disapproving.

"Hey, listen, sometimes I sort of run off at the mouth, you know. Jesus, I never thought, I mean no one who ever comes in here would—listen, Ma'am, you don't happen to be acquainted with the president or anything?"

"No, I never met him."

The man seemed relieved. "You know," he said, "he only works a coupla blocks away but I've never met him, either. Shows you."

Dolby thanked him for his service and walked to the door.

"Have a good day," he shouted after her.

She cleared White House security at 7:20. Dr. Jones was already in the Emergency Group's conference room. On the table was a tray of stale coffee cake and a solitary pot of coffee with stacked plastic cups. "I think we'll need a food committee," Dr. Jones greeted her.

"At least that one might accomplish its mission."

The others arrived shortly. Last to enter were the vice-president and Drognan Kowalski, deep in conversation. The others stopped talking. The vice-president looked around as he took his seat. "I think we had better wait for Corbin Williston. He's driving in with our Israeli agent. Anyway, they'll be here presently, and it doesn't make much sense to start before they arrive. So help yourself to some breakfast." Before they could, Williston entered the room with Avram Tal. After the introductions, the vice-president stood. "You have all heard about Chicago, I assume?" A chorus of yeses, gravely now. "El-Wasi is taking credit for it. I heard him on a newscast on the way here. Is it a coincidence, do you think, Will, a bluff, or was it really his operation?"

"It would be too great a coincidence, I think," Watkins said. "I don't doubt that it's the first of their threatened actions. It sounds like something they'd dream up, all right. And a nice touch, that, coloring the water red, so that people would be scared off drinking it."

"Not everyone was scared off," Williston interjected. "The last word I had was that 42 people have died so far, apparently drank the water in the dark. We have no idea how high the death toll may go—or when it will stop."

"I guess we know where that extra Arab went," Pinckney said. "He sure didn't stay around New York."

"It would take a lot more than one man, I assume, to poison the city water system," Watkins responded.

General Sykes cleared his throat. "No, not necessarily.

Wouldn't take much. Anyone could do it, actually. All it takes is a pump to deliver poison into the system at a pressure higher than the flow from the water main. A very simple principle. In 1976, a couple of federal employees tried to extort a million bucks from the city of Philadelphia. Threatened to pump a thousand gallons of heating oil into the water supply. They didn't do it. Got caught first because they were stupid. But they could have. Right, Tal?"

"You are correct, General. I have seen it done. Not a whole city. But the principle is the same. When the job is finished, you simply cart the pump away or blow it up on the spot."

"How many would it take to do such a thing?" Dolby asked.

"One could do it, but two or three could do it easily if they knew what they were doing."

"So it could be the seventh Arab alone, or working with another guy or two?"

"Well, maybe," said Sykes, "but it doesn't seem likely, does it?"

"Why not?"

"Seven men get into limousines at the airport. None could've got out along the way. Who would've let them? If anyone had, we would have had a report. So the one guy must escape detection in New York City, get back to the airport, arrange for a flight, get to Chicago, find a pump and poison and whatever else he needed, hide out until some hour of the morning, do the job, get rid of the pump, and disappear. Not likely."

"The flight, maybe, but not the rest of it. And besides, who? If someone else is cooperating, then we have more than one man to worry about anyway."

"And where could the guy have gone? Staying in Chicago is risky. The FBI is crawling all over there by now. If your hypothesis is that the one man from New York is el-Wasi's only operative, then it would be careless to chance being discovered. Whatever else el-Wasi is, he isn't careless."

"Only in the large sense," said Tal.

"Only if we do our jobs," Sykes shot back. "No, I don't

buy the theory that the seventh man flew there. El-Wasi must have had someone there already."

"Then he must have people in other places," Doolittle said, packing tobacco into his pipe.

"Why?"

"Because otherwise the theory would make no sense."

Doolittle stopped talking while he brought his pipe to his mouth, lit a match and watched the flame as he puffed, until the reassuring cloud of smoke surrounded his head and the sweet odor of Mixture 62 from Artie's Smoke Shop had gone halfway across the room. He puffed twice more, then removed the pipe and holding the bowl between two fingers, pointed the stem at Sykes.

"It's not a question of where they come from but of how many he has deployed. And two or three men, even if they started out in Chicago, wouldn't be enough for what he says they're going to do."

"That depends on what he has in mind."

"Do we believe that he really has other episodes planned?" Watkins asked.

"I think so," Tal said. "If he can pull off something spectacular like poisoning a city water system, then he has to do something for an encore or we'll know the rest is bluff. And he does not want us to think he is bluffing. That isn't the way they play it. Don't you agree, General?"

"Yes. I think we can assume at least this much—el-Wasi is not bluffing. He is in deadly earnest. He has men, how many I don't think we can say, planted in many places. Probably around the world, because if they had all come here I think someone would have noticed it. No secret of that dimension could be airtight. We can't know whether there's a pattern—how regular they will be—until the second one happens. But I think we must anticipate more attacks."

"That's awful," said Pinckney.

"Do you believe what el-Wasi said about the acts of violence being uncontrolled?" the vice-president asked.

"It sounds like a doomsday machine."

"Doomsday machine?" Dolby asked.

"A device that will destroy the world if it is set off,"

Sykes explained. "It is put in place and cocked as the ultimate deterrent. The theory is that no one will do whatever will set it off because then the world will be destroyed with certainty. You can't outbluff it because the actors place it out of even their own control. That's why there's no way to turn it off once it's set."

"What kind of device? You mean like a bomb?"

"Yes, or a series of autonomous terrorist attacks."

"But if they get their way, there would be no point in continuing with them. So there must be a way of turning them off."

"It would seem so. Therefore el-Wasi must have some kind of control."

"But perhaps only at the end—perhaps 'victory' is the only signal," Tal said. "Gentlemen, I fear that we have not brought out on the table the most critical element of all. That is time. How much time do we have?"

"Until the next attack? We have no way of knowing."

"I agree. But I was not referring to that time sequence, as critical as it is. I mean how much time for Israel? How much time until the assembled delegates begin to vote for her abolition?"

"But surely, that's no problem," the vice-president said. "The United States will never tolerate any interference with the sovereignty of Israel. You know that. Any such vote would be meaningless."

"I thank you, sir, for your statement. But some day—a week from now, two weeks, maybe more—the world will weary of this game. The world will not want to wait for us to remove the terrorists, even if we ever could. The world will just want to go back to its normal routine, and Israel will seem a minor sacrifice. Others may take action that you cannot stop. The final UN vote will be a thing for show, to lend a mask of respectability to a final act of genocide."

"You don't really suppose that the world would permit the destruction of Israel? They would see the illegality of that."

"It would be comforting to think so, Mr. Pinckney, but I am not so confident." Pinckney was flattered that Tal remembered his name. "May I show you something that suggests why your reliance on legalities is unrealistic?"

Tal removed his jacket and rolled up his left sleeve. The number 349576 was burned in purple on his forearm.

"Every day I see this number. When they branded me like a cow, Mr. Pinckney, it was done according to the laws of the Reich. That is why, you see, I feel no great confidence in legalities when the noose is tightened."

The ensuing silence was finally broken by a knock at the door. Pinckney started, his knees coming up under the table making a hard rapping sound. He winced. It was the Marine sergeant with a folder. He handed it to Williston wordlessly. Williston skimmed it while everyone waited.

"There was an explosion and fire in an armory two blocks from a water pumping station," he said, looking at the paper. "By the time the fire department got it out, there wasn't much to be found. The heat must have been intense. A trailer truck was blown up; must have had a full gas tank. Some kind of machine was found melted down, next to a steel drum, about 500-gallon capacity. It was plugged into some pipes on the wall. Lots of metal hoops lying around on the floor."

"That's how they did it," Sykes said. "Job completed and they put a match to a gasoline trail. Run like hell and boom."

"Apparently they didn't run like hell," Williston said, puffing at his pipe.

"What do you mean?"

"In the center of this warehouse, they found two skeletons, burned clean."

"Oh, my god," said Pinckney, covering his face.

"Any weapon found?" Tal asked.

"Why a weapon?" Watkins asked him.

"Because they're not likely to have simply tripped after setting this fire."

"Maybe the explosion was an accident."

"I doubt it."

Williston looked up from the file. "There was a metal lump across the room. Police think it was a Smith & Wesson .45."

Tal frowned. "Very neat."

"You mean they were murdered?" Pinckney asked, shock on his face.

"Of course."

"That is not the usual modus operandi of the Arab terrorists," Watkins observed.

"That is true, sir," Tal replied. "El-Wasi would not send in his best agents and then have two of them murdered by the third."

"Perhaps it was suicide?"

"The gun would not have been across the room. No, I think the pathologists will find that they were shot from behind, probably while they were soaking the room in gasoline. When they finish checking the dental records, I'm sure you'll find they were locals, not Arabs, recruited for the job. El-Wasi obviously means to stop at nothing. We must expect the worst. A time bomb, a series of time bombs, have been activated."

"We must eliminate el-Wasi," Pinckney said.

"Yes, my friend, we must, but not just yet, and anyway, how? We can do nothing to upset el-Wasi until we determine whether he has the power to shut off this madness. I think he has. He is too meticulous a planner to become a captive of a scenario, even if it is his own. But we must make sure. When we know for sure, then perhaps we will know also how to eliminate him."

"But how do we find all this out?"

"We need a psychological profile," Dr. Jones said.

"We have enough of a profile," Dolby replied. "Perhaps we need some action now."

"Not yet," said Williston at once. "There is only one way for us to go about this, and that is systematically. All we know about this operation so far are surface things. Not nearly enough. We have to go below that.

"We have a rather large budget," Williston continued, "larger than any of you might suppose, and certainly larger than el-Wasi could ever guess. I mean to use it. We will solicit and process all police and intelligence information on a continuing basis worldwide. That is step number one.

We in this room will study all this information every day, continually."

"All of it? That must be a lot of material."

"Langley headquarters will first go through it with a fine-tooth comb. They will give us whatever, I stress, whatever may conceivably be relevant."

"How are they going to know that?"

"We'll have to tell them."

"But we won't know unless we see it all."

"It's not quite that much of a problem. There are ways of siphoning out the garbage. But I agree with what you are implying. We will be burdened, especially at the start. But in time it will be winnowed down."

"If we have time," Tal said.

"If we have time."

"But that's not all," Dr. Jones added. "We must begin to formulate a negotiating position. We have to figure out what we can offer him."

"I venture we can offer nothing," Tal said.

"You may be right. But we can't discount the possibility."

"And another thing," said Tal.

"What's that?"

"We must study these events as they occur, otherwise we may miss their significance. I am assuming that there will be a pattern to what el-Wasi has planned. It is very difficult for the human mind to design a completely random series of events, at least at the level of action that el-Wasi has set in motion. A computer can spin out random numbers to give cryptanalysts plenty of headaches, but el-Wasi is not a machine. He's working under handicaps—logistics, supplies, communications, resources. His plan must have a pattern."

"I hope you're right, but I must say I'm not very optimistic about that," Watkins said. "The whole point of terrorism is confusion."

"This isn't simple terrorist action," General Sykes said. "The acts are terrible enough, and they may seem unpredictable and aimed at those who have no connection with them, but they have been planned by someone with a fixed goal in mind. This is a rare kind of tactical guerrilla warfare."

"Agreed," said Dr. Jones. "As I said before, el-Wasi is not crazy and he's not acting irrationally. In my judgment that is a big plus for us. All we have to do is find the method in his madness."

"That's all?"

"That's all."

The table fell silent again.

The vice-president looked around. "Very well then," he said, "let's take a break until two-thirty. From then on it's steady work. Will, I want you to have your people start putting together a functional history of Arab terrorism. I think we ought to know the details of everything they've done before. Corbin, I assume you can begin supplying us with intelligence information?"

Williston nodded.

"Dr. Jones, perhaps you can begin to consult with Colonel Tal. What patterns of terror might el-Wasi have in mind?"

"Jennings—"

Pickney's head perked up. "Yes, sir?"

"You put a list together of sanctions that are available to us on a worldwide basis against anyone that it might make sense to do that to."

"Yes, sir."

"And Art, you're in charge of analyzing for us all the cable traffic that you and the CIA can get your hands on."

"Right."

"Nancy, you start putting together a report on everything that is going on in New York—"

"That's a lot—"

"—relevant to the situation. I think we have to be updated constantly about anything that happens around the UN, inside and out."

"Yes," she said, and then added, "sir."

"Mr. Vice-President," Tal interjected. "I have a request."

"Yes?"

"I would like to be able to study everything that el-Wasi

has said so far. Is it possible to bring videotapes here so
that we can view them whenever we wish?"

"It's possible, yes, but is it necessary?"

"Nothing is necessary until it works, sir. We are working
with obviously limited data about this operation of el-
Wasi's. One can never tell what hidden, apparently incon-
sequential clue may be buried somewhere. We must make
maximum use of all data that is available, and so far el-
Wasi's speeches are our only source. I'd like to get videotapes brought here on a regular basis."

"Very well, you'll have the first one by this afternoon.
The Marines can see to the machine."

"One more thing," Tal added. "Have we looked into
what the police are doing in New York to keep the situation
under control?"

Sykes answered. "I have obtained through channels a
copy of a special police report detailing all phases of the
police response, everything from their deployment of men
to their weapons. I feel it is adequate."

"I'd like to look at that report," Tal said.

When Sykes hesitated, the vice-president answered.
"Let's defer that for awhile, Colonel Tal. It is rather sensitive material, you must understand, and really quite removed from our province as a group. Anything else?" The
vice-president looked around the table. Silence.

He stood. "Until two-thirty."

As the room cleared, Williston edged his way toward
the vice-president, who remained standing by his chair, a
distracted look on his face.

"An odd request," Williston said without emotion.

"Which?" the vice-president asked, turning to face him.

"Tal's, for the New York police report."

The vice-president nodded.

"I suggest," Williston said, "that we stick to your answer.
I don't see giving him anything relating to tactical options.
He's here to help us, but he's still an agent of a foreign
government."

"You've got no quarrel from me," the vice-president
replied.

They left the room together. On the table, lying open,

though neither happened to notice it, was Dolby's yellow pad. In a bold, angular hand, she had written: "Second day, no plan."

BONN

West German officials met all day under extraordinary security measures at the Chancellery. There were two separate concerns. The first and most immediate was whether Germany was vulnerable to el-Wasi's terrorists. The consensus was that the security police could prevent any major hit from being carried out within the national borders. Some had misgivings about such optimism, but, having no alternatives to suggest, they remained quiet.

The second concern was more global: How far might el-Wasi really go, and what should Germany be prepared to do about it? Here the pessimists carried the day. "He's in too far now not to burrow in further," said the vice-minister for foreign affairs. "He will come out dead—or the head of a new state."

It was agreed after considerable discussion that the latter possibility was dangerous to Germany's security because it would, in the long run, strengthen the Russian position. The minister of justice opined that the last thing Germany needed was to appear to have turned against the Jews once again. The majority agreed that resistance to el-Wasi's demands should be the German position, but for a different reason: Internal security is the paramount concern; symbols come later. German policy must thus be to oppose the terrorists. El-Wasi had extended an invitation to all governments to communicate with their captured representatives by the simple means of public television, and Germany would now accept the offer: The German ambassador to the UN would be instructed to continue to vote no.

But that was as far as Germany could go. Perhaps she could try to persuade others to vote no as well—or at least to abstain—but the military decisions were for the Americans. "We can help them buy time, but that is all we will purchase. It's their problem."

ℵOCTOBER 7:ℵ
TWO DAYS LATER

WNET-TV STUDIO,
NEW YORK CITY

In the middle of reading a news item on the continuing fall of the Dow Jones industrial average, Tyler Johnson was momentarily distracted by commotion behind the camera. An assistant producer waving a paper in his direction caught his eye. She was pushing aside crew members who blocked her path toward the light-drenched studio set. Johnson finished the item. The red light winked off: station break.

"Tyler!" She was running between the cameras, jumping over cables. She leaped onto the platform that held the dummy news desk.

"What is it? This is a short break."

"Sorry. You've got to scrap the rest. This just came in."

From the gloom of the studio someone yelled out: "Ten seconds." Johnson scowled.

The woman dropped two pages on the desk and hurried off the set, ducking as she scurried behind the camera.

Johnson picked them up and scanned the first page. He had not finished it when the red light went on again. Johnson looked up at the camera. He put on a serious face. "I have just been handed this late bulletin and have not read it fully myself. So please bear with me and I will read it exactly as it has been prepared in our newsroom.

"'The *S.S. Rotterdam*, docked at the French port of Le Havre, was destroyed by a powerful explosion at three forty-five in the afternoon local time.'" Johnson looked up at the studio clock. "That's just forty-three minutes ago," he said, returning to the typescript. "'The ship was filled with vacationers bound for a pleasure cruise that would have carried them to three continents. No count has yet been made of fatalities, but rescue workers at the scene have reported that the number may go as high as five hundred. At this very moment, all available ambulances and fire trucks have been dispatched to the site to transport the wounded to hospitals.

"'Several witnesses who were waiting on the pier report having seen two rubber boats heading away from the ship toward a boat anchored far offshore shortly before the blast. French police surmise that the unknown assailants, thought to number no more than four, lined the ship's hull with time-set underwater explosives, such as used by naval demolitions experts. The exact nature of the explosives is unknown. French divers are still clearing the waters of mines that were apparently laid by terrorists to retard any chase after them. There are no further details at this time.'"

Johnson looked back up at the camera. "The report does not say so, but it is not inconceivable that this tragic event may be the latest act of terror in the campaign of Hashim el-Wasi and his Palestinian party, now holding 156 United Nations ambassadors and others captive in New York, to dismantle the State of Israel. If so, the situation has become much more treacherous than feared. Some intelligence sources have speculated that the acts of terror would be confined to the United States. Others have thought that there would be nothing to follow the spectacular poisoning of the Chicago water supply. But all these theories may now be proved false.

"We will interrupt our regular programming to bring you

more details of this bombing as we receive them.

"And tomorrow morning we will bring you a look, promised for today, of that special restaurant that opened in New York, exclusively for dogs. I will be back at six tonight. Until then, this is Tyler Johnson."

GENERAL ASSEMBLY HALL

El-Wasi's instincts and his sense of the delegates' desires prompted him to recognize the Israeli ambassador "in the spirit of fairness which, as you know, has long been denied us by your rulers." Ambassador Ben-Eshai had been periodically calling for the floor for much of the last two days. Now he walked forcefully to the rostrum, turned his back to el-Wasi, and spoke.

"I address you in the spirit of truth, and as the representative of a people which has seen six million of its sons and daughters extermiated in the greatest catastrophe ever endured by a family of the human race. I come to this rostrum to speak for a united people which, having faced continual danger to its national survival, is unshakably resolved to resist any course which would renew the perils from which it has emerged."

Though his voice rang out clearly in impeccable English he appeared haggard. His face was gray with stubble. His grayish hair was unkempt, his suit a bundle of wrinkles. His tiredness exaggerated the creases around his eyes. Without a toothbrush, his mouth felt sour. But Ben-Eshai was a professional, he was at a podium, the microphone was on, the audience was his, and he spoke forcefully.

"I speak not to attempt to justify Israel's existence, for its existence is both justified and a fact, but to place on the record before you, as counterpart to the cruel fiction to which you have been held captive audience, the truth, not only that it shall be known but that nobody, inside or outside this Hall, will doubt Israel's resolve to endure irrespective of the capitulation to terror and hatred of some member countries of this institution."

As Ben-Eshai spoke the several clusters of delegates who had been talking quietly among themselves turned to face the rostrum. After the first day the terror had subsided and boredom became the Hall's dominant motif. Few had patience for el-Wasi's oratorical flights under the best of circumstances; from now on, little that was said at the rostrum would be of compelling interest to those in the room. Ben-Eshai was an exception. Even those who opposed his cause recognized in him a commanding rhetorical voice; listening to him was always instructive from the professional's point of view—and especially this day, after more than seventy-two hours without telephones, newspapers, letters, or books. The seats of the General Assembly, already causing serious backaches in many delegates, and the aisles in which stretching and pacing were permitted but briefly, had already become unendurable. The absence of any beds heightened their discomfort. The only recreation was the repetitive conversations with colleagues. Against that, a speech—or even a lecture—by Ben-Eshai was welcome relief.

"During Israel's life, from the moment of her birth, the intention to work for her destruction by physical violence has always been part of the official doctrine and policy both of Arab states and of Arab terrorists working outside any official national umbrella. At our birth we were viciously attacked by hordes of Arab armies. It was at this moment that the 'Palestinian refugee problem' was born. Why? The Israeli government urged the Arabs of Palestine to stay, yet they fled at the exhortations of our Arab neighbors, who encouraged them to flee and later return with the conquering Arab armies that would feast on Jewish blood. For decades these Arab refugees were confined to camps as virtual prisoners of Arab governments, for inhuman use as ammunition in a ceaseless propaganda assault against Israel.

"Indeed," Ben-Eshai continued, "from 1948 to this very day, with the sole exception of our recent negotiations with President Sadat, there has not been one statement by any representative of a neighboring Arab state, or by any among the so-called Palestinian freedom fighters, indicating readiness to respect existing agreements or to recognize Israel's sovereign right to exist." Ben-Eshai looked pointedly at the ambassador from Saudi Arabia. The latter affected to sleep. Ben-Eshai mopped his forehead with a rumpled handkerchief extracted from his back pocket, and glanced quickly at his notes on the lectern.

"In June 1967 Israel was encircled by tens of thousands of massed Egyptian, Syrian, and Jordanian troops. And when Egypt at that time called for the total removal of the UN Emergency Force which provided a buffer between our two countries, the United Nations acceded with obscene speed, without carrying out lawfully mandated procedures and without consulting Israel on the consequent prejudice to her military security and her vital maritime freedom, and without seeking ways to prevent a dangerous confrontation of hostile forces."

The Moroccan ambassador was beginning to itch all over. He scratched his legs and the itch moved to his chest, then to his back, then unbearably, to the soles of his feet. He tore at himself frantically, oblivious of Ben-Eshai's words.

"Yet notwithstanding their vast numerical superiority, we thrashed our adversaries. But is it surprising that we are firmly resolved never again to allow Israel's very security to rest on such a fragile foundation as this organization's whim? Our faith in the international sense of justice will never be recaptured. It is a fact of technology that it is easier to fly to the moon than to reconstruct a broken egg."

El-Wasi was conferring with one of his aides, taking no apparent notice of Ben-Eshai's speech until, looking out at the Hall, he saw that the audience was listening. He felt anger: When he, Hashim el-Wasi, a hero of history, spoke, they stood around in clumps of five or six and seemed not to care. But now his adversary had given him an audience. He would take it.

Ben-Eshai felt a body against his, pushing him aside. He turned to his left and saw, inches from his face, the face of El-Wasi, who took the microphone and addressed the Hall.

"We have heard enough of lies. You all know, deep within your hearts and souls, where the truth lives. We shall have no more of meaningless words. Instead, I have news to deliver to you.

"We have struck again, in France. It is an unfortunate fact that in war many people are killed. This is war, war for the survival of the Palestinian people, who wish to have their sovereign right to exist recognized. This time, in Le Havre, we used explosives. We have more, and worse, in store. Please stop us—by your votes. I will share your pain if we are forced to continue these unfortunate acts which fate and the Israeli presence have forced upon us.

"All things have their time. The time for debate and procrastination is over. Now is the time for action. It is late now, and you may sleep. I hope you are managing to bear the discomforts of these quarters. I hope you will not, by futile stubbornness, subject yourselves to greater discomfort.

"Tomorrow, we shall vote again."

CABINET ROOM, JERUSALEM

From the outset of the Arabs' takeover at the UN, the Knesset's Foreign Affairs and Security Committee convened daily and remained in informal session throughout each day. The participants were hurriedly convened by the committee secretary at 5:10 in the afternoon, Israeli time, when the report of Le Havre reached Israel.

The prime minister called upon an officer in the Mossad, Israel's secret service, for an update on the events in America.

"I have just spoken with Colonel Tal over the scrambler. The situation there, he says, is tough. The Americans are fearful of the diplomatic consequences if they attempt any attack on the terrorists. They believe the explosives which the terrorists claim to have wired are real, and the American government does not seem willing to bear the international impact if they storm the building and foreign delegates die as a result. Tal says the Americans are full of theories and meetings, but are so far very slow to action. In fact, they will not even discuss plans for action."

The foreign minister nodded in agreement. "I can understand that. America feels it has a responsibility not only to us, but to the international community as well. They will be very slow, I predict, to risk the deaths of the world's representatives."

The minister of defense interrupted. "Our friends may smile on us during sunshine and sell us umbrellas when the rain begins, but in a storm we must protect ourselves. In the final analysis, I believe the problem is not really America's or the world's, but ours, and the solution will come from nobody but ourselves."

"But even if we could conceive of a solution," responded the foreign minister, "we are rather helpless from this distance to implement it. For better or worse, we must depend on the Americans, and take no steps and make no noises which will alienate them."

The chief of operations spoke up. "We have no friends but ourselves. How long will the world hold out? Tomorrow there will be more horror elsewhere, and no government in the world will dare alienate its electorate by running the risk of the terror striking there. To the world outside, a vote against our existence will seem a cheap price for the security of one's own country. To them, we are a small patch of sand inhabited by Jews, and of no great consequence. We must end the terror ourselves."

"But how? By flying F-15s across the Atlantic and into midtown Manhattan? El-Wasi was smart this time. What military option do we have inside the United States?"

"The foreign minister is right, perhaps we should negotiate."

"Negotiate? We cannot negotiate our own destruction. And have you heard the terrorists demand negotiation this time? They do not want money or release of prisoners. They want us to lay down our arms, pure and simple, so that they can inherit the country. Are we to negotiate about the colors of the Palestinian flag that will fly over this building?"

The prime minister interrupted. "Our ambassador will

be meeting tomorrow with the president in Washington. He will impress upon him the urgency of the situation as far as we are concerned, and seek a commitment from the president that the United States will use its good offices to persuade its allies to vote against el-Wasi's preposterous resolution. That, at least, will buy us time."

"This time, time is against us," said the chief of operations. "Time will wear down the delegates inside the Assembly Hall, and time will permit the terrorists outside the Hall to continue with their operations. And the more that happens, the less will the world's resistance to duress endure."

"But even if el-Wasi's resolution passes," the chief justice commented, "it has no legal effect, as having been obtained under duress."

"You are a fine jurist but a poor soldier. Do you think that after the terrorists occupy our country and take over our arms they will succumb to a judgment of eviction from Israel?"

The prime minister called on the chief of the Mossad for a report.

"In the last twenty-four hours, we have dispatched several teams into active guerrilla camps in Lebanon—in Quia, Tyre, and Kafr Chuba. I myself was in Tyre less than three hours ago. We have questioned, in a most compelling manner, many dozens of the terrorists and have taken a great number back with us. We have used our most persuasive means of eliciting information from them. Yet none admits to any advance knowledge of this operation, nor to any idea of what the future holds. We have been most successful in the past, as everyone in this room knows, in convincing these terrorists that it is in their best physical interests to cooperate with us. Their unflagging failure to cooperate in this instance leads me to conclude that this time the terrorists involved have seen the strategic wisdom of operating with their mouths shut. In short, I believe that nobody outside the active participants in this operation had advance knowledge of it, and that only they know what the future operations will be. But I must confess that except for having reached this conclusion and having captured some killers whom we had previously been searching for, our operations in the terrorist camps have produced nothing.

"We have considered certain military options. We shall present them to this committee as they are refined, for your consideration."

"For our approval," the foreign minister cautioned.

FORT BRAGG,
NORTH CAROLINA

A section of Fort Bragg had been off limits for two days. It was common knowledge at the base that the special commando squad trained there, so the assumption was that assault maneuvers were being planned. But no one without a special pass could confirm the rumor at first hand.

Within the special compound, three construction teams were erecting the skeleton of a large domed building on an around-the-clock schedule. Assault techniques and strategy sessions consumed an inordinate part of the day, while demolitions specialists experimented with their arcane art on a plywood structure expressly wired from the inside for verisimilitude. The Pentagon special weapons division had been beseeched for exotic gadgetry in the forlorn hope that technology would provide the fix.

Colonel McDougal slept three hours a night. If he was to lead his men, he knew he would have to ease his pace, but too much was unsettled. Perhaps after the fourth day, when the outlines of a strategy might be worked out.

He talked every evening with General Sykes, who, to McDougal's great relief, seemed delighted to chat. It did not occur to McDougal that Sykes's particular interest in him at the moment was to discover what he could about the present operations of K Detachment. Sykes seemed unusually generous with his time. They both had a common objective, of course, in the present crisis. Nor did McDougal wonder why Sykes would only come to the telephone after 9:00 P.M. or why he was so reticent about his assignment in Washington.

When McDougal had first phoned Sykes and asked what he was up to, Sykes had replied that they did not have time to discuss the general's duties. Other things, he said, were more important. In the second call, McDougal ventured the suggestion that perhaps, as a tactician, Sykes could find out about strategy debates in Washington and keep him advised, a necessity, McDougal thought, because of the confusing lines of authority under which K Detachment operated. Sykes said tersely that he could not, adding that these telephone calls were strictly off-the-record. Sykes's tone meant that it was an order. McDougal recognized the tone. He would not ask again. He was too tired to realize that in pouring out his frustrations to Sykes, he was telling the general a good deal.

Pursuing the leaks—for that was what they were—from McDougal was a matter of some urgency for Sykes. It had become clear to Sykes that no one would talk, not even to him, about what the mysterious K Detachment was up to. Although it was not part of the Emergency Group's task to plan military strategy, Sykes was too thorough a strategist to be content with his ignorance. The U.S. military option was part of the president's ultimate responsibility, and the Emergency Group was a presidential unit. Unless Sykes knew what K Detachment's operational limits were, he could not give sound advice. So, though the initial call was fortuitous, Sykes was determined to foster McDougal's dependence.

Had McDougal known all this, it might not have mattered. He was growing increasingly depressed at the lack of clarity from his superiors in Washington. McDougal needed encouragement, and he would take it on any terms he could get.

ℵOCTOBER 9:ℵ
TWO DAYS LATER

HOSPITAL ASSUNÇÃO,
RIO DE JANEIRO

Two white-coated figures scurried down the long corridor toward the staff elevators. "What is wrong, Ramon, did they say?" one asked.

"I do not know, Luis. Dr. Melhado said only 'on the double' to the emergency ward. He said the duty nurse called to inform him that long lines are forming outside the door. The people appear to be quite sick." They paused in front of the main elevator, then one waved to the other and they ran toward the stairs, taking them down two at a time, panting. Footsteps from above. A face hove into view. "Simon!" Luis shouted. "You too?"

"Everyone who can be spared, Luis. There are hundreds of people outside."

They yanked open the stairwell door and made the sharp right turn to the emergency annex, attached to the hospital by an enclosed but unheated metal awning. Through the windows they could see lines of people, leaning on one another, many holding their heads in apparent agony. They burst through the two-way doors.

"Nurse, what is it? What is going on?" Ramon cried across the room.

The small dark-haired woman looked around. On her desk were two stacks of printed white forms. The larger stack contained blank forms. To the smaller stack the nurse was adding a scribbled report of a new patient every other minute. She pointed to the completed forms. "They are all the same. Fever, chills, many complain of pain behind the eyes, some have it in their joints."

Ramon grabbed the wrist of the nearest patient, who sat moaning softly next to the nurse's desk. "Pulse very high. Temperature?"

"One zero four point three," the nurse replied. "I have never seen anything like it."

The other doctors were examining the patients in the room. They passed quickly from one to another. All the symptoms were the same. The faces of some appeared swollen. Luis shook his head. "What do you think?"

"I wonder how the contagion spreads, and how quickly? How can we isolate so many people?"

"If it spreads by direct contact, Luis, it is too late for us. But I am not sure."

"You have a theory?"

"I remember something like this from the jungle. Nurse!" Ramon was yelling across the din of anguish that rolled across the room in waves.

"Yes, Doctor?"

"Where are these people from? All over the city?"

"Mostly from the northeast, Doctor Valdez."

Ramon Valdez looked puzzled.

"Doctor?"

"That's very odd. Look here, Luis, Simon, this I think is a tropical disease. If it is what I think it is, it is spread by mosquitos. But they do not breed where these people live."

"Well, what is it?"

"It's just a guess at this point, but I think it's breakbone fever."

"Breakbone?"

"Dengue."

"Ah."

"Nurse," Dr. Valdez said, "alert the public health authorities immediately. Tell them to send someone here quickly. If it's what I think it is, it could spread all across the city unless the mosquitos are eliminated. It is highly contagious."

"Ramon, please forgive me, old pal," said Simon, "but I forget the prognosis for dengue patients. It's been so long since my last one."

Valdez greeted his friend's remark with a derisive smirk. "Hah, you old fraud, admit it, you have never seen this before."

"Okay, okay, enlighten me then."

"It is rarely fatal, Simon."

Simon seemed visibly to relax. He was nodding: "Good, good."

"Not so good, Doctor," said Ramon.

"No?"

"No. It produces an exquisite pain."

"Which is treated how?"

"Which cannot be treated at all. Come on, let's get to work."

GENERAL ASSEMBLY HALL

El-Wasi smiled, switched off the television, approached the rostrum, and reported the Rio fever to the delegates.

"You should know that although our approach is now a more active one than we have previously followed, with somewhat more startling results, there is a reason for everything we have done in the last several days. The discomfort, shall we say, that the world is now experiencing is not being inflicted at random.

"You may ask, why was Brazil selected as a target of our operations? After all, it has been previously uninvolved with the question of Palestine.

"The answer, my friends, is simply this. In our struggle for liberation, there is no longer any such concept as uninvolvement or neutrality. If you are neutral, you are our enemy." He shouted the last word into the mike. "Since the illegal establishment of Israel on our soil, the only result of thirty years of talk has been preservation of the status quo and the spilling of Palestinian blood. Neutrality has helped preserve the status quo. Today we have served notice on mankind that inaction and indifference are votes against us. Thus the target of Rio. No longer may any nation on the face of the earth feel secure in its position of so-called neutrality on the issue of the Palestinians' right to return to their homeland.

"Accordingly, as we vote again on the resolution which I have introduced on behalf of the PLO, there will be no further abstentions. You will vote yes, or you will vote no, but you will vote a position. And until the result of the vote is one that reflects principles of justice, you will keep voting, and your peoples, all over the world, will feel our fists.

"I ask the Brazilian ambassador, since your vote of abstention is no longer viable, whether you vote yes or no on the resolution?"

The Brazilian ambassador rose. "Señor, I must communicate with my government."

El-Wasi answered, "We have at our disposal the quickest form of communication known to man. Your government, like every government in the world, has heard your request." El-Wasi turned to the television camera. "There will be no private communications. The government of Brazil has three hours to deliver to its representative whatever instruction is deemed appropriate. We and the rest of the world shall hear it simultaneously.

"We are aware that the representatives in this Hall are not themselves governments, and our respect for the rule of law demands that we permit the governments themselves, outside this Hall, to make those governmental decisions. We do not wish to accomplish the re-establishment of the

State of Palestine by means other than votes of the delegates in this Hall reflective of the lawful mandates of the governments they represent."

Three hours later, Brazil cast its vote in favor of the Palestinian resolution. The final vote stood 51 for, 98 against, with no abstentions. The entire Arab bloc, and a considerable number of their African and Latin American friends, had seen the wisdom of el-Wasi's position.

GRACIE MANSION

A few minutes before the scheduled arrival of U.S. Deputy Assistant Secretary of State Elihu Pitt, the mayor met with his appointments secretary and Police Commissioner Andrews. Captain de Petri sat silently at the commissioner's side, under strict orders to say nothing unless spoken to.

"There will be serious repercussions to the city because of all this," Manny Newman said. "In fact they've already begun. The sanitationmen's union says its men want parity with the police because when they clean up after all these crowds at the UN they're near a danger area."

"But Mr. Mayor," Andrews objected, "my men are constantly in the line of fire. There's a big difference between picking up garbage and dealing with the armed terrorists inside the UN. I don't think you should do anything that will alienate the PBA, not just now anyway. We all know they're capable of calling a strike whenever they decide."

"Commissioner, I didn't call you here to discuss municipal salaries," the mayor snapped. "The liaison officer from State is on his way over, and if we don't act responsibly Washington may burn us on our next call for money. I don't want any fighting here. Whatever he says is fine."

At that moment an intercom buzzed. The mayor pressed a button and told the receptionist that Mr. Pitt should come right in.

Elihu Pitt walked straight to the mayor and shook his hand dourly. Newman and the commissioner, both ignored, let their outstretched right hands drop uncomfortably back to their sides.

"Well, Mr. Mayor, Washington wants to know what you intend to do."

The mayor said nothing at first, then asked Pitt if he'd care for some coffee. Pitt waved him off, without uttering a word. After a momentary silence, the mayor asked:

"Is it our problem, or Washington's?"

Pitt stared in disbelief. "We're trying to weigh alternatives down in the capital, but we did think that since this is all going on in your city, as you know, you might have given a few moments of thought to what can be done."

After a pause, the mayor said, "You know we do have my special emissary down in your neck of the woods, working day and night, though I hope not all night, with your special group. We're getting regular reports from her, and we're analyzing them thoroughly." A pause. Then: "It was my understanding based on conversations I have had with the highest authorities that New York City's police anti-terrorist unit should defer to Washington. Does Washington now want us to take action on our own?"

"No, no, of course not," Pitt replied. "However, we did think there should be some shared responsibility here, some input from you people, since these terrorists did pierce through New York City's security, and that was, after all, your responsibility."

The commissioner spoke up: "You know that we were given strict orders not to search the delegates."

Pitt ignored him. "Mr. Mayor, I must say that we in Washington are most surprised that you didn't have some kind of contingency plan."

Manny Newman answered. "We had plenty of contingency plans. Absolutely. Trouble was, we got the wrong contingency."

Pitt ignored the jest. "I have been asked, personally, by the first deputy assistant secretary in charge of federal-state relations of the State Department, to tell you that if you have any suggestions they will be appreciated."

Captain de Petri, exhausted from the last week of tension,

spoke up. "My men can charge that building and blow those bastards back to Arabia in two seconds."

"Don't worry about the Captain," the commissioner interrupted, glaring at de Petri and then turning to Pitt. "He's a brilliant field tactician, and is well trained to follow only civilian commands in crisis situations."

The mayor turned to Pitt. "Do I correctly understand that although Washington would, as you say, appreciate our suggestions, we are still to undertake no action without direct orders from Washington?"

"That is correct." Then turning toward de Petri, Pitt added: "We don't want the world to come to an end through some trigger-happy functionary."

"Very well. You needn't worry about us up here. We will try to keep the situation under control, but will not act unless you people tell us to."

"And what are you doing in the meantime?"

"In the meantime, Mr. Pitt, we are doing our best to keep eight million people from going completely berserk, and to keep this city running smoothly as possible under the circumstances."

"I mean about the terrorists."

"Our representative is in Washington. And as soon as these Arabs struck I commissioned a study group to come up with possible alternative courses of action for us to recommend to Washington. The group has already recommended that a permanent study group be established to devise systems for avoiding recurrences of similar situations. I've sent them back to the drawing-board."

"I can only hope," said Pitt, standing, "that your study group finishes its report before your administration ends. If it does come up with anything, please let us know." That said, Pitt turned and headed for the door, without handshakes or goodbyes.

The mayor shook his head after the door closed. "Manny, it looks like he didn't come here to offer to pay for our police overtime."

"I guess not, the sonuvabitch. We've just got to keep doing what we've been doing."

"What's that?" Captain de Petri asked.

The commissioner turned and ordered him to stop talking.

"To keep doing nothing to hurt the situation, Captain," Newman said. "There may be very grave dangers to this city because of the whole situation, not to mention the survival of the world. There's also the next election to think of. It would be nice to have the president in our corner."

"Commissioner," the mayor asked, "do you think they may strike somewhere in the city?"

The commissioner hesitated, then said, "They already have, they're holding the UN."

"No, no, I mean another strike, like in Chicago or Rio."

"Maybe. But what can we do? There are so many ways a real crazy can mess up the city. Suppose they have agents who call every office building in the city and empty them with bomb threats? All they need are some phones and dimes. Or call the police and make subway threats? Or call here and say all the air in the city is poisoned? There's no way we could stop them. These guys may even have missiles with warhead launchers. Do we want to seal off all air traffic at Kennedy and LaGuardia to prevent a catastrophe? I think we've just got to sit tight and try to carry on as normally as possible."

The mayor stood. "Okay, gentlemen, we've talked enough. Commissioner, you'd better give some more serious thought to how to end the situation, so I don't have my pants down next time this guy Pitt calls."

"Me, Mr. Mayor?"

"You."

At that, the mayor and Manny Newman left the room. Commissioner Andrews turned to de Petri. "We'd better go." Before they left Gracie Mansion, the commissioner turned to de Petri and said, "Captain, you'd better come up with a plan." Then, quickly, "But don't do anything with it until we've all discussed it."

Captain de Petri said he'd try his damnedest.

GENEVA

The president of the Federal Council of Switzerland settled back importantly in the rear of his Fleetwood as it rode slowly down the rue de Lausanne. He paid no attention to the chatter of the five aides with him. He leafed again through the typed speech that had been prepared for him. The NATO countries, communicating by telephone on short notice, had agreed that the representative of a neutral country might stand a chance of convincing el-Wasi to negotiate an end to the siege. Certain Arab countries had first been approached to make the overture to el-Wasi, but had, in diplomatic language, refused.

Switzerland's offer to serve as negotiating conduit would be broadcast live by satellite from the European headquarters of the United Nations, based in Geneva. The speech had been prepared by the West's foremost military psychologists, and was designed to open a two-way line of communication with el-Wasi. Every sentence, phrase, and word had been analyzed for nuance and context. It was most important to entice el-Wasi into beginning a dialogue, any dialogue, with the outside world.

The psychological subtleties were of no concern, and were not apparent, to the Swiss president. The tone of the speech seemed right, proper, conciliatory, reasonable, and convincing, and the role the Swiss government would now play would reinforce Switzerland's status as a significant nation in world events. It was a satisfying prospect.

The limousine turned left at the Avenue de la Paix, and stopped at the UN headquarters. The president was ushered quickly into the main chamber. The makeup woman applied powder to his face before he strode to a regal chair in the center of a battery of bright television lights.

His speech was aired live in New York on several stations. When the Swiss president stopped speaking fifteen minutes later and the TV lights were shut off, his aides told him as gently as possible that el-Wasi had announced after twenty seconds that he would not listen to the speech, that he was not interested in dialogue, that he knew all about psychologists' tricks, and that he was switching channels.

THE WHITE HOUSE

"Read it to me again, will you, Nancy?" Tal asked. He leaned his chin on the videotape machine, still warm from its ninth running that day of el-Wasi's takeover speech at the UN.

"Christ," Dolby said, jabbing her pencil against the table. "You've heard it six times. It's almost eleven o'clock. I'm starving. The rest of us are starving." Only Doolittle and Dr. Jones were left. She had removed her jacket two hours earlier. Despite the implacable air conditioning her blouse was damp with perspiration and she had opened the first two buttons.

Pausing momentarily at her uncharacteristic dishabille, Tal looked sternly at her. "You can leave."

"No, no, I'll stay until we're through. Until you're convinced there's nothing in it."

"But there must be something. There must be a connection. Look, just read it one more time, then we'll go get some dinner. Dr. Jones will treat us, yes, Doctor?"

"We'll put it on the White House tab," Jones answered.

"They'll never stand for it," Dolby said.

"Nancy, we four can do anything," Jones replied.

"Except figure out this puzzle," Tal reminded them. "Read it, Nancy, read it."

"Okay, it says—I quote—'Dengue or breakbone fever is an acute, infectious, febrile—'"

"What's 'febrile' mean again?"

"Feverish."

"Please continue."

"Where was I? Yes—'infectious, febrile disease which temporarily is completely incapacitating but is almost never fatal. It is caused by a specific filterable virus and may occur in any country where the mosquito vectors breed, although it is endemic only among inhabitants of warm climates. The vector incriminated throughout most endemic areas is the yellow-fever mosquito *Aedes aegypti—*' "

"There is that *aegypti*. Egypt. What does that have to do with it?"

"Probably nothing."

"You are probably right. Go on."

"Look, hundreds of people have died," Doolittle interrupted. "This is getting us nowhere."

"Let's think again of what we have," Tal insisted.

"Oh God, we've said it so many times I could say it in my sleep," Dolby said.

"Try it awake."

"So far they happen every other day. They have each taken place in a different country, each on a different continent. One appeared to be a warning and the others were in earnest."

"But the 'warning' killed some, and the epidemic has not."

"Not so far."

"Yes, that's true, but the epidemic is causing a great deal of excruciating pain."

"There doesn't seem to be any pattern to it," said Doolittle. "Are we supposed to watch out in all countries next time, or just on the remaining continents?"

"Or anywhere. What about the weapons?"

"Well, the first was poison, of course. The second, explosives. And the third is a virus. Germ warfare."

"So what does that tell us?"

"Nothing. Go on to the victims, Nancy, review that."

"Okay. The first involved an entire city. Only eighty-nine dead directly from drinking the water, but several hundred thousand thirsty people. And no telling how many sick people might have died because they couldn't take a drink. The last count from Le Havre was—what was it, Art?"

Doolittle picked through a wad of papers on the table. "Five hundred fifty-two, plus the wounded." He paused. "Quite a haul those frogmen got."

"Those what?" Tal asked.

"Frogmen. The underwater terrorists at Le Havre. Sorry, an American word." Then he finished the count: "And thousands suffering from dengue fever."

They tried to read a pattern out of it, but couldn't and shortly ran out of speculations. Dr. Jones ended it. "Know what I suggest? That we eat. Have we exhausted this forty-third run-through?" he asked, looking at Tal.

Tal did not respond. "Hey, are you still with us? Let's eat." Tal shook himself, as if waking up.

"What?" Then: "Yes, yes, I think that's a good idea."

"Pizza, anyone?" asked Dr. Jones.

"Whatever. That's probably all we can get at this hour."

"No," said Tal. "I think we need a meal. Besides, Corbin Williston won't allow me outside in Washington. Too great a risk, he says. I'll have to sneak out with you as it is. I don't think he would approve our dining in a pizza shop. Dr. Jones, don't you know a quiet, dark little place that serves food very late?"

"Harvey's, I think, 'restaurant to presidents,' about ten minutes from here."

"Good. And on the way, Dr. Jones, I would very much appreciate your going over that theory of yours again about el-Wasi's possible delusional structure, I believe is what you called it."

"Delighted," said Jones, to a low chorus of groans from Doolittle and Dolby.

"Don't you ever stop working?" she asked Tal.

"In my line of work, very rarely, Nancy, very rarely. How do we get there, Dr. Jones?"

"We can walk."

"Wouldn't a limousine be safer?" Doolittle asked.

"I don't think so," Jones said. "If we arrive in such a car, people will assume we are somebodies. If we walk at this hour, no one will know us or care."

They encountered only one passerby as they departed the northwest gate of the White House opposite Lafayette Square. They crossed Pennsylvania Avenue, entered the park, and headed north for Connecticut Avenue. The streets were nearly deserted. Tal turned to Dr. Jones, who was leading the way, and invited him to repeat his psychological theory once again.

"To spare our friends," Dr. Jones began, "I will omit a good deal of the detail that leads me to my conclusions. In essence, what emerges from the intelligence reports is a man who is nursing a monumental obsession. He is obsessed with the notion of the Palestinian people. He believes that they are the direct descendants of a people who held claim to land that is now in Israel thousands of years ago. He does not recognize national populations as such. Syria, Jordan, Egypt, and so on are just conveniences, as far as he is concerned. They are lines on maps drawn by old kings and potentates. But they don't represent a people as truly as he represents the Palestinians. And he believes that the Biblical borders, whose location has come to him as if by revelation, must be restored not so much as a political act but as an act of piety. Now that is where his obsession turns into a delusion, you see. For he is convinced not merely that the cause of reclaiming or redeeming his homeland is a righteous one. Even more important in his mind is the thought that he is the only person who can accomplish this mission. In other words, he is the redeemer."

"Yes, but this afternoon you were suggesting something even more, something about the emotional overtones to this belief in himself as a redeemer."

"You mean the religious aspect of the belief?"

"Yes."

"Well, I am not at all sure of this, but I think it is at least plausible that el-Wasi sees himself as on a par with Mohammed himself. That el-Wasi is the second Prophet of Allah."

"Is that a fairly, what would you call it, a high-flown belief for an Arab?"

"Such a belief is downright blasphemous."

"Is el-Wasi sane?"

"'Sanity' is a very loose term. It isn't really a medical term. Properly speaking it belongs to the lawyers and judges, for whom sanity-insanity is the line dividing those who are to be held accountable for their deeds and those who are not. In medical terms, we would say that el-Wasi is suffering from a delusion, a false but fixed belief that he holds as not merely true but self-evident. In fact—" Dr. Jones said, hesitating.

"Yes?"

"Well, I didn't want to suggest it this afternoon. But I think it not impossible that el-Wasi suffers from a much deeper delusion than that of being a second Prophet of Allah."

Tal stopped walking and grabbed Jones by the arm. His eyes were wide as he stared Jones in the face. "Much deeper?"

"Yes."

"As deep as believing himself the Son of Allah?"

Jones shook his head. "You read me very well, Col. Tal."

Dolby, who had been standing patiently, though shivering in the cold night air, now could contain her puzzlement no longer. "What is all this? What do you mean, son of Allah? Do you mean that el-Wasi thinks he is literally the son of God?"

"It is just a hypothesis, Nancy," Jones said, beginning to walk again.

"But a very interesting one, Doctor," the Israeli said. "In fact, it is a fascinating delusion. But tell me, since you have gone this far, might we not push a little further? Is it not possible that el-Wasi's belief is even more extreme than that?"

"What could be more extreme than that?" Dolby asked.

"Come now, Nancy, that's not hard. What is more extreme than thinking you are the son of God?"

"Thinking you are the daughter of God, perhaps?"

Tal laughed. "Yes, yes, we will concede you that. Then even more extreme than being the daughter of God?"

"Being God?" she asked in a whisper.

"Precisely."

They were at K Street now, where Seventeenth and Connecticut meet. They stopped walking and stood, looking at each other. That el-Wasi thinks himself God! Tal reminded them of the cold, and they resumed their walk. Finally Dolby spoke. "Where does that get us?"

"In itself, nowhere," Tal answered. "But I think it might have something to do with the three acts of terror that the world has suffered."

"How?"

Tal did not answer.

They were nearing the restaurant. "Art, you have been uncommonly quiet. What do you think?" Jones asked.

"I think our friend has a theory. Is that right, Tal? You connect the three acts logically?"

"I'm not sure. Something is not complete."

"But if you are right?"

"If I have thought this out correctly, Art, then I would be prepared to hazard a guess as to the next act."

"What?" he asked.

"This is only tentative, but I think the next strike may be on an airplane or at an airport. Something to do with flying."

"Why?" Doolittle asked, as they arrived at the restaurant door.

"Please don't press me. I'd rather not say now until I am sure."

"But shouldn't we alert someone?"

"There is nothing that we can do now. The attack could take place anywhere and it may just be hours away."

"When will you be sure?"

"I may never be. But I have some studying to do this evening when we have finished dining."

"Studying?"

"Yes, I think I have a book that has the answer."

"What book?"

"I'd rather not say yet. Let's forget it. And no talk about this matter inside here."

He reached for the door and held it open for Nancy Dolby, who did not argue this night about being accorded such a privilege. "Come," Tal waved the others in, "let us dine—with the president's blessings! Or at least on his expense account, eh, Doctor?—suddenly I have an appetite—and Nancy, since you asked the other day, let me tell you about the role of women in our armed forces."

The door shut after him and he followed the others in.

ℵOCTOBER 11:ℵ
TWO DAYS LATER

SHIBUYA, TOKYO

The Shibuya section of Tokyo contains some of the city's busiest boulevards. At most times, and especially from noon until two o'clock, it is crowded with pedestrians, automobiles, buses: anything that can move. Shoppers, businessmen hurrying to and from lunch, and thousands of others daily. They scurry: ceaseless motion. Seen from above, they appear like automata, lifelike figures making their perpetual rounds in an elaborate clockwork designed by fastidious craftsmen. Seen from way up, atop the tall buildings that line the avenues, they appear as specks, ants crawling one way, then the other, never stopping; ants, vulnerable to forces from far off, forces unseen and unimaginable.

The Tokyo commissioner of police sat alone in his office, apprehensive. Though most of his countrymen assumed the danger to be remote, he drew little comfort from the fact that the terrorists had acted on three other continents. He could understand the pattern no better than any of the others, but he sensed that the strikes might occur around the globe. Japan, and especially Tokyo, seemed a more promising site for such terror than, say, Sidney or Jakarta or other Pacific points. Besides, the Japanese had an indigenous group of terrorists; the Red Army was ruthless and sadistic. He had begun to squeeze hard against the underworld community in Tokyo. Those thought to be prone to violent crime were being rounded up, and even those suspected of regularly associating with them were being hustled in for questioning. He needed only a pretext, interrogate them for a few days, let them go later. The idea was to disrupt whatever plans might have been hatched, to throw them off schedule. No one was going to take liberties with his city.

But Tokyo is large: more than eleven million. No police force in the world is capable of safeguarding such a city against an urban guerrilla force determined to wreak some unknowable kind of havoc. Who could guess when they would strike, or where, how many there would be, how hard the city would be hit? The commissioner knew he should have retired last year as his daughter who lived in America had begged, moved in with her and her husband. They had room. He had argued: Who wants to live in Los Angeles? Now, he wasn't sure. If he could live through the next week or two, he would consider it.

There was an insistent rapping at his door. How extraordinary! Even in times of greater stress, requests for his attention would be made more decorously. But now? "Sir," said a police lieutenant, "I think we have found what you are looking for. A man caught in the roundup last night said he has heard there is movement in the Red Army cell to the north. Explosives, he says."

"Where?"

"We do not know that yet."

"But why not? Does this man not know?"

"He is not in a, shall we say, position to talk further at this time."

"Fool."

"It could not be helped, sir. He was uncooperative

enough. We were lucky to get this out of him."

"Will he live?"

"Yes, sir, but it will be a few days before he can talk intelligently."

"We do not have a few days. What else do you have?"

"Nothing."

"Keep pressing. It will be in Tokyo. Have your men look into every alley, every sewer, every corner. It is almost two o'clock now; report to me every hour."

"Yes, sir," said the lieutenant, bowing and backing out his chief's door.

At that moment, twenty-one separate explosions sounded simultaneously along the unnamed streets of the Shibuya. The roar was immense, like a retort of thunder electronically amplified a thousandfold. For an instant, the ants stopped moving; from the building tops where the explosions occurred the picture below was like a frozen tableau. Then motion began again—the motion of panic and hysteria. People inside took refuge outside; people outside ran instinctively to the nearest doorway.

The tops of a dozen office buildings were blown apart. Huge chunks of concrete spewed out like a volcano erupting with all its primal fury. Jagged boulders plummeted to the ground.

A dense rain of debris began to pour to the streets. Shards of glass stung some of the lucky ones; larger slivers slashed the less fortunate. Rubble from stone facades tumbled down, crushing some pedestrians outright. Bits and pieces of office accoutrements—handles of filing cabinets, slabs of wood from desks and drawers, tons of paper blown to bits, stems from plants, pencils, pens, paperclips, pieces of ceramic teacups—were flung out and fell. Thousands of fragments of human bodies descended at the same speed. What would later stand out in the consciousness of survivors was the feeling that the skies had come alive with dozens of species of flying creatures descending en masse upon the earth. The sun was blotted out; a vast cloud of dust stayed in place for hours after the last solid remnants of the explosions splattered on the ground.

When the immediate crisis was over, 37 floors had been

demolished, leaving gaping holes at or near the tops of 18 buildings. The death toll stood at 2,162, and more than five thousand others were seriously injured. Subsequent investigation showed that the cause of the explosions was a series of radio-controlled plastique bombs that together had more force than any single man-made explosion up to the time of the first atomic bomb at Hiroshima.

GENERAL ASSEMBLY HALL

Several delegates were in pain. Arthritic conditions were exacerbated. Spines ached, legs throbbed. Other delegates had taken sick with fever; there were no blankets, and suit jackets were all they had for covers. It was too early in the season for the UN heaters to be turned on, so the air conditioning continued its steady drone. Delegates shook with chill.

Some had not eaten well for days and were weak with hunger now. The New York City caterer had provided prepackaged kosher meals for the Israeli delegates, but the Arab who brought the serving cart in had removed the six aluminum pans and crushed them underfoot before the first meal. There were to be no more kosher deliveries.

The ventilating system no longer sufficed to rid the Hall of the stench that emanated from the portable lavatory in the rear. The delegates, who had originally spread out, now moved forward day by day toward the front of the Hall. Although he had not planned this effect, el-Wasi was pleased by it, because it forced the delegates at least to see him more clearly when he took the rostrum, as he did several times a day to give orders, make demands, and issue harangues.

El-Wasi awoke at 6:30 to the news of the Shibuya success. He was exuberant. "The plan progresses," he told an aide near the podium. The aide had been up all night, on guard. It was time now for him to exchange places with one of the five who had been sleeping in a restricted section of seats. "We will pray," el-Wasi said, "and then you may sleep and I will prepare my talk. Today the squeeze inside begins."

The food was due in at 7:30. He would deliver his speech first, then enjoy his breakfast. At 7:20 he rose to the podium and turned on the microphone. Several delegates were milling about, but most were asleep. The mike's squeal roused them. Except for the latest act of terror, however, they had heard this speech before: El-Wasi was patient, the Palestinians were patient, but time was growing short and it was time to act. It was time to discontinue all the televised pleas by governments to institute a dialogue. He had read all the standard works on the psychological profiles of terrorists and on the tactics of the police and he would not be fooled by their tricks.

Then his voice changed. Speaking with a new intensity, el-Wasi announced that food deliveries would be reduced to two a day, at 7:30 in the morning and the same time at night. And if that did not prompt a more realistic sense of how to vote, rations would be cut to one meal a day, then none. After that the lavatory would be taken out. Soon, he said, the delegates would feel firsthand what it is like to live in the squalor of refugee camps in which the Zionist imperialists had confined the Palestinian people for thirty years. And after that, unless the world took his demand seriously, the delegates would begin to die.

LONDON

The two men sat at a corner table in Claridges, ignoring the pâté de fois gras, the salad greens, and the lamb en brochette that the waiter, with an unobtrusive sigh, served and cleared, course after course. They pushed at their tea cups. Their conversation was low but animated, punctuated with silence whenever the waiter approached.

"I tell you, Maurice," one man said, "we must be on his list. How can you doubt it?"

"Because I have no evidence, none whatsoever, and you have none, either."

"I have told you—I have political evidence."

"You mean your bloody political logic."

"Same thing. Point is he needs our vote. If the U.K. goes for his resolution, the Commonwealth will fall into line. If that happens, he gets very close to his absolute majority."

"And we won't capitulate without an attack against us."

"Exactly."

The man addressed as Maurice glumly cradled his jaw in his palms. "Very well, I will cancel all leaves, and we will begin work around the clock tonight."

"Good chap. We cannot afford to have this thing strike us."

"We cannot afford to capitulate if it does. I am depending on you to convince the P.M. of that logic, too."

"I see him tonight."

"Persuade him tonight."

THE WHITE HOUSE

"Have you all heard the news?" the vice-president asked glumly, convening the meeting. Everyone had. "It's getting worse, much worse."

"Strange, though, that the damage seems unrelated to the nature of the act," Tal said in a voice so soft he seemed to be talking to himself.

"Seems pretty related to me," responded Watkins, who was sitting next to him.

"Of course it's related," General Sykes boomed, irritated. He was on edge continually now. He didn't like inactivity, sitting in a cramped room with the same people for days that would seemingly never end, listening to the increasingly irrelevant comments from the Israeli spy, no matter how good he was supposed to be; the discomforting news from McDougal at Fort Bragg; worst of all, not knowing what the meaning to this whole madness was.

"That wasn't quite what I meant," Tal said firmly.

"Well damn it, say what you mean and let's get on with it."

"What I meant to say is that the damage appears unrelated to the metaphor of the act."

"That's a worse riddle. What in hell is the metaphor of the act?"

"Why don't you give him a chance to explain?" Dolby answered. Tal cut short Sykes's rejoinder to her.

"What I mean by 'the metaphor of the act' is the reason why the specific acts have been committed."

"Are you saying what I think you're saying?" Jones asked.

"What's that?" said Sykes, now thoroughly puzzled.

"Maybe that he's solved it, if you'd listen," Dolby answered for Jones. Then she turned to Tal: "When I heard it wasn't airplanes—"

"What in hell is going on?" Sykes demanded. "What has been solved? What airplanes? There weren't any airplanes involved last night."

"Exactly, General," Jones said affably. "But last night, just outside the restaurant, Tal ventured a prediction that the next attack would have something to do with airplanes."

"Restaurant?" Corbin Williston interrupted. "What restaurant?"

Dolby answered. "We were hungry, Mr. Director."

"Goddamn it, I told you not to go outside. That was a damn fool stupid thing to do."

"Nothing happened, Corbin," Dolby said.

"Who else was there?" Williston demanded, swinging his head around. Doolittle raised his hand, puffing silently on a pipe.

Williston threw up his hands and shook his head with disgust. "I thought I had made it clear to you, Colonel Tal, that as a guest in this country you are responsible for abiding by necessary security precautions. And that does not include dining out on a whim."

"It wasn't a whim, Corbin," Dolby said in her sweetest voice. "We were hungry." Her smile could soothe any bureaucrat in New York—but Williston was having none of it.

"You could have been killed! Or overheard!" A vein along Williston's neck pulsated visibly.

"But we weren't, Corbin," Dolby answered. "We were just four friends out for a walk and dinner." She brushed a loose strand of hair from her face.

"You walked?" Williston's jaw dropped open.

"A car from the White House stirs discussion," Tal said. "At least, that's what the indispensable Dr. Jones suggested. Security precautions after all, you see."

"Gentlemen, please," the vice-president cut off Williston's retort. "You can deal with this later. We seem to have lost sight of Colonel Tal's claim to a modest accomplishment."

"Jesus Christ, yes," Sykes snarled. "Let's hear it." Dolby doodled the name "Sykes" on her pad, and entered next to it the letters "S.O.B."

"Indulge me if you will while I trace through the reasoning. Perhaps I am still not correct but the facts do seem compelling."

"What facts, man?"

"General," the vice-president said, frowning at Sykes. The officer slumped back in his chair.

"You all recall that Dr. Jones gave us yesterday afternoon an eloquent lecture on the psychological makeup of el-Wasi. He told us then that el-Wasi had an obsessive belief in the divinity of his mission—in fact, Dr. Jones said it is not unimaginable that el-Wasi believes himself to be the equal of Mohammed and that his role in history is to aid the divine plan for the Palestinian people. That started me thinking. Suppose el-Wasi is so obsessive that he has—how do you say it, caught?—an even worse delusion. Suppose he thinks that he is God or, at least, close enough to God to be doing God's work."

Pinckney dropped his coffee cup on the table with a loud clatter. The hot liquid rolled off the table onto his lap. He jumped up, frantically brushing himself with a napkin.

"It's just a delusion, Mr. Pinckney," Sykes snapped. Pinckney tried to ignore the burning pain.

Tal continued. "Dr. Jones elaborated on this hypothesis on the way to dinner late last night. So it is not just my theory. Now let us work from there. What is it God would do if he wanted to gain a homeland for his people?"

"Christ," said Sykes, "it was bad enough when we were just trying to figure out what el-Wasi would do, now we have to figure out what God would do. How in the hell can we do that?"

"There is a precedent."

"A precedent? Where?"

"In the Bible, of course. All the signs were right there, but I just couldn't connect it before. Not until yesterday evening when Art Doolittle used a word for the terrorists at Le Havre."

"Frogmen?"

"Yes."

When nobody spoke, Tal continued. "Remember, we know far more of el-Wasi, factually, than Dr. Jones' psychological study. His background—educated, proficient in several languages—extremely verbal, in fact, and extremely religious."

Sykes interrupted. "Tal"—he glanced momentarily at the vice-president and said "excuse me" in his direction, then turned back to Tal—"we don't have time for bullshit."

Tal returned the stare. "General, are you interested in my telling you the key to these acts of terror?"

Sykes did not respond, and Tal paused long enough to emphasize the general's silence. Then he turned away from him and looked around the table.

"What did God do when he wanted Pharaoh to let the Jews out of Egypt?"

Doolittle stopped puffing on his pipe. "He sent the plagues."

"Exactly. And perhaps our friend from New York can tell us—how many of them?"

"Ten," Dolby answered.

Tal sat back in his chair and savored the silence. "Gentlemen," he finally said, "el-Wasi has recently smitten us with the first four plagues."

"The what?" Sykes demanded.

"The plagues. El-Wasi is reenacting the ten plagues, only in his script the plagues are modernized and the goal is not to get the Jews out of Egypt but to get them out of Israel and to get the Palestinians in."

Nobody spoke. Tal continued.

"It struck me when Art Doolittle mentioned 'frogmen' yesterday. Don't you see it yet?"

Again, silence.

"Let's start with Chicago. What was God's first plague? Turning the waters into blood. That was easy for el-Wasi to duplicate, and obvious, too. I should have figured it out earlier. What was the first terrorist act el-Wasi contrived? Turning the waters red, but in Chicago instead of Egypt."

"What was the second plague?" Sykes asked, leaning forward now, his curiosity obvious.

"I'm surprised at you, General," the vice-president scolded. "The second plague was frogs—frogs everywhere, in the houses, in the streets, in the waters, everywhere."

"I am impressed," said Tal. "No, el-Wasi couldn't produce a bunch of real frogs, and even if he could the act would be ludicrous, and not harmful. So he used a metaphor or an expression. The Bible speaks of 'a multitude of frogs upon the beach.' El-Wasi sent his frogmen to the port at Le Havre. 'Frogmen'—we have the same idiom in Hebrew, *ahnshay tz'fardayah*. It struck me as soon as Art used your word."

"Astounding," offered Pinckney.

"The third biblical plague was gnats or lice," Tal continued. "Remember last night I said I had to do some research? What I had to find was a connection between the third plague and the fever outbreak in Rio, and I found it. Talmudic scholars believe that the effect of the swarms of insects in the third plague was an epidemic of dengue fever. And that, of course, is what el-Wasi visited upon his victims in Rio."

"That leaves the airplanes," Dr. Jones said.

Tal smiled. "Well, yes, I have to concede my error there. I was overconfident. In the Bible most frequently used in this country, the King James Bible, the fourth plague was the overrunning of the land with flies. I confess that I underestimated el-Wasi. I assumed he would build his act on the English Bible, and it seemed obvious that the target for a plague built around flies would be airplanes. Silly of me. He obviously planned everything within the context of his own Mideastern heritage, and is sticking much more closely to the original version. In the Hebrew, the fourth plague was a visitation by all manner of small insects. So what he did was more consistent with his theme than my guess had been, and more subtle than I gave him credit for. He produced a situation in which the skies were full of flying particles; the paper said this morning that there were also tremendous dust clouds so thick the sun was blotted out, as though night had fallen. Isn't that what would happen if there were swarms of insects so thick you couldn't see? And what his assassins accomplished in Tokyo was even more than that. The Bible says that the land was ruined by reason of the swarms of insects. The land along the streets of the Shibuya was surely ruined by reason of el-Wasi's perfectly executed catastrophe. The streets are a shambles. So I think that everything that has happened so far is explained by the plague hypothesis." Tal sank back into his chair.

Sykes raised his hand to his forehead. "I salute, you, sir, congratulations." Pinckney began to applaud, and instantly the table erupted into applause and the laughter of nervous release. Although the vice-president rapped on the table for quiet, they would not stop their mutual congratulations. Everyone realized, instinctively, that a corner had been turned, even if no one knew what would be found round the other side.

They crowded around the coffee urn, talking all at once. Jones wanted to know whether Williston wanted to know where they had gone for their infamous dinner. Pinckney asked Watkins how el-Wasi could possibly believe he was God. The vice-president clapped Tal on the shoulder. The others stood in a circle around them. Dolby extended her hand. Tal shook it, and held it an extra moment to tell her he had also enjoyed the dinner. She told him she had, too. They looked away from each other at the same instant, each conscious that they had nothing more to say.

"Now all we need to do is predict the next six plagues," Williston finally offered.

"That won't be very easy."

"But at least we have something to go on, a framework, for God's sake."

"Does anyone know what the rest of the plagues were?" Tal asked impishly.

"I remember the last one," Watkins said. "Killing of the first-born of the Egyptians."

"Very good, Will, but what was the fifth one, which is our more immediate concern?"

The circle fell quiet. Williston and Jones, conversing to the side, suddenly became aware of the sound of their voices. Jones stopped in mid-sentence. "What's wrong?"

"Do you know the plagues? Can you list them?" The two men shrugged. "Can no one list them, even the next plague?"

The vice-president shrugged when Tal looked at him, and Tal smiled.

"I thought so." Tal stood up and walked to the closet farthest from the door. He opened it, reached into his overcoat pocket and withdrew a Bible.

Tal resumed his seat. He opened the Bible to a page marked by a piece of scrap paper and began reading aloud. "'Behold, the hand of the Lord is upon thy cattle which is in the field, upon the horses, upon the asses, upon the camels, upon the oxen, and upon the sheep: there shall be a very grievous murrain.' The Fifth Plague. Exodus, chapter nine. Mr. Vice-President, I suggest you order a Bible for everyone in this room, and that each of us study every word of these plagues. From now on, everything in there can be a clue."

The vice-president walked to the door and left the room for several seconds. When he returned to the table, he said, "The secretary says she hopes we're doing more in here than praying."

With the foreknowledge that each succeeding act of terror would be based in one fashion or another on the biblical plagues, said Tal, it was the group's task to predict and if possible prevent each from occurring. Tal explained the difficulty of their job. The next plague, for example: If el-Wasi meant to kill only cattle, the symbolic place to do it would of course be in India. Ideally, an alert should be passed along to the Indian government, but the chances of detecting a few saboteurs bent on poisoning cattle somewhere in a country so large was miniscule. Besides, the plague could be appropriately fulfilled in metaphor by poisoning any of a number of types of animals consumed by humans anywhere in the world. With probably only 36 hours before the next plague would hit, it was unlikely that anything anyone did would result in prevention of the act.

Dolby suggested they warn the rest of the world against eating meat.

To do so, Williston answered, would be to inform el-Wasi that his plan had at least been partially unraveled. "In this business," the director said, "you never give away such a secret. If you know something about the enemy's secret plans you never let him know that you know it. World War II might have had a different outcome if that principle had not been scrupulously adhered to."

"But people might die and we can try to save them," Dolby remonstrated.

"That is the problem with war," Williston said. "You can save some people, but at the expense of how many others? Churchill made a painful decision in 1940 not to alert the people of Coventry that there would be an air attack. He knew that there would be because the British had cracked the German code. But any alert would give that fact away. It had to be kept secret, the Ultra secret, at any cost. The cost turned out to be 400 dead, and many more wounded. That was a high cost. But it was a necessary one if we were to continue to read the German communications."

"Did we need to read them?"

"Oh, absolutely. So the bottom line is you do what you have to do and you don't do what you must avoid, no matter who gets hurt. If that puts you in a position of being party to death, so be it. It's on your head."

"Then we are murderers."

"I wouldn't put it that way."

"I'm sure you wouldn't."

"No. El-Wasi is the murderer. There is no moral absolute

when the enemy puts you in such a position. Otherwise he could simply blackmail you into surrender."

"Very hardboiled."

"Very necessary."

"I agree with Mr. Williston," Tal said. "We kill when we need to kill and we let die when we need to let die. That is our only means of defense."

"I had hoped for better from you," Dolby said.

"I am an Israeli agent," he replied calmly. "I have risked my own life many times for my people and if necessary I will risk other people's lives for them, too."

"So the end justifies the means?"

"Not always. But sometimes it does. Especially when the means are relatively small and the ends are inconceivably large."

"But how can we know when the means are small enough in relation to the ends? With what assurance do we act?"

"We act with the assurance that we are right. I know—in this case. Do you honestly want to risk any chance we have of anticipating el-Wasi's plans and neutralizing his agents? Unless we do that, we can't get el-Wasi out of the UN. And we have to do that if we want to avoid the possibility of—well, whatever the possibilities are. I leave that up to your own imagination. But I take it you don't want to jeopardize what we have already accomplished?"

She shook her head.

Tal smiled. "Good. You have solved the equation as I have. As I think we all have. Moral uncertainty is the natural estate of man—and woman. Besides, el-Wasi may have something else in mind altogether rather than killing cattle or poisoning meat. That's what we have to figure out—and fast.

"Let's define our problem. El-Wasi has hostages inside. Their room is wired. We've got to capture el-Wasi and get the hostages out, alive. We've got no immediate plan for accomplishing that. Meanwhile, el-Wasi's men are positioned all around the world, preparing greater horrors. That, perhaps, we can stop. At least we may be able to stop some of it, if we can anticipate their acts. I suggest we work on the plague hypothesis, and divide ourselves into a series of 'plague teams,' each with responsibility for trying to predict plagues five through ten."

"And if there are more than ten?" Watkins asked.

Tal's eyes narrowed. "Then the basis of our hypothesis will have expired," he said evenly. "Once el-Wasi runs out of plagues, we'll have to begin again. I suggest we not let that happen."

In the euphoria, Tal repeated his previous request for the New York City report on deployment of its police force. Sykes shook his head sideways.

"Colonel Tal, since your partial solution to this puzzle was so insightful, perhaps you can answer this, too: why are you so interested in that report?"

Tal thought for a moment, then offered: "One must have all the facts in a crisis."

"If one plans to act," Sykes responded. "I'm sure you are aware, Colonel, that you are not in your country and decisions as to actions will be American decisions. Our role here is to come up with ideas, not to execute military operations."

"Really, Colonel Tal," the vice-president continued, "this detailed blueprint of the city police response and deployment can't be of much help to anyone unless he's planning to storm the UN. And I'm sure you'll agree that would be premature for consideration now. I think you'll have to let us decline this one request." He glanced at Williston, who nodded in agreement.

As the vice-president divided the group into plague teams, Nancy Dolby got up and walked to a telephone at the rear of the room. The dial was missing. "How do I make a call on this thing?" she asked out loud, to no one. She had been making her calls from the hotel.

"Just pick it up," the vice-president responded.

"Your call, please," said a voice.

"Oh, uh, Emanuel Newman, please, area code two one two, two four nine four one nine three."

"Please hang up."

"Hang up?"

"I will ring when Mr. Newman is on the line."

"I see. You don't need my credit card number or something like that?"

There was a slight pause. "This *is* official business?"

"Oh, yes."

The operator answered: "We pay for our own calls here."

Dolby hung up the phone and, moments later, it rang. "Mr. Newman on the line. Go ahead," said the operator.

"Manny?"

"Jesus, Nancy. You're down there less than a week and already they're making calls for you. I'm surprised you have time to remember your old friends."

"Oh, Manny, cut the crap. Listen, I need something."

"Name it."

"A copy of the police department's report on its deployment of men at the UN."

"Forget it. That can't fall into the wrong hands. And doesn't the group already have it?"

Dolby's face reddened. "We're not the wrong hands. And *I* would like a copy."

"Listen, sweetheart," Newman said. "That's too hot to be passed around by a phone call."

"For an old friend, Manny?"

"Sure. Just get the group to ask for it in writing. And check, I think they've already got it." A pause. Then: "By the way, Nance, do you have a code name or something?"

"Goodbye, Manny. Say hi to the mayor."

Tal was sitting alone at the videotape machine and pushed a button. By now, the others in the room ignored him when he turned off lights in a corner and began watching the videotape replays. He turned the sound low in order not to interrupt the vice-president's orders to the rest of the group.

Then, the same picture. He had already watched it so many times before that every word and gesture was familiar: The camera, at first panning around the room, suddenly zeroing in on the delegation of Palestinians, their white robes appearing in a cluster at the front of the Hall. After a few minutes, el-Wasi mounting the rostrum and delivering his speech. The Israeli delegation attempting to walk out, stopped by the Arab weapons. Then the camera beginning to swoop about the room showing the Arabs at the back of the Hall apparently stringing their explosives, and a corner of the booth shown as the camera dropped.

Then came that crazy collection of sequences: almost a full minute devoted to the ceiling of the TV booth, then the same jerky movements as the cameraman picked up his minicam, the floor, dirty with wadded paper, cookie crumbs, and paper coffee cups, moving back and forth in a jerky manner, then random and peculiarly angled shots of walls, ceilings, floors, stairs, doors, crevices, and windows, as the cameraman was brought out of the booth, down the stairs.

Tal pressed the "fast forward" button: he had seen the meaningless kaleidoscope of floors and walls and windows and crevices so often, it could all be skipped over this time. He switched the machine back to "play" at the point where the cameraman entered the Hall and focused back on el-Wasi. Then the closeup of el-Wasi, smiling and waving, as the cameraman was instructed to focus on the podium. Then the same unvarying picture of the center of the stage, the focus on the rostrum. El-Wasi resuming his speech.

Tal pushed the "stop" button. He thought: nothing. Not a clue. El-Wasi had done it all perfectly. Then he noticed a strange quiet in the room.

Tal looked around him. Nobody spoke. They were all reading the Bible.

ℵOCTOBER 13:ℵ
TWO DAYS LATER

DOBBYNS RANCH,
NORTHERN TERRITORY,
AUSTRALIA

At 2:27 A.M., a twin-engine jet lumbered down the runway of Penang airport. Chartered to the Malay Trading & Export Co., Ltd., its dull gray exterior was almost completely invisible along the ground. It carried a crew of three and, ostensibly, a cargo of leather goods en route from Bangkok. The flight plan filed with the Malaysian authorities listed the Philippines as the final destination, but once the sturdy craft crossed over the Malay peninsula to the east, the pilot took her off course, veering southeast, through the South China Sea toward the Java Sea.

The plane had been built more than twenty-five years earlier by the British air force. It was a Canberra bomber, intended to fly at 50,000 feet, but the bomber could perform handily at extremely low altitudes, and now the pilot kept it only a few hundred feet above the water. At 540 knots, it would take about five hours to reach destination.

At 4:14, the pilot turned eastward again, having skirted Java and Borneo. A half hour later, the pilot again put the plane on a southeasterly course, crossing the eastern Indonesian islands and over the Timor Sea. Now it was open water for at least an hour. Course corrections kept the plane from crossing over Australian territory too early.

The crew remained silent most of the way, except for occasional routine discussions between the pilot and navigator. The third man sat behind the cockpit, staring from the window. The pilot stayed alert. Flying below radar could be a tricky business, especially when you are cut off from radio contact with the worldwide air controllers' network.

At 6:25 the plane left the sea behind and streaked over land for the first time (except for the brief pass over the Indonesian blips that passed for islands in those parts) since it had left the Malay peninsula nearly four hours before. The pilot spoke excitedly to the third man; the navigator was already busy, poring over the charts that he had spread out around him. The game would get a bit dicier now.

The pilot took his plane up to 800 feet. He could hold it there for about thirty minutes on a nearly exact southeast course; then he would have to come up another two hundred feet, due to the increased elevation in the interior of the Northern Territory. At that he would only be flying about 300 feet above the land, which, fortunately, was largely unpopulated. There was a good chance he could get all the way to his target undetected; if not, he had a cover story ready.

The pilot began to decelerate at 7:12. The bombardier wanted the plane down to 200 knots as they approached the target area. The navigator continued to call out course corrections, though at this point his visual sightings would count for about as much as his instruments. The pilot became aware of the perspiration that drenched his shirt. They flew on for twenty more minutes.

"There it is," the navigator suddenly called out. The pilot looked down; it was 7:30 exactly. Ahead below loomed the large buildings that housed the giant feedlot of the Dobbyns Ranch, on which more than 600,000 head of cattle were fattened for market. The ranch lies midway between Borroloola and Brunette Downs, though a couple of hundred miles to the west. The pilot passed over the ranch, climbing rapidly until he was about twenty miles out. Then he turned back, heading due west. He began a steep descent, to be in position as rapidly as possible. It was imperative to do it right; they would have only one chance and little time. The sound of the aircraft was sure to alert someone, and then the police and later the military authorities would be called.

The Dobbyns cattle were spread over an expanse of nearly 6,000 acres, more than 9 square miles, too much ground to douse thoroughly. But thoroughness was not required: Immediate panic and then political caution would lead the Australian authorities to finish the job for them.

"One minute to target," the navigator called out.

The bombardier sat tensely before a console of buttons that controlled four dozen nozzles fitted into the bomb bay. These were attached to large steel tanks containing what would appear to be pesticide, if inspected. The plane, at 250 feet, was now going as slowly as it could without stalling out. Luckily the air was calm, the wind less than three miles an hour.

"Ten seconds."

The cattle were clearly in view now, immense numbers spread out across the green grazing land. Large, healthy cattle, soon to die.

"Commence firing."

The bombardier activated the nozzles. A fine spray was released, as though the plane were seeding clouds or dusting crops. But inside the tanks were hundreds of gallons of a specially grown culture containing *Brucella abortus*, a microorganism that causes a disease which in cows is known as brucellosis and in humankind is called undulant fever. It is not a pleasant disease. The patient sweats, feels pain in the joints, complains of constant fatigue, suffers from a fever that rises and falls each day—all of which may last for months. Humans can be infected by cow's milk or by eating the meat. Although cattle can be immunized, this large herd had not been. For such a herd, there was but one course: destruction. Most of the cows would be infected, and isolating the healthy ones would not pay. Once it became known that the Dobbyns herd was infected neither the ranch nor the government would have any alternative but to kill them all outright and to put them into the largest mass grave ever dug.

When the plane had swept across its three and one-third mile run, the nozzles were shut down and the pilot banked sharply to the left, reversed direction and began the run again a quarter-mile north. The nozzles were opened and the spraying began anew. The plane repeated this process twelve times; on the thirteenth and final run, seven minutes after it began, its tanks empty and the fine spray settled onto flank and grass, the pilot took it up to a thousand feet, accelerating quickly to over 500 knots, and retraced the course over which it had flown. As it passed over the living quarters, the bombardier ejected a small buoy that would take five minutes to land by parachute. To it was attached a crudely painted sign: "These cattle infected with brucellosis." By the time the message was read the plane would be more than forty miles away, still flying below radar, heading for the sea. By the time the Australian authorities understood what had happened and notified airports around the Pacific, the Canberra bomber was at the bottom of the Timor Sea and the crewmen had become vacationers aboard a pleasure yacht bound for Port Moresby.

PARIS

The cabinet meeting at the Elysée Palace exhausted the patience of every man in the ornate room. Table thumpers, shouters, finger pointers, and hecklers were on steady display late into the evening. The issue was whether France had done everything possible to avert further damage to her national sovereignty and injury to her citizens.

One faction, vehement but distinctly a minority, expressed its outrage that France would not resist el-Wasi's pressure.

Another faction contended that a decision to vote "yes" on el-Wasi's resolution would be not only munificent but under the circumstances all that could be done.

Against these positions, a third group argued for more. The principal proponent of this view was a high-ranking official in the Service de Documentation Exterieure et de Contre-Espionage (SDECE), the French secret service. The voting in the UN was a farce, he explained. It was just a cover. The critical question was the mechanism by which Israel would be dismantled when the time came. Outside the Arab bloc, thirteen nations in Europe and Asia were developing a plan of invasion timed to coincide with the moment that the majority of UN ambassadors acceded to el-Wasi's demands. It was imperative that France be among that group, to insure itself a prominent place at the prize table thereafter. The booty, of course, was oil.

It would be the end of French honor, one minister shouted. It would be the beginning of French power, another replied.

The president of France had remained silent throughout the meeting. Now he rose and a hush fell across the room. "My mind is not made up," he said, "but it is clear that there must be no more attacks in France. Something must be done. You," he pointed to the SDECE man, "come with me." They left the room.

MIAMI

The El Al 707 touched down in a hangar in the rear of the Miami International Airport. Among the passengers were forty-three men and four women dressed in business suits, who walked down the ramp off the plane, carrying their own suitcases. Immediately after clearing customs and passport control, they boarded a waiting DC-8 that had been chartered for their mission. It departed soon after the last man shut the door behind him.

Two and one-half hours later, the jet landed at Westchester Airport in the town of Purchase, thirty miles north of Manhattan. The group disembarked, carrying their baggage, and walked through the terminal to the parking lot, where they entered a row of cars which had been waiting for them, each with a driver.

Within an hour, the Aleph commandoes settled into the Hotel Tudor on Forty-second Street and Second Avenue in New York City, in nine rooms prepaid and registered in the name of the "Electrical Appliances Salesmen of America Convention."

Maj. Mordecai Ofir left his room, went down to the street, and located a telephone booth half a block away. He put through a call to a phone booth in Washington, D.C. Tal came on the line.

"Avram, how are you?"

"Tired, but under the circumstances I would be ashamed to complain. Did everybody get in?"

"Everyone."

"Unnoticed?"

"Unnoticed."

"The Arabs seem to have used some intelligence in planning this operation. I have been confining myself to Washington. They like to talk here and hold meetings, but they are very difficult to deal with when it comes to action. Everything by them is international this and domestic that. And they don't know the Arabs. But we have to work with them, at present. I'm going to stay here for a while longer. I'll reach you at the hotel when I need you."

"Where should we begin?"

"Learn what can be learned over at the UN. I've been unable to get hard information down here about the city police units surrounding the UN. My colleagues don't quite trust me. But we must get the hard facts about how they've deployed their forces—it will be crucial. Scout them out as best you can yourselves."

"Avram, has anyone down there guessed we might be coming into the country?"

"No one. They don't know the Israelis, either."

"That's what's made them such impartial arbiters through all the years—they understand nothing."

"Shalom, Mordecai. Don't be such a cynic."
"Shalom."

THE WHITE HOUSE

"It will take the Australian army unit about a week to bury the cattle," Williston said when the morning meeting convened, fifteen hours after the destruction of Dobbyns Ranch. "Trading in beef futures has been suspended on the London commodities market and the Commodities Futures Trading Commission will consider such action here. The experts tell me that beef prices may double in a week. And we can look for all meat prices to start shooting up. Gentlemen, what do you propose?"

"I say we recommend an assault on the UN and bring this madness to an end," General Sykes said after a moment. "This latest raid shows that there is no way we can outguess the plans el-Wasi has drawn up. If we can't nip the plans we have to nip el-Wasi."

"I said that a week ago," Dolby, seated next to him, reminded the table without looking at Sykes.

"With all deference, Madam, your experience with this type of affair is no doubt less than your experience with other types."

Tal spoke up before she could reply. "If we attack now, we risk killing all the ambassadors and not stopping el-Wasi's assassins in the field."

"He can't have an infinite number of them. This has to stop sooner or later," Sykes argued.

"But it could be much later."

"Well, there were only ten plagues," Pinckney said unexpectedly. "We've already had five. That means in ten more days we can all relax." He smiled.

"I'm afraid it may not be that simple," Tal said patiently. "Ten plagues did the trick for my God, but el-Wasi may need more. The Lord stopped after ten because the Egyptians could not hold out any longer. But I think we can hold out longer, and el-Wasi must be prepared for that contingency. I don't think we can take it for granted that this madness will stop after ten acts of terror."

"Then?" Watkins murmured.

"Then we have to keep working. One of our teams is bound to predict correctly. If we can just catch one of these groups of terrorists before they commit their atrocity, I think we can stop the whole chain of acts."

"Do you really think so?" the vice-president asked.

"I have faith."

"It's as thin a hope as that?"

"Faith is not so thin, Mr. Vice-President," Tal said.

"No, I suppose not, at least not in this administration."

"Shall we get on with it, then?" said a dour Corbin Williston. "Who was assigned to the Plague Six Task Force?" He looked around the table. Doolittle raised his hand.

"Very well, Art, what have you come up with?"

"Well, as you know, the Sixth Plague was boils. The Bible says—and I quote—'And the Lord said unto Moses and unto Aaron, "Take to you handfuls of ashes of the furnace, and let Moses sprinkle it toward the heaven in the sight of Pharaoh. And it shall become small dust in all the land of Egypt, and shall be a boil breaking forth with blains upon man, and upon beast, throughout all the land of Egypt."' End quote."

"The King James Version," Tal noted.

"That's the one I quote from," Doolittle said.

"Following your suggestion, Tal, we have checked through about two hundred commentaries on that particular text, in Hebrew, Greek, Aramaic, Latin, French, Arabic, and English. And we have come up with thirty-seven possibilities."

"That's all?"

"I mean thirty-seven categories of possibilities—thirty-seven main topics. The possibilities, I grant you, are limitless. Shall we go through them?"

Four hours had been established as their limit of endurance at any one sitting. They talked and argued incessantly all morning and came to no firm conclusions. At noon a tray of sandwiches was rolled in, along with stacks of newspapers, the late morning editions of the *New York Times*, the *New York Daily News*, the *Washington Post*, early afternoon editions, the latest London papers, *Ma'ariv* from Jerusalem, and the Australian papers that day. As usual the headlines were large and depressing. "Eight months supply of cattle gone," Pinckney commented from a sofa, surrounded by newspaper sections. "How did they pull that off?"

"Stolen or disguised plane," Sykes explained. "Not too hard. The amount of military hardware floating around this world is colossal. Anyone who wants to start his own little army and air force, not much of a problem, not if someone is bankrolling you, anyway."

Williston was studying the latest intelligence memos that were rushed to him periodically during the day. "A plane left Penang about two-thirty in the morning; that's ten AM our time yesterday. Filed a flight plan to Manila and broke radio contact about twenty minutes after it took off. From a description of the plane it could have been an old British bomber. That's probably how they did it."

"Penang? Where the devil is that?" Watkins asked.

"It's on the Malay peninsula," Doolittle told him.

"I don't even know where *that* is. How can we solve this puzzle in a world as big as this?"

"Gentlemen," Williston concluded, "we've really got a king-size problem."

Dolby slowly pencilled the word "w-o-w" onto her pad. Sykes spotted it from over her shoulder. He slammed his fist down on the table.

"I think Miss New York City here takes this as a joke," he announced. "She sits here doodling while we've got the gravest of responsibilities to undertake, and I'm damn sick of it."

Dolby flushed, then turned to him. "You and the rest of this group seem to me to be accomplishing approximately nothing." Her voice cracked slightly.

"Calm down," Williston interjected. "Control yourself. If you can't take the heat, get out of—or should I say, get *into*—the kitchen."

As a woman in a profession filled with men, she had long ago grown used to the breed of supercilious male. At Harvard Law, on Wall Street, and then in City Hall, hard work had made her at ease with her abilities, and sure of herself. Her accomplishments made her impatient. She wanted to confront problems, make decisions, and implement them. Those who prattled about how helpless they were, or she was, she regarded with contempt.

She turned to Williston. "Cut the chauvinism."

From Sykes: "Sweetheart, you may have come out summa cum laude from Radcliffe, but you could still be my daughter."

"Mr. Sykes—" she began.

He interrupted. "*General* Sykes."

"Mr. General Sykes, who do you think you're talking to?"

Sykes ignored her. "I had hoped," he said to Williston, "that New York would send us someone more experienced in dealing with matters of such grave importance."

Dolby grew furious. "Your idea of 'dealing with,' Herr General, is talking things to death. You've helped make this group entirely incapable of action. A bunch of murderers, financed by ignorant oil-drunk sheiks dictating American foreign policy and international morality from the pinnacle of rigs in the middle of the desert, have effectively taken over control of the world, and the most positive thing you've been able to suggest is that I put down my pencil!"

Sykes began making noises, none of which formed a word.

"General Sykes," she continued. "You are a—bureaucrat." She spat the word out.

Williston told her that kind of talk was neither nice nor productive. She glared at him. Then he added: "Shut up." Her face reddened.

"Mr. Williston," she said, very softly, "this whole group is counterproductive. Your inability to conceive of a plan of action, or to implement one, is scandalous. The world is being blackmailed by savages, and this group has not yet even recommended that we stop feeding them full rations."

She looked at Tal. "He's the only one here capable of doing anything positive beside talk."

Sykes spoke up again. "Then young lady, I don't know why you stay here."

Dolby stood. "For the first time, you're right. I quit."

She stood, removed her coat from the closet, and walked to the door. She opened it, then looked back at the conference table.

"Good luck, Colonel Tal," she said, and left with a toss of her head.

NEW YORK CITY

A youngish man, well-built, raised the window facing east in a twelfth floor office at 809 First Avenue, and looked down. He could see the General Assembly building completely surrounded by buses, touching nose to rear, keeping the thousands of curious onlookers away. Within the circumference formed by the buses was a forbidding assortment of police cars and heavy-duty military equipment of the NYPD Special Operations Division: tanks, bulldozers, armored personnel carriers, and a mobile command van. Several dozen policemen were milling around in this area, shielded from the General Assembly building by the heavy vehicles. The area between those vehicles and the building, was deserted.

The young man on the twelfth floor had nearly finished snapping a roll of film when the building custodian came up from behind and asked if he needed help. The young man shook his head sideways, turned away quickly, and hurriedly left the office.

A taxi continuously shuttled across the Forty-second Street ramp off the East River Drive south of the UN. The men inside all kept staring north while crossing First Avenue. They, and their driver, spoke Hebrew.

The Circle Line, a tourist boat that sails around Manhattan several times a day, was confined for security reasons during the first few days of the siege to the Hudson River on the west side of Manhattan. Later, permission for it to resume its tour completely around the island was restored. Today, two large men began snapping photographs as the boat, heading north, cruised up the East River past the UN.

In the personnel office of American Rivertronics Company on the thirty-seventh floor of the building at the corner of Forty-eighth and First Avenue, the receptionist was having a hard time filling out the man's form. The job applicant, a strongly built young man, seemed to be paying little attention to her. His gaze was fixed southward, out the window over her shoulder, downward, toward the northern end of the building under siege. He seemed preoccupied, barely answered her questions, and, when he did, he spoke with an accent she could not quite place. She finally had to tell him there was no immediate opening but they would call him. He did not seem very disappointed when he thanked her. Before leaving, he walked over to the window, complimented her on the view, and began snapping photographs.

An attractive brunette stood peering through the thin space between two buses. At last, the officer who had been giving orders and was very obviously in charge walked away from the police van bearing license tag SOD-1. She called to him to come over to answer a question, and he smiled at her and approached. She asked for some directions, and he answered. He asked if that was a French accent, and she answered yes. Then he told her what a pretty girl she was, turned, and walked away. Before he did, she noted that the nametag on his chest said "Captain de Petri."

At the New York Public Library, a man spent several hours ordering and poring over old books about the UN. He seemed particularly interested in its architecture, and photostated whatever blueprints and architectural designs he could find.

The five Israelis in the car all noticed, when they entered the underpass of the East River Drive that curves beneath the UN gardens, a large screened vent in the wall. They returned in a pickup truck, stopped it in the right lane beneath the vent, and placed "Con Edison" placards on the ground behind their truck. The paint on the placards had not yet dried. They placed a ladder against the wall, and one of the men climbed up, unscrewed the vent, and crawled into the shaft. It was dark and filled with the filth and soot of too many years gone by. With his flashlight and an ice pick, he made his way forward through the shaft on his belly. Thirty-five yards later, and nearly under the General Assembly building, he found that the shaft terminated in impenetrable concrete. He crawled back out, blackened, and the group left.

A man wearing a tag on his jacket that read "Press— *New York Daily News*" picked his way through the crowd, snapping pictures of the people, the buildings, the buses, everything: nine rolls of film.

The hotdog vendor stood at the corner of Forty-fifth Street and First Avenue. His instructions were to spend a day there and look the crowd over, get to know the people.

It was a ragtag lot. Always thin in the morning, the policeman informed him when he came over to inspect his food purveyor's license. Gets bigger in the afternoon, at its peak between four and seven. For the most part, the morning group comprised the regulars. What an odd assortment they were, too: as diverse a segment of eccentric humanity as could be found anywhere. Several caught his eye. A short woman, she looked in her sixties, wearing a ruffled gray muslin skirt, sweaters, loops of gold link necklaces, a bright red bandana wrapped over her forehead and tied at the back of her head, paced back and forth exhorting those whom she passed to trust in Jesus and be saved. As she walked she kicked up her skirts, revealing a dirty pair of white sneakers and red, swollen ankles. On the corner, squatting against the building, a panhandler. He wore a white yachting cap with the initials N.Y.A.C. in blue on the front. He held out a set of cheap pens and asked a quarter of every passerby.

Two old, thin blind men, one black, one white, with dogs, cups, and canes, stood at opposite ends of the street, each wearing signs blessing the givers. Several members of the Hare Krishna sect danced around, heads bald, reddish frocks swirling in the slight breeze; sandal-footed, they chanted, beating on tambourines. A giant black man, nearly seven feet tall, in a dizzying pink suit, leopard-colored spotted shoes, and a bright orange stetson, hurried by every half-hour, each time going in the opposite direction. An odd woman with long golden curls, lips puffy with lipstick, burly looking legs protruding from a miniskirt, mincing as she walked. A hooker? On the third pass, the hotdog man concluded that he had finally seen a genuine transvestite.

And the unshaven, old sad-faced man with baggy pants that he kept hitching up at the waist. At his left ear he held a small square radio and moved his lips as if in time to music, but the radio was silent. The man came and went, looking now at the ground, now across the street at the building, again at the sidewalk beneath his feet. He wore strange-looking green shoes. Endlessly he paced. Once the vendor watched him make his rounds. He saw him down to Forty-second Street, where he disappeared around the corner; but five minutes later the man was heading back.

There were normal looking people, too, who walked along, past the crowds who stood and gawked at the scene across the avenue. Two of them stayed a long while; men in their thirties, stocky, wearing checked sports coats, clashing striped ties, and brown hats. FBI agents, he later learned.

But the crazies were the special attraction. They warded away the boredom of the lookout. Crazy, yes, but peaceable enough, allowed to roam the streets because no one supposed they were capable of harm. Harmless as the lizard.

Uri Shir, who had never sold a hotdog before, drifted into a reverie, still watching, one part of his brain still active here in New York, but another remembering that morning years ago, that crystal-clear morning in the Sinai—camping out; alone at what seemed the sandy base of the universe, the world stretching out and up around him. Comforting somehow to be so small and unnoticed in the dry heat of that summer day. How small was man, how insignificant must he seem to the world that held him up and succored him. A movement. A lizard scurried toward his belongings. He took his long knife from the sheath, held it out, waited motionless. The lizard within reach: arm out and down; in an instant, the lizard, headless, lay wriggling—the dance of death. In a few weeks he would join the army and learn to kill men as he had killed the lizard, or even more efficiently—he shuddered at the memory of the thought that began to sicken him in the white glare of that summer day. Killing: He had learned to do it; he had done it to help save his country. But it was wrong, nonetheless. Killing was contrary to man's law and God's law, no matter what they said, no matter how they rationalized, no matter that he had done it and would do it again if he had to. A bad business: He would resign. Join the kibbutz: learn the arts of war no more.

The lizard had been harmless, but it had got in his way. He moved his cart back a few feet, withdrawing from the path of these swarms. Just watch and report. That was his assignment. Stay invisible. Let the lizards go by.

FORT BRAGG, NORTH CAROLINA

Nine days had come and gone. The men of K Detachment were ready—physically they were as alert as they would ever be. But ready for what? They had never been battle tested. They strutted about in the mess hall and engaged in the cocky banter of special forces men everywhere, but underneath it, Colonel McDougal felt the unease.

There was no clear plan. Without one all their bravery would be wasted, all their braggadocio empty. But whose job was it to plan? The colonel could not make the decision to invade. He could not even get permission to send three men to New York to reconnoiter. Stay in place, he had been told by his various superiors in Washington, each still fighting for direct command of K Detachment.

He had begun, nevertheless, with dozens of plans. The planners within K Detachment talked about tear gas, sleeping gas, other poisons, laser beams, stun lights, sound grenades, flooding to short the circuitry, helicopter descents, "subterranean encroachments," but none of these nor other schemes avoided the primary risk—that of blowing up the Hall and its 156 hostages. At some length, they discussed the feasibility of an "incursion" into the "outer perimeter"— the areas inside the General Assembly building that surrounded the Hall. Getting in would be manageable. The TV camera guarded the delegates' entrance, but there were other means of ingress to the vast lobby and spaces outside the Hall. But what purpose would be served by that? If their entry wasn't one hundred percent secret, TV would report their doings directly to el-Wasi. There was no way to shut up the broadcasters. And even if "total cover" were achieved in the initial assault, what then? To have a hundred men outside Action Zero and not be able to act would be useless. He needed outside help and wasn't getting it.

McDougal's professional calm during the week of preparation was giving way to dejection. He complained to Sykes that the Washington snafu was greater than usual. Sykes was mysterious. "There may be a break," he said but would not elaborate. Then Sykes said something that made McDougal jump. "Forget the Pentagon. Forget the strategists. You create the plan. Eventually it'll be up to you anyway. Because what can they do? You're the experts down there. This thing will be in your hands—my God, Arthur, the world may be in your hands."

McDougal's skin grew clammy. He had never been told by higher authority to disregard the orders of higher authority. They never taught this kind of reality in the army.

CITY HALL, NEW YORK

Though Nancy Dolby had expected the worst, the mayor's vehemence surprised her.

"I will accept no explanations, Nancy. What you did was not appropriate behavior for the representative of the greatest city on the face of the earth."

The mayor slumped into the leather chair behind his large mahogany desk. He had been pacing back and forth across the room, frenetically, since Nancy had entered his office and reported her resignation from the Emergency Group. It had taken ten minutes for Manny Newman to quiet him down and, finally, coax him into his seat.

"I'm sorry you feel so strongly about it, Mr. Mayor," she repeated, "but I've still got some ideals left and those bureaucrats—"

"Cut the 'ideals' bullshit," Newman interrupted. "Do you know how thoroughly Washington must be pissed off by what you did? Do you have any idea—I mean do you have *any* idea—how much money your idealism is going to cost this city? And how many votes that is going to cost this administration in the next election? You have betrayed your trust."

"I have principles, Manny."

"Let me tell you what you can do with them—"

The mayor interrupted. "Look, Nancy, you've got responsibilities quite apart from your personal principles. I sent you down there not just because I believed you were bright—there are many bright people on our payroll. I thought you'd have a significant contribution to make, and I certainly thought you'd act responsibly. That was not responsible behavior, storming out that way."

"Like a pouting child," Newman added.

"Like a person of principles," Dolby attempted to correct him.

The mayor held up his hands for some temporary peace. "Nancy, this matter is really too serious for further discussion. There are no alternatives. You simply must return to Washington, at once, and apologize your way back into those meetings."

"I can't. I won't."

"You must."

"They're clowns down there, all but the Israeli. He's the only real man in the bunch; the rest are just windbags. If they'd left him to his devices I'm sure the whole thing would be solved by now."

Newman turned to the mayor. "I warned you not to send a broad down there." Then, to Dolby: "This is not the time, darling, to become a philosopher or a teenie-bopper, but to get your adorable little ass back down to the capital."

The mayor cut off Dolby's response. "Look, Nancy, Manny, let's not waste more time with more words. The whole world may be blown up any minute, right in my backyard, and when they write the obituaries I don't want it said that this administration was fiddling, so to speak, while the world burned. Nancy, the bottom line is you've got to return. Someone from here has got to be there, and it's too late for them to accept a newcomer from the city. You simply can't afford the luxury of your ideals."

The mayor was trying to control himself, but his face was red. He pointed to two large stacks of paper in the middle of the matching mahogany credenza behind his desk. "See those? Every day I'm getting reports from every major municipal agency on how they're responding to this crisis— the police, firemen, garbagemen, everyone." Dolby turned to look. "Believe me," the mayor continued, "there are headaches enough without additional problems erupting from people I thought I could trust."

The mayor paused for emphasis. Nancy Dolby thought: reports. Tal wanted a report.

Newman's voice filled the silence. "It's costing this city plenty of millions of dollars every day to cope with this situation, honey. And I can tell you that when this is all finally over, if any of us are still alive, we're going to have to ask Washington to reimburse us for all this, and we can't let them say New York walked out when the sledding got rough. And if you don't get your ass back in gear down there, it's going to be lots of dough flushed down the toilet, kaput."

"But it's not only the money, Nancy," the mayor said. "It's not responsible behavior for a city like this to remove itself from the decisions being made in Washington. We can't do it, period."

Silence. Dolby finally sat down in a chair across from the mayor's desk. She draped her pocketbook across one of its arms. The mayor smiled at her, then rose and began walking toward her. She glanced at the papers on the credenza.

"Think about it, Nancy. I've got to meet with the head of the sanitationmen's union now. Stay here with Manny and talk it out. But remember—this city, and I personally, need you back on a plane to Washington today. And don't worry about having to eat a little crow by going back." He turned to Newman. "Talk some sense into her." Then, to Dolby: "There'll be a car waiting outside to take you to the airport." He walked toward the door, then turned.

"And Nancy?"

"Yes, sir?"

"Good luck when you go back." The mayor left.

Manny Newman walked over to Dolby and put his arm around her shoulders. "There are things in life, Nancy, that one does even though they're unpleasant."

"Please, Manny get your sweaty hand off me and don't give me any of that 'things in life' bullshit."

"If I can't give you that bullshit, what can I give you?"

Nancy looked at him and smiled for the first time that afternoon.

"How about some of that good Johnnie Walker that His Honor keeps in the closet? If I'm going to eat crow in Washington for him, I'd like to loosen up here first at his expense."

Manny said he considered that an absolutely fine idea. He did not stop to consider that he had never seen her take a drink before. He removed a bottle of scotch and two shot glasses from a closet in a corner of the room, set the glasses on the mayor's desk, and poured.

Newman offered a toast. "To your dignity." They quaffed off the glasses in a gulp. Dolby felt her insides burn. She asked for another shot. Manny filled both glasses.

Dolby lifted hers: "To the budget of the City of New York, may it never lose its balance." Newman drank down the glass quickly. He kept his head tilted back, waiting for the last drop to spill into his mouth. Before raising her glass to her lips, Dolby emptied it with a quick flick onto the mayor's carpet. Loudly and from deep within, Manny Newman belched.

"Manny, that's the cleverest comment I've ever heard you make." They began chatting. She told him of the members of the Emergency Group, one by one.

Half an hour later, Newman refilled the glasses and lifted

his. "A toast to Jennings Pinckney," he said and began sipping. He noticed that Nancy was talking more to him now than she ever had. He felt happy, flattered. She knew him well, and she kept chattering.

"Manny, you're persuading me. Let's pour another one before I go."

"I'll drink to that," he answered, and did.

She refilled his glass and made a pouring gesture toward hers. Newman lifted his glass: "To a sensible woman. And a sexy one." He began sipping again, but his body no longer would take more. He saw Dolby raise her glass to her lips and tilt it toward her mouth. He did not notice that her glass was empty.

Newman removed his tie and flung it onto the mayor's desk. He was pleased by her attention. Soon, his arm again wrapped its way around Nancy's shoulder, but this time he hardly seemed to notice when she slipped away from it. Indeed, he now hardly seemed aware that he had put it there. Nancy Dolby learned that Manny Newman thought it extraordinarily humorous to belch in different keys from deep within his guts. He tried another sip, then began to belch the melody of "Yankee Doodle," but midway through the tune his inspiration and energy began to flag, and he lay down, smiling broadly, hands clasped across his lap, on the couch of the mayor of the greatest city on the face of the earth. And in those circumstances he began snoring, loud and repeatedly. His jaw dropped down and mouth opened and his oversized belly began rising and falling rhythmically.

Dolby walked over to the sofa and put her hand on Newman's shoulder. Nothing. She shook him slightly. Nothing but the continual open-mouthed snoring.

Quickly she walked to the credenza behind the mayor's desk and began sifting through the documents piled in two foot-high stacks. Midway through the second pile she spotted the title "N.Y.P.D. Response and Deployment at UN" on the cover page of some half-dozen sheets of typewritten paper stapled together. She glanced back at Newman. Still out. She skimmed through the report, then slipped it out of the stack and tiptoed to her pocketbook on the chair facing the desk. She folded the report and stuffed it inside.

A glance back at Newman. Asleep. Dolby found a pad of paper on the desk. Printed in italics at the top of each sheet were the words "From the Mayor's Desk." She tore off a page and wrote:

> *Dear Manny:*
> *Tell the mayor you convinced me. I hope he appreciates the job you did. For my sake, I hope crow tastes good.*
> *Love and kisses,*
> *Nancy*

She curled the piece of paper into a cylinder, picked Newman's tie off the desk, and knotted the tie around the paper. She placed it gently on his stomach. Dolby tiptoed to the door and eased it open. She hurried past the secretary in the outer office, walked to the street, and climbed into the waiting limousine.

ℵ OCTOBER 15: ℵ
TWO DAYS LATER

WINDSCALE, ENGLAND

Before the sun rises, the road along the Irish Sea coast at Windscale, where the British government operates a nuclear fuel reprocessing plant, is almost always deserted. A large truck was in low gear as it climbed the slight rise in the road seven miles from the facility. The driver could see the lights of a small car coming toward him from a distance. The car suddenly veered into the northbound lane a quarter of a mile away. At first the truck driver thought the car was turning around. But as the car backed up it stopped, overlapping both lanes, facing crosswise and pointing toward the field that surrounded the road. "What in blazes?" the driver remarked to himself, as he braked his heavy truck in time to avoid a collison. It would not do to get into an accident. Not with the cargo on this truck.

He stopped about thirty feet in front of the car. It was a Citroen; the motor was still running, lights on. He put on his high beams. He saw two figures. "Hey, what do you suppose they're up to?" he asked, turning to the trucker in the passenger seat.

"I don't know, Charles, but I don't like it." He reached into the glove compartment of the cabin and removed a .44 Magnum. It was loaded. The driver pushed a button on the dashboard and picked up a microphone. "Ed," he said, "something strange ahead. I don't like the looks of it. Gaffney's going out. Cover him."

As Gaffney opened the door and swung to the ground, a rifleman in a concealed compartment atop the truck pulled a visor four inches to the left. From thirty feet the motion would not have been perceptible. He could see Gaffney walk toward the car. The driver of the car sat on the far side. Gaffney walked up to the passenger on the near side; the window was rolled down. "What's the problem, blokes?" he said.

The passenger pointed to the driver, who was holding his hand over his chest. "I think he's had a heart attack." There was something slightly foreign about the accent. It wasn't midlands, for sure.

Gaffney walked around the front of the car to reach the driver. "Where are you from?" he called out.

"Brighton," the man said. That might explain it. The man ambled behind Gaffney.

He reached for the door handle. "I'm going to lift him out," he said. He opened the front door and reached in to touch the man's arms when he felt a sharp pain through his neck. The driver rolled out, keeping low, and kneed Gaffney in the crotch. He crumpled to the ground, unconscious.

From the truck, the man in the topside compartment saw Gaffney go down. He squinted through a telescopic sight attached to his Webley & Scott 728, but he couldn't get a bead on either of them; they were crouching behind the car. "Gaffney's been hit," he said softly through the mike to the driver.

"I'll radio for police," Charles said.

The Citroen driver had a bullhorn in his hand; he raised it to his mouth and his amplified voice, breaking the eerie silence of the still-dark morning, cut across to the truck.

"We have your man. He will not be harmed—if you co-operate. Come out of the truck with your hands up. No weapons."

"Go ahead, Charles," the man up top said. "I will cover you. Try to get Gaffney brought around front."

Charles opened the driver's door and climbed down slowly. He put his hands over his head and stood by the truck.

The voice from the far side of the car ordered: "Now walk slowly this way. Keep those hands above your head."

"What do you want?" Charles called out.

"Your truck." Charles now saw that the man had a pistol in his other hand. The man walked around the side of the car, dropping the bullhorn. The other man brought Gaffney up to his feet and shoved him around the side also. "Tie them," the first man said.

"Why don't we just shoot them now?" the other asked.

"Not until you're sure you can drive that thing. Get the gear out."

The other man deposited Gaffney in front of the first man, still holding the gun. Gaffney sat down dazed. The second man retreated to the car, pulling out what appeared to be two space suits. "Put them in the cabin."

The hidden rifleman in the truck waited until the man carrying the suits was within ten feet. He fired, and the man toppled over backward. A second shot rang out, hitting the body again, but it was already dead. Charles dived to the ground when he heard the rifle's first retort, lunging against Gaffney and pulling him flat.

The driver of the Citroen panicked. He could see nothing through the glare of the truck lights. There were supposed to be only two men on the truck, but obviously there was at least one more, firing from somewhere. He rolled on the ground himself, then scurried on his belly toward the front of the car. A bullet glanced off the bumper. He picked himself up and dashed to the far side, staying low. The door on the driver's side was open. He got in; he had left the motor on, as instructed. He kept his head below the seat and put the car into gear. It lurched forward; he cut the wheel sharply to the right and recovered the pavement before the car ran altogether into the field. The rifleman was still firing. A bullet tore into the trunk. He steered a zig-zag course and gunned the car. After a bend in the road and a slight depression, he was out of sight and beyond range.

Charles picked Gaffney up. He was groggy but standing on his own. They collected the suits that had fallen to the ground and while Gaffney carried them to the truck, Charles inspected the body of the man lying on the road. Two tiny pools of blood were forming under his head and back. "He's dead all right," Charles called out.

A patrol car arrived within minutes. The police had discovered the Citroen two miles down the road, abandoned. No sign of the driver. He had apparently parked an escape vehicle nearby for just such an emergency. The military helicopter landed two minutes later. The agent had a brief conversation with one of the police officers, then collected the body. "You'll have police escort," he said to Charles. "You'll dump your cargo, then we'll fly you in to London for debriefing. Not a word to anyone. We cannot allow this to be breathed about. If the papers get wind of this—well, the home secretary will not stand for it."

"It goes that high?"

"It goes higher."

"I understand."

"What are those?" the agent asked, pointing to the suits draped over the seat in the cabin.

"Radiation suits. They took them out of the car, apparently to put them on."

"How long are they good for?"

"About an hour if they're close to the radiation source."

"Could they handle your cargo with them?"

"Yes, if they meant to carry it around like a baby in a basket. They'd have to have them. And then they would have to leave the baby on somebody's doorstep and run like hell. But why would they want to do that?"

"That's what we want to find out. Come on, let's go."

ℵ OCTOBER 16: ℵ
ONE DAY LATER

WNET-TV STUDIO

Ever since the siege had begun twelve days earlier, Tyler Johnson had stayed at the studio. He would be nearer the news, he had told his producer. He could function at a moment's notice. So a small room adjacent to Studio 3 became his bedchamber and housed a cot, to which he retired every night promptly after watching the other local news programs on different TV sets, at 11:30. Last night he had gone to bed reluctantly, nervously, aware that the acts for which el-Wasi claimed responsibility had come every two days and that the end of the second day after the bombing of Dobbyns Ranch was now at hand. Had actually passed, in fact. It had been 54½ hours since the attack in Australia. The next event was overdue. It would probably come as he slept. Consequently he slept poorly, dreaming fitfully that a huge AP ticker kept announcing that el-Wasi had taken credit for an unceasing stream of bizarre antisocial acts: bombings, killings, lootings, pulling the plug on his TV show, pulling the plug, pulling the plug. . . .

He got out of bed at 5 A.M., unable to turn off the demons and unwilling to confront them. It had all seemed so real. He shook his head, pushed his way into the studio. It was pitch black. He groped for a switch, found one, fumbled with it, finally turned on a solitary light along the back. It lit up the ticker. The ticker was typing. He ran to it, a dread inside, his heart pumping hard, his mouth dry. Local news. He pulled up the long scrolled sheet that had fallen over the front of the machine. He scanned it going back to 11:30. Nothing. Quiet at the UN. Quiet around the world. Quiet in New York. Nothing unusual seemed to have occurred. A shooting or two, a freak six-car accident on the Los Angeles freeways, a school busing demonstration in Boston, shark sightings, meat prices out of sight, Utah man claiming to have conversed with aliens from space who arrived in something shaped like a Bentley—none of that was out of the ordinary; with the exception of meat prices, none could be attributed to terrorists. Was there a change in el-Wasi's plans? Some worse event planned for today? Had the countries that counted, the big powers, secretly decided to dump Israel? Maybe that was it. God, wouldn't that be something. What a story. Headline: "El-Wasi Wins: Israel Destroyed."

"Jane." He yelled for his chief writer. No answer. Of course not. Only 5:15. He would write it himself. He shuffled sleepily to a desk in the corner, swept a mass of papers and old coffee cups to the floor and began writing.

"It is now the beginning of the third morning," he wrote, "since the poisoning of the cattle at Dobbyns Ranch in northern Australia, the last act of terror perpetrated by the Palestinian commando el-Wasi, the self-proclaimed 'kidnapper of the world,' who with five of his cronies is holding the United Nations ambassadors under siege in New York. Since the poisoning began eleven days ago, there has been a remorseless, two-day cycle to the terrorist attacks that el-Wasi has described as 'self-triggering' and as necessary to induce the world powers to dismantle the State of Israel. But now that cycle seems to have been interrupted or at least suspended. There has been no apparent major catastrophe during the past 24 hours that would qualify—"

He struck out the word "qualify": too sententious. ". . . that would put it in the big leagues of international terrorism.

"As usual, no one is talking. It has been impossible to get any statement from el-Wasi other than those that he chooses to deliver at his own time. The networks have repeatedly asked for direct interviews, and at this time I repeat the request directly to Mr. el-Wasi, if you are listening, sir, but so far he has spurned all offers. He has said he intends to control all news going out of the General Assembly chamber, in which 156 people are being held hostage. The mood in the chamber is grim. Many of the ambassadors are ill; with food rations cut to twice a day, doctors are predicting that manifestations of malnutrition will soon appear among the delegates.

"The mood in Washington is no less grim. The White House has so far refused all direct comment, saying only that the president is in close daily contact with the heads of the major nations. Dr. Drognan Kowalski, national security adviser to the president, has stated that the United States 'stands unequivocally behind Israel, come what may,' in his words. He has also said that the United States is 'considering its options.' But this sudden departure from the two-day cycle of events has caused a number of high officials to wonder whether some deal is now being negotiated."

Johnson paused. He wasn't sure whether Jane would let him get away with that last comment; at the least he'd have to find one or two such officials to do such speculating. That shouldn't be too hard. People were always anxious to have their speculations, if not their names, used on the air; and if their names weren't mentioned they usually didn't much mind what speculations were attributed to them.

GENERAL ASSEMBLY HALL

El-Wasi kept staring at one of the televisions, the one not permanently switched to Channel 7. He did not smile. As each newscast ended, he switched to another channel. Then there were no more newscasts and the only news on the tube was what he could see directly: the scene inside the General Assembly itself.

In disgust he turned off the television and hurried off the podium to his guard at the front door of the Hall. After a brief whispered conference, he repeated the procedure with the four other commandoes. Then he strode briskly to the rostrum and grabbed the microphone.

"Time is passing," he began, "and our patience is rapidly wearing thin. You, the world outside this Hall, have been very lucky today. You do not know how lucky. But let me assure you that your luck is very temporary. Be assured that we are completely in control.

"You call our actions terrorism? So be it. The reign of terror shall continue until you halt it by vote of this tribunal. Be assured that there is no way you can stop us. You will learn within twenty-four hours how brief a respite your luck has brought. Do not suppose that this surcease will avail you anything. The commentators are wrong, desperately wrong. You should proceed as if your expectations yesterday were fulfilled. There are no negotiations—yet. There can be no negotiations until this Assembly has voted the principle that we seek: the recognition that Israel is a rogue nation that must be dismantled. This is your last chance—the last chance of the superpowers, and I say it again, the last chance even of my Arab brothers."

The ambassador from Morocco stood up. He could contain himself no longer. He was afflicted, he confided to his few friends in the Hall, with a severe psychological handicap: he was a claustrophobic. In ordinary times the vast space of the Hall would not disturb him. But he had been cooped up nearly two weeks. Worse, the room kept effec-

tively shrinking, as the ambassadors retreated from the
stench in the rear. For the three days past, he was coming
slowly unhinged. He felt an enormous weight pressing
on his head and face. His ears had started ringing two days
ago. His skin was crawling; something inside him was
straining to break through. To stay any longer would mean
suffocation—or madness.

"I'm going," he said to the Algerian ambassador.

"My friend, I beg you, do not. Stay with me."

"I cannot."

"But you cannot get out. You will blow us all up."

"I do not think so. I tell you it is a bluff. I must go."

The Moroccan walked slowly toward the rear. At first
it appeared he was heading for the lavatory. The system of
raising one's hand to obtain permission to walk back had
broken down. The smell was a more effective regulator: No
one walked back unless absolutely necessary. But well short
of the lavatory, the ambassador veered to the left. When
he was fifteen feet from the side door he lost his anonymity.

"You!" an Arab across the Hall shouted. "Where do you
think you're going?"

The man kept walking, not looking up, his eyes fixed
on the door.

El-Wasi stared in disbelief. "Stop," he shouted into the
microphone in Arabic and English. Everyone turned to
watch. The man kept walking toward his salvation. When
the Moroccan was three yards from the door, el-Wasi
screamed at Bekr, his associate nearest him: "He'll blow
us sky high! Shoot him!"

Bekr swung his Ingram 10 into firing position. He
squeezed the trigger twice. The first burst hit the Moroccan
ambassador in his right side and ripped through his lungs
and chest, penetrating the UN wall beyond. The second
burst exploded in his head. He toppled forward, two feet
from the door.

His body was dragged to the rear of the Hall and left on
the ground.

MESSAGE INTERCEPTED AT CIA HEADQUARTERS, LANGLEY, FROM JERUSALEM
(translated from the Hebrew Code)

Classification: TOP SECRET
To: Avram Tal
From: Mossad
Date: 16 October, 1630 Hours
Reference: Big Ears
Action Requested: Information Only
Herewith, operational update on Operation Big Ears, French sector. Senior staff in the French High Command are preparing plans for military invasion of Israel. Code name: Survival. Although these plans are still being formulated and have not been officially broached to Elysée Palace, informal discussions suggest impetus stems from highest civilian ranks. Especially ominous is report that plans call for coordinated attack with military units from at least 13 other nations, now being contacted at intelligence levels. Contact with Riyadh, Amman, and Damascus rumored but not substantiated at this time. Nuclear probability: negative. French concern said to be "world survival" and "normalcy." Alternatives being discussed include secret asylum for select number of ranking Israelis— as a bribe. Plans could be readied by October 23, or within five days, pending increase in size of UN affirmative vote to 75 nations. Hurry.

ASSOCIATED PRESS "A" WIRE, TRANSMITTED FROM NEW YORK

XT1020
12:22
By AP
Cairo (Oct.16) -- A four-alarm fire broke out near government headquarters here in the central section of the Egyptian capital just after 7 PM (12 noon EST). Firemen are devoting most of their attention to what is said to be a police precinct headquarters, where fire is reported to have spread throughout the three-story building.
XT1020
12:31
By AP
Cairo (Oct.16) -- Fire fighters have so far been unable to subdue what city officials are calling a "freak" fire in central Cairo. An alarm called in at 7 PM (12 noon EST) brought four truck-and-ladders racing to central police headquarters, where fire had already spread through the three-story building.
XT1020
12:37
By AP
Cairo (Oct.16) -- A second fire alarm has brought fire fighting equipment to Hafanda, two miles away from the site of a spreading fire in the center of the Egyptian capital. The mayor's office says the two fires are unrelated and that firemen "are already bringing both under control."
URGENT URGENT URGENT URGENT URGENT
XT1020
12:42
By AP
Cairo (Oct.16) -- Fire is sweeping throughout the Egyptian capital. With more than 20 alarms sounded since 7 PM (12 noon EST) this evening, all city fire fighting

equipment has been dispatched. The mayor's office, which at 7:25 declared no relation to exist between two fires then discovered, now refuses all comment.
URGENT URGENT URGENT URGENT URGENT
XT1020
12:44
By AP
Cairo (Oct.16) -- The Egyptian capital tonight is a blazing inferno. Apparently uncontrollable fire is sweeping through all sections of the city. Officials at fire department headquarters have called upon the Egyptian army for emergency assistance. During a 30-minute period from 7 PM (12 noon EST), operators at department headquarters logged 86 alarms in widely scattered parts of this ancient town. Unconfirmed reports suggest widespread panic.
XT1020
12:50
By AP
New York (Oct.16) -- The Associated Press has temporarily lost computer contact with its Cairo bureau because of the fire that is sweeping the city. The AP regrets the inconvenience, and expects to re-establish contact momentarily.

THE WHITE HOUSE

It had been three days since the vice-president had told Nancy Dolby they would accept her apology and had shook her hand. But not until this morning had she decided what to do with the police blueprint. She draped her coat onto a windowsill and sat in the empty seat between Sykes, who ignored her, and Dr. Jones.

Watkins brought the discussion into gear. "I just don't get it," he complained. "Why do they wait three days and then all of a sudden try to burn down a city? What the hell does that have to do with boils? Not another one of el-Wasi's metaphors, Tal? Do you think this madman is a poet?"

"Yes, and why Cairo, eh?" Pinckney asked. He had learned to speak up only after someone else had led the way.

"The Cairo part is easy, Jennings," Watkins responded. "El-Wasi's threat that this is the world's 'last chance' must include Egypt in the warning."

"He especially means to include Egypt," Tal added. "That is his sorest point. That is what brought all this to a head. If Sadat had not gone to Jerusalem and if there had been no Camp David, el-Wasi might have continued to hope he could extort a homeland through a big-power agreement. But Sadat doomed his chances. So I'm not surprised. I'm only surprised he didn't strike there sooner."

"But how can the Cairo fires relate to boils, the sixth plague?" Watkins asked.

Sykes looked smugly at Tal. "Do you suggest el-Wasi, our mastermind, concluded that fire causes boiling?" Tal stared back at him without speaking.

Jones broke the silence. "But fire can certainly pucker up the skin."

"That's it!" Pinckney cried.

"Then why the three days?"

"Maybe they had trouble with whatever they used to start the fires."

"I don't think that's likely," said Tal. "Egypt is perhaps the easiest place in which to commit such an act. There's something wrong. The three days is troubling. El-Wasi is too methodical. And there would be no reason for him to inject uncertainty at this stage."

"Then what do you suppose?"

"Perhaps it's another plague," Sykes said. "Like maybe Number Seven. Who has Seven?"

Tal nodded. "Yes, General, I like that. But if—"

"How could that be?" Dr. Kowalski interrupted. He had not attended the meetings regularly. He was sitting in now because the president was becoming very impatient at the lack of plans. "The Seventh Plague is hail, so how could it be symbolized by fire?"

"Yes sir, hail, but also fire," Watkins said. He was in charge of the Seventh Plague and he was excited. "Actually it wasn't one plague, it was three—thunder, hail, and fire, and the land was scorched and people died."

"So Cairo was the Seventh Plague?" Kowalski asked.

"Seems so," Tal said.

"Then what happened to Number Six?"

"That is the question, isn't it? Let's find it."

"What in hell for?" Kowalski asked testily. "I really don't think we have the time to worry about things that didn't happen. May I remind you why we are here? The president wants answers."

"And this is one answer we cannot afford to do without," Tal replied. "Why not? I'll tell you why not. Because if we can find out what the Sixth Plague was and why it didn't happen, then we are sitting on our most important discovery since we discovered that these acts represent the plagues."

"What, that they can happen out of order?"

"No, no," Tal answered. "That the series can somehow be restarted even if one incident fails. Remember, el-Wasi claims that they are a self-triggering series. But suppose they are not. Now that I think about it, why should they be? There is always the chance of failure. The commando chief for Number Six, or for any plague, could be killed in an accident completely unrelated to all this. He could be hit by a bus. Or they could be detected and prevented from acting. There are too many things el-Wasi can't control."

"So?"

"So, how can I put it more plainly? El-Wasi must have devised a backup system in order not to have to rely on the success of one venture in order to activate the next one. He must have some way of starting the chain again if for some reason something slips."

"Maybe. But so what?" Sykes challenged.

"Don't you see? This piece of information—which you don't seem to regard as important—helps us define our tactical objectives. We must stop el-Wasi not only in order to free the hostages, but also to prevent him from reactivating the sequence of terrorist activities around the world."

"But sir," Sykes interjected, "by your theory the sequence has already been reactivated, hasn't it?"

"Certainly. Which means we must anticipate and prevent

one of the next plagues. Only then can we capture el-Wasi. But then we must do it quickly—before he can reactivate the chain."

"Colonel Tal," said Dr. Kowalski, "there's no way you can get the hostages out of that hall—alive—unless el-Wasi leaves a door open and invites you in. Look, this group has been in almost constant session for two weeks, and I don't hear anything worth communicating to the president."

"Then don't waste his time yet," Tal replied. "Perhaps we'll have some reason to take up his time in the future."

"The near future, I hope, and not just with theoretical talk," Kowalski answered.

"I hope so, too," said Tal. "Meanwhile, let's see if my theory is correct." Tal turned to Williston. "I suggest we try to discover if el-Wasi had a plan for a sixth plague that went wrong."

"How do you propose to do that?"

"You have the answer."

"You mean in here?" Williston tapped his briefcase.

"If that's where you're keeping this morning's intelligence reports, then that's exactly what I mean."

Williston opened up the thick maroon pouch. He had collected some four-hundred pages of reports that morning. The highlight memo suggested nothing that immediately sounded like the Sixth Plague. He began to pass the folders out.

"I doubt you'll find anything in there," Jones said between puffs on his pipe.

"Why not?" Dolby asked.

"Because the Sixth Plague would have occurred sometime no later than yesterday, would it not, if they were following the scenario. I think we ought to look through that material as well."

"Of course—you're right. Corbin, where are yesterday's files?"

"Burned."

There was a groan from the table. Williston drew twice on his pipe, then added, "That is, the copies I had here were burned. We can retrieve copies if we need them."

"We need them," Tal said.

Williston went to the telephone. The others began reading through reports. Tal asked them to call out anything that might remotely be representative of the boils of the Sixth Plague. For an hour there was the steady sound of paper being shuffled; ten piles of paper became twenty as the materials that were read became a discarded pile, until the discard piles absorbed the original and only ten were left.

Dolby finished reading her stack, then muttered, "I can't believe you really collect all this stuff."

"Every day," Williston answered, staring at her.

She caught herself. "Terrific job. I mean, really thorough. Must make you feel proud to do a job like this, doesn't it?"

"Security, young lady."

"You really do a wonderful job uncovering how a local politician in Burundi made an anti-American speech yesterday."

"It goes in files; it will be remembered," Williston boasted.

"And uncovering a theft of pencils from the Peace Corps office in Sarawak. You do a remarkable job!"

"We don't ask our agents to evaluate every shred of data. We want it all."

"And seem to get it."

"Everything we hear."

"And you have lots of ears."

"Oh lots."

After an hour nothing turned up conceivably related to a plague of boils. The group sat silently, with nothing left to say, until twenty minutes later duplicates of the previous day's reports arrived, having been helicoptered directly to the White House. Williston passed them out.

Ten minutes into the second reading, Doolittle said: "I think I've got it." Everyone looked up. "Radiation was pretty high up on your list for Number Six, wasn't it, Dr. Jones?"

"Yep."

"Well, listen to this. A truck carrying spent uranium fuel

from a nuclear utility in England was almost hijacked yesterday morning about six o'clock London time. The truck was intercepted by two men in a car along the road. They conned the guard out of the truck by feigning illness, then knocked him out and forced the truck driver out. He heard one of the hijackers say something about driving the truck. Then somehow, it doesn't make this any too clear, one of the hijackers began carrying two suits to the truck but was shot and killed. The other hijacker got away. British authorities still haven't found him."

"Who did the shooting?"

"It doesn't say how it was done."

"Obviously there was a third man," Sykes said.

"There are certain details," Williston noted, "that they won't put in these reports, even to us. Good reason, too. We wouldn't tell them, either. Came in handy, that little secret. Who was the dead man?"

"Don't know. No identification. No prints. They're still checking."

"And what were those suits?" Dr. Jones asked.

"Well, that's the interesting part. They were radiation suits."

"Let me see that," Williston said. Doolittle passed it over the table. Williston scanned it, went to a telephone on the sofa behind. The call to Langley was held, then patched through to London.

"Hello, Maurice," Williston said, after two minutes. Then: "You did, eh? I suppose you know why also? Yes, that little item about the truck. Yes, we do—very crucial. I can't say, but you might be able to help. Where was the cargo headed for? What? And how potent—I see. You're sure? Never picked up the other fellow, I suppose? Yes, a nasty business all right." He listened while the man in London spoke. "All right, Maurice; I owe you at least a dinner. Next month, shall we say? Oh, it will be over by then. If it isn't, God save us all. Goodby, Maurice."

Williston studied the telephone for a moment. Then he looked up. "That was definitely your Sixth Plague. There was enough nuclear material in there to irradiate a hundred thousand people, at a minimum. All they had to do was to remove it from the sealed container inside the truck."

"It would have given more than boils, Corbin," Jones said.

"True, but the effect on the skin alone would have been dreadful, they say. It would have been one helluvan affliction on the skin."

"Where were they taking it?"

"The British were taking it to a reprocessing facility. Where the terrorists planned to take it is anyone's guess."

"But how far could they have got with that truck?"

"Probably pretty far. The truck was disguised as an ordinary moving van. The radiation shields were all inside."

"London?"

"Maybe."

"What difference does it make?" Tal said. "We've found it; that's what counts. Our theory is confirmed. Almost. But there's another connection we have to make. Was el-Wasi aware that his plan had failed? Were the others in the field aware of it? I think someone must have been. There was no news released about any radiation poisoning or even an attempted hijacking. But somehow the Seventh Plague occurred. How?"

"Maybe el-Wasi has a communication link with his commandoes," Watkins said.

"It would be convenient—convenient for him, but more convenient for us, if we ever caught on and intercepted it. No, I don't think so. It's much too risky. I take him at his word—his only link with the outside must be through the television. Mr. Vice-President, have last night's tapes arrived?"

The vice-president pressed a button. A Marine sergeant entered the room and the vice-president whispered several words to him. Discussion around the table stopped until the Marine had returned with two reels of tape, placed them on the video recorder, and left the room. Tal pushed a button. An image of el-Wasi flashed on the screen. "Let's put it at the beginning of his harangue," Tal said. He depressed the "fast forward" button, making el-Wasi appear to gesticulate in rapid motion. "Try it there," Tal suggested, pushing another button. El-Wasi suddenly froze on the screen. Tal again pushed the "play" button.

". . . the last chance of the superpowers," el-Wasi was saying.

"Let's back it up a bit," Tal said, doing so. El-Wasi moved backwards, his arms ascending rapidly and floating more slowly to his sides. After one or two more tries, they caught the beginning of the speech.

"Time is passing, and our patience is rapidly wearing thin. You, the world outside this Hall, have been very lucky today. You do not know how lucky. But let me assure you that your luck is very temporary. Be assured that we are completely in control.

"You call our actions terrorism? So be it. The reign of terror shall continue until you halt it by vote of this tribunal. Be assured that there is no way you can stop us. You will learn within twenty-four hours how brief a respite your luck has brought. Do not suppose that this surcease will avail you anything. The commentators are wrong, desperately wrong. You should proceed as if your expectations yesterday were fulfilled. . . ."

Tal hit the stop button.

"You think that was the signal?" Sykes asked.

"It must be," Tal said. " 'Proceed as if your expectations yesterday were fulfilled.' That's not a warning to the world—what I thought it was when I heard it yesterday, what it seems to be in context. No, it's a command to his own men."

"In other words—"

"In other words, when the Sixth Plague was interrupted, the Arabs in charge of the Seventh Plague did not get the signal for which they were waiting. Nothing happened, no Sixth Plague. So the seventh team did nothing. The chain was snapped. The self-triggering mechanism failed. The trigger to any plague must be the actual occurrence of the previous plague. What el-Wasi did was to restart the chain. He pulled the trigger."

"So what is the way out of the mess?"

"We have to break the chain again and keep el-Wasi from pulling the trigger."

"Swell. How the hell do we do that?"

"We anticipate and stop the others before el-Wasi can start them up again."

"We haven't anticipated anything yet."

"There is always tomorrow. Which will come all too soon if we don't start anticipating. Who has the Eighth Plague?"

"I do," Sykes said gruffly.

"Proceed, General," the vice-president said.

For several hours, they debated the findings of General Sykes's Plague Eight team. The Eighth Plague was locusts, which "covered the face of the whole earth, so that the land was darkened; and they did eat every herb of the land, and all the fruit of the trees which the hail had left; and there remained not any green thing in the trees, or in the herbs of the field, through all the land of Egypt." Sykes's theory, to which he steadfastly clung, was that the terrorists would attempt to defoliate a major forest or in some other way eliminate a major plant or vegetable supply. Sykes dismissed all alternatives; his worry was the place and the means of execution of the defoliation that he was sure would come.

While the others debated Sykes's prediction, Tal sat quietly, doodling intricate traceries of mazes on a pad. He was not callous to the destruction that would follow the day after the next, but he was not sanguine about their ability to stop it, no matter how canny a guerilla theoretician Sykes really was. Tal was concerned, instead, with a larger matter that had suddenly come to seem more pressing: the elimination of el-Wasi. The voting margin was becoming uncomfortably narrow, and Mossad's message earlier that morning had depressed him. Time; he needed time. But it was, as el-Wasi had warned, rapidly running out.

The discussion droned on until the vice-president excused himself late in the afternoon to attend a regularly scheduled cabinet meeting. The rest talked a while longer, until finally Williston turned to Sykes and said: "All right, I can't say I'm convinced, but I have nothing better to offer. Let's put together a warning around the world about defoliation, but classify it 'eyes only' for intelligence chiefs. We cannot afford this getting into the papers."

They decided to break late in the afternoon. As everyone headed for the coats, Tal announced he would stay on a bit to review the tapes again. Dolby took her coat and walked over to Tal.

"I hope you don't think I let your country down by walking out," she said. Before he could answer, she withdrew a magazine from her coat pocket and handed it to him. "There's an interesting article I insist you read, today, on page 8." Then, lower, "And please don't show this to anyone else before you read it." Then she and the others left Tal alone.

He watched her walk out of the room. Feisty woman, he thought. All to the good. America could use a few more like her. He put the magazine down on the table. The tapes came first.

Dr. Kowalski had been right, Tal thought: How could the hostages be rescued unless, as Kowalski had put it, el-Wasi left a door open and invited a rescue party in. Unless, of course, the doors weren't wired. But el-Wasi claimed they were, the TVs had shown it, and the Moroccan ambassador had died for it. Perhaps el-Wasi was bluffing. Unlikely. Nothing in el-Wasi's scenario had been a bluff. Perhaps he could spot phony wiring on the video rerun of the takeover. Unlikely. He had watched that half-hour dozens of times. He wouldn't have been fooled. And el-Wasi would have known, before the takeover, that the scene would be rerun many times after he was in; he'd have permitted nothing artificial to show up on a television screen. But: maybe one more screening. One more screening couldn't hurt. Anyway, Tal could test himself: He thought he'd already memorized el-Wasi's entire speech. Tal buzzed the Marine sergeant, and asked him to set up "reel number one" on the video recorder.

Tal ran it through. The delegates standing. El-Wasi and his entourage enter. El-Wasi walks to the rostrum. El-Wasi speaks. Tal anticipated every word. The Israeli delegation begins to leave. The Arabs race to their stations around the

Hall. El-Wasi continues speaking. Then, those kaleidoscopic minutes when the cameraman is captured and his
camera drops—the ceiling of the TV booth. Then some
corners and the wall as he is escorted out. Then the walls
and corners and stairway and steps, a bouncing picture, as
he is brought down to the first floor. Then a door. Then,
inside the Hall, el-Wasi again speaking. Then el-Wasi's
orders, through the television, to the outside world. Then
that commentator Johnson.

Tal switched off the machine. He rubbed his eyes, then
rested his head on the table. That damned tape! El-Wasi
had been so perfect. Nothing there. Tal had memorized it.
Nothing. Dozens of times. Memorized. Nothing. He pushed
the fast rewind back to the beginning of the tape, watching
el-Wasi's absurd gesticulations in rapid reverse. Then fast-
forward, in disgust. Maybe the tape will break. Half trying
to snap it. Fast re-wind again. Fast forward. Back again,
and forward, fast, dizzying. Now the whole scene was a
kaleidoscope. The absurd gesturings of el-Wasi in fast-for-
ward, fast rewind. Absurd! Like a caricature. Ridiculous!
Like those ridiculous kaleidoscopic minutes where the cameraman is out of commission. Ridiculous shots! Dropping
the camera. Ceiling. Crevices. Walls. Stairway. Steps.
Door. El-Wasi.

Steps. Door. El-Wasi.

Door. El-Wasi.

"Jesus goddamn Christ." Tal didn't hear himself utter
the words. "Jesus goddamn Christ."

Steps! Door! El-Wasi! That's it!

Tal pushed the "fast rewind" button. He pushed "stop"
before the reel returned to its beginning. He switched off
the sound. Then he pushed the "play" button and sat back.

El-Wasi gesticulated noiselessly on the screen, for thirty
some-odd seconds. Then, suddenly, only a ceiling showed
on the screen. Harold Saperstein had just been attacked,
and had dropped the camera. Tal pushed the "slow" button.
For long seconds, the screen showed only a ceiling. Then
it showed the crease between the ceiling and wall of the
TV booth. Then the floor and the door of the booth. It

opened. The landing outside the booth. Then a staircase. Then, closer to the staircase. Then each step, as they descended. A left at the foot of the stairs. Then a turn to the right. A closed door.

Then the door opening. A door sill. And then el-Wasi again, inside the Hall.

The door had opened. After the televisions had shown all of the doors in the Hall being wired, one particular door had opened, and there had not been an explosion. And the precise door could easily be identified by tracing the camera's path from the television booth against a floorplan of the inside of the building.

Of course el-Wasi had wired the Hall. He had left nothing to chance. But one door had opened. That meant either that that door had not been wired, or had been wired in a manner easy to unwire. And that would be the door, most likely, that the food was being carted in through every day.

And between the time that el-Wasi's henchman left through the one door that would be unwired for that purpose, and the time he always returned with the food cart, presumably through the same door, only a few minutes would pass. The door would probably not be rewired within that few minute period, but would be rewired only after the food had been carted in.

Most likely. Nothing could be certain. But that was more than likely. And it was likely that they would always use the same door for the wiring-unwiring process. Not certain, but likely.

Tal re-wound the reel again. This time, he took a pen and paper, and made notes. He ran the middle of the reel through another eight times. Forty-five minutes later, he was satisfied that he had written down all that could be gleaned from the most important witness he had. He ripped the pages on which he had scribbled his notes from the pad and stuffed them into a pocket. He pressed the buzzer for the Marine sergeant. The door opened; a new sergeant was on duty.

"Sergeant, you may remove the tape."

"Very good, sir, thank you, sir," the sergeant said, saluting, and turning with the tape in hand. When the door closed, Tal walked to the telephone on the sofa. He sank into the soft seat and picked up the receiver.

"Your call, sir," the operator said briskly.

"New York, please," he began. Then he recovered his wits. The White House could not afford not to tape calls leaving that room. "Excuse me, operator," he said. "I'm sorry, never mind." Cursing at himself, he slammed the phone down and walked outside.

The cold air snapped at his face. He had been cooped up too long. If he was right, his sedentary life would not last much longer. He cleared the White House guard, returning the salute unconsciously, and headed for Seventeenth Street. On the corner he found a pay phone. He placed a collect call to a New York City number.

"General Hospital," said the male voice answering the ring.

"A collect call from Dr. Ableman," the operator said.

"I will accept the call," the voice said.

"Good evening, Dr. Betterman," Tal said.

"Good evening, Dr. Ableman," the voice answered. "You are calling about the patient?"

"Yes, and about the surgeons."

"The surgeons are standing by. They await your orders. What is the prognosis?"

"The disease is severe, but it can be arrested with the proper treatment. It is time to plan for Operation Hightower. You must assume control of the operating room. But we will also require special operating equipment, which I shall describe to you now."

They talked for fifteen minutes, while Tal gave his orders. "How much time do we have to prepare all of this, Dr. Ableman?" the voice in New York asked.

"I am not sure," Tal answered. "We should be ready to enter the operating room for surgery within two or three days' time."

"Very well, Dr. Ableman."

"Dr. Betterman?"

"Yes?"

"I am concerned about Uri Shir. Since his last operation he has seemed on edge. Have you observed the signs?"

"I have noticed an air of disquiet."

"I think he should not have his hands on the knife."

"I agree."

"Assign him to observer status."

"I understand. But should he perhaps be confined to his office during Hightower?"

"No, I think not. His eye is keen. His confidence needs bolstering. He should be used, but on the periphery."

"Very well."

"Good night, Dr. Betterman."

"When shall we see you? Or will we see you?"

"I plan to be the chief surgeon, Dr. Betterman. I will notify you on my arrival."

"I understand. Good night, Doctor."

"Good night."

Tal hung up the phone. He could see his breath now from the street lamp down the block. But he no longer felt the chill. His body was refreshed. Approaching combat always tuned his muscles and his mind. He walked back briskly to the White House to summon the car that would take him to Langley for the night.

As he walked, the faces of his Washington colleagues flashed through his mind. The one that lingered was Nancy Dolby. And as it lingered, he remembered that he had forgotten her magazine.

A marine escorted him back into the room. It was dark. He switched on a light. The magazine sat where he had put it. What page had she wanted him to read? He couldn't recall and began thumbing through it. Nothing of apparent interest in the table of contents. As he walked toward the door, leafing through the pages, a stapled sheaf of typewritten papers fell out. On the cover page were typed the words "N.Y.P.D. Response and Deployment at UN."

Had her angry departure been contrived?

Tal hurried to phone more information to Dr. Betterman.

GENERAL ASSEMBLY HALL

El-Wasi called for another vote. Seventy buttons on the panels in the front of the Hall lit up green, and 79 red. In the regrettable absence of the Moroccan ambassador, el-Wasi cast a yes vote for him. As soon as the ambassador from Zambia cast his vote, el-Wasi spoke again, loudly.

"There are those in this room who have plainly grown from our shared experience of these last two weeks. To you, we offer our congratulations and our hand of friendship. Your act of courage in the pursuit of justice will be well honored by the pen of history.

"But there are those of you who continue to turn deaf ears to our cause. Remember—you bear the full responsibility for your own continued presence here, for that of your brother delegates, and for the suffering that you cause us to keep inflicting on the world outside. You bear full responsibility at this point not only for your acts, but for ours, and the blood that spills is on your hands."

Ambassador Ben-Eshai rose stiffly. His short-sleeved shirt, open at the neck, was by now dirty brown and wrinkled. Two weeks without shaving had given him a beard. He shook a finger in el-Wasi's direction and began to speak.

In mid-sentence, there was a thud, and Ben-Eshai stopped and slumped to the floor with scarcely more sound than a footstep. Behind him, looking down at the crumpled body, was Musaab Umair, both hands holding the barrel of his gun, whose butt had thudded against Ben-Eshai's skull.

None of the delegates moved as Musaab Umair quickly transferred his gun to firing position and rapidly traced an arc across the room. The Hall was silent. Ben-Eshai moved slightly on the floor. Umair looked down at him and spat on his face. Then he returned to his place near one of the doors.

El-Wasi continued. "Time is growing short, quickly. Do not think we can exercise restraint forever. I have been warning you—the time for stalling is over. Time is now on nobody's side. I shall soon order your food ration cut down again. If your collective vote does not then change, I will be forced to announce most reluctantly that there will no longer be any food. There will no longer be toilets. There will no longer be water. For we the Palestinian movement have long arms, and we shall strike again, and again, and you shall feel our fists soon, and often, and with all the wrath of God."

From the rear seat, a dignified diplomat nearing eighty years, his tie knotted smartly at the collar, began to wail.

NEW YORK CITY

The SoHo district, south of Houston Street in lower Manhattan, has become one of New York's avant-garde neighborhoods. The spacious lofts that cap its buildings are rented by artists for their showings, by acting troupes for improvisational theater, and by rock bands for rehearsals.

Posing as New York University graduate students, two of the Aleph commandoes rented adjoining lofts on a quiet block on Spring Street. They paid two-month deposits in American currency. Within an hour, ten of their colleagues had come to visit, carrying sledgehammers, and all that remained of the wall dividing the two lofts, and of the walls that had partitioned each loft into rooms, was a dusty assemblage of broken plaster lying on the floor. There was now one gigantic room. Most of the Israeli contingent gathered there that night.

"Avram has given us orders," Mordecai Ofir said. "A crisis point is near. It may soon be necessary for us to liberate the Hall."

He opened up one of several large manila folders, removed a group of snapshots, and handed them to one of the men.

"Danny," he said, "study these pictures carefully. Take four men back to that lumber and supplies yard I pointed out to you on the way down here. Buy whatever you need to reconstruct the front of the delegates' entrance."

"Reconstruct it?"

"That's right. You are going to build a prop, like in a play. The scene you will be creating is the front of the delegates' entrance. Take a large slab of plywood, and paint onto it the delegates' entrance and a few yards of the wall around the door. Don't forget to add the overhang. We've brought a TV here, it's in the corner. Turn it on to the channel carrying the picture of the delegates' entrance. I want your scene to include everything that you see on the TV."

"How large?"

"Life-size, as large as the entrance area itself. I've written the actual dimensions onto the photos."

"Fine. Why?"

"You'll know soon enough, but right now time is of the essence, so just do it. And I also want you to paint another large board, too. On that one, I want you to paint everything the screen shows of the ground, beginning where the ground meets the base of the building."

"Also life-size?"

"Right, same as the actual dimensions of the portion of the ground visible on the TV screen. And everything should be painted the same colors as the colors on the snapshots."

"The painting is no problem, but two pieces of wood large enough for that won't fit through the door into this room so I can work on it."

"Then have it sawed into panels, but make sure the panels can be hinged back together into the two large surfaces."

"Easy enough."

"And one more thing."

"Oh?"

"I want you to cut out the door of your picture after it's painted, so it actually opens and closes."

"Hinge it back in?"

"Correct."

"So someone can actually walk through it?"

"That's right," Ofir nodded.

"How much time do I have?"

"Almost none."

Danny Nahteev walked quickly to the door, calling out

as he went the names of four men to help him. They closed the door behind them and raced down the steps. Ofir ran to the door and called out after them. "And bring back a few dozen long wood beams."

Ofir returned to the group and spoke again. "The rest of us have to plan a takeover of the building."

Everyone suddenly began speaking out at once. Ofir raised his hands and called for quiet.

"I do not know when we'll be going in. I do not even know for sure if we will. I know only that Avram has told me we should get ready to take the Hall. I don't know if the Americans approve, or if they know. Frankly, I doubt it. Avram has told me that we are now operating against not only el-Wasi and the terrorists' chain that has been set in motion, but we are also operating against time. He wants to be certain that we will be ready, if and when he gives the order, to take over the building and the Hall.

"Let me rephrase that. He does not *want* to be certain that we will be ready. He *is* certain. Now we must prepare."

Ofir got down on his knees. He opened the other manila envelopes, and removed a mass of photographs from them, which he spread on the floor. He began pointing at each of them, in sequence. The other men hovered over them.

"Everyone study these, in their order," Ofir directed. "This is the path we will be taking, from the delegates' door, into the building, to the staircase, up the stairs, to this door to the Hall. And this is what the inside of the Hall looks like from the door we will be entering."

"What about the wiring?"

"Avram believes that this particular door will not be wired when we reach it."

"How does he know?"

"He believes he knows."

"And if he's wrong?"

"Then he'll be wrong," Ofir answered. "Isn't that obvious? Now let's get to business, fast. Look at each picture. Study it. Commit it to memory. Study the sequence of these photos. Commit it also to memory. Know everything about these photos as if your lives depend on it. And Israel's."

"Will Avram be with us?"

"He will enter the building with us. But he will enter the Hall before we do. He will be in the Hall for a time without us."

"For how long?"

"He doesn't know. Maybe half a second. Maybe seconds. Maybe a minute. Maybe more, but that's unlikely."

"Even if we get inside the building, and even if the door Avram has picked out is not wired, and even if he gets in okay without blowing us all to pieces, how can he be in there for more than an instant before they kill him?" The man who asked the question crouched down and put his finger on a doorway of the General Assembly. He dragged his finger along the picture, emphasizing by the slowness of his movement the impossibility of taking cover in the vast Hall.

"You'll get all the details soon," Ofir replied. "Let's take things one step at a time. And we must act quickly."

Then: "Something else you should know. Avram will be wearing a tiny transmitter, and we'll have a small receiver outside the door. I have already obtained a body transmitter for Avram, as he requested, and a receiver for us. Both are of the highest quality, extremely sensitive. When Avram gets inside the Hall, he'll try to spot the Arabs. If he can, he'll transmit their locations to us, through the usual 'clock' code. The door he enters through will be 'six o'clock.' That door is in the rear of the Hall, near the center. The middle of the wall opposite that door, across the Hall—where the podium is—will be 'twelve o'clock.' The middle of the wall to the right where he enters will be 'three o'clock,' and so on. If any of the Arabs are not against the walls, he'll try to describe in more detail where they are, though that may not be possible. He will also try to let us know if the delegates are seated."

"After Avram has done all this, is he going to ask the Arabs to please drop their guns, and then ask us to come in to handcuff them?"

"Knowing Avram as we all do, that wouldn't be surprising. But don't worry, if that doesn't happen we'll know when to come in. Either Avram will signal us through his transmitter or, if he doesn't have time—and he doesn't think he'll have even time enough to say one word—we come through the door at the first sound of shooting."

"I hope the shots we hear come from Avram's gun."

"I'm sure he hopes so, too. Okay. First, memorize these pictures. When Danny Nahteev gets back here to begin his painting job, we'll take those extra beams I told him to get, and build the mock-up. This place"—he took in the whole loft with his arm—"isn't as luxurious as the room Ben-Eshai is sweating it out in. But the floor area is large. That's the key. And we have to be quick. We won't have much time to rehearse. No more joking. Now we work like we're working for our lives."

ℵOCTOBER 18:ℵ
TWO DAYS LATER

TRANSCRIPT, TELEPHONE CONVERSATION, DIRECTOR, CIA, and CHIEF, OFFICE OF STRATEGIC PLANS, UNITED STATES ARMY

W(illiston): Hello, General. Bad news.

S(ykes): They beat us, I assume.

W: They did.

S: Somewhere in Africa?

W: Christ, yes, you were right.

S: Where?

W: Ghana.

S: Ghana? What in the hell would they—oh, shit. Cocoa. Ghana has only blacks and cocoa.

W: (inaudible)

S: Shit, why didn't I think cocoa. How bad?

W: Pretty bad. They had at least six planes; maybe more. They—

S: Same as Australia?

W: Pretty much. They covered about two-thirds of the current production with cacodylic acid.

S: Bad stuff.

W: Yes.

S: Salvageable?

W: Very little. Probably destroyed forty percent of the total crop. Ghana figured the cocoa production to be close to three-quarters of their total export this year.

S: So it—

W: Ruins the country. It will go absolutely bankrupt.

S: Loans?

W: Sure, but what the hell. You know, General, that there will be trouble in Ghana long before loans will do any good. Already is trouble, in fact.

S: How did they get those planes in there?

W: Apparently they didn't. All the pilots who were shot down were black. Planes must have originated locally, pilots were revolutionaries undoubtedly, African fanatics.

S: Secondary reactions?

W: The Africans are pissing green. There's open talk of invasion.

S: Preposterous.

W: Sure, but they're hotheads. Some of them may actually mobilize.

S: The Israelis would cut them to ribbons.

W: Right, but we don't need that right now.

S: Christ, no. It would—

W: Exactly.

S: All I can say is we're going to need better intelligence fast. Damn fast. This shouldn't be happening to us.

W: Let's not go into that now.

S: I don't know when else we can. Certainly not in front of the Jew.

W: No.

S: So?

W: Africa is being reorganized.

S: A little late, wouldn't you say?

W: If this thing keeps going, Africa will get another crack before long.

S: If it goes on that long we're all dead.

W: Yeah. I will see you at 0800 hours, General.

S: (inaudible)

NEW YORK CITY

Captain de Petri left the subway and began the two-block walk to his apartment in the Bensonhurst section of Brooklyn. It had been a difficult two weeks. The goddamn Arabs were worse than blacks or Puerto Ricans. What balls, to hijack the UN! If he had his way, they wouldn't be there long though—no job too big for Special Operations, and they could clear the building out in minutes if the politicians would only let them. Two weeks of fighting the Arabs, the mayor, and even goddamn Washington. Time was when people respected the law, and that was because the police were allowed to handle criminals like criminals, instead of babysitting for them. It wasn't easy, sitting outside the UN 16 hours every day for the last few weeks. Thank God for a nice quiet apartment, and the wife and daughter.

The moment Captain de Petri closed the front door behind him, he could feel two cold metal barrels pressed against his temples. A male voice to his left told him not to move. The accent sounded French to him. He didn't dare try to move his head. Two more men stepped out of the hallway closet. Both carried guns capped with silencers.

"Captain de Petri, my name is Ba'ar. We are officers of the Israeli Secret Service. We are not here to hurt you, but if necessary we will blow your head off. Do you understand?"

Captain de Petri barely moved his lips for fear of disturbing the two guns pressed against his head, but murmured he understood. The young man standing near Ba'ar walked over to de Petri, frisked him, and removed his .38 police revolver, ammunition belt, and a smaller pistol he found in a leg holster strapped to de Petri's left calf. Then he removed de Petri's handcuffs from his belt, and cuffed de Petri's hands behind him. De Petri felt the guns leave his head.

Ba'ar again spoke. "Come with us into the kitchen. Do not be alarmed by what you will see there. Do not scream. Do nothing. Nobody has been hurt, and nobody will be hurt if you cooperate. We are here to save lives, not end them." Ba'ar took de Petri by the arm and led him into the kitchen.

De Petri could not restrain a gasp, but did not shout. His wife, a frumpy little woman, and the de Petris' only daughter, fifteen years old, were seated on kitchen chairs. Their mouths were gagged with dishrags. Their hands were free. Two Israeli men stood leaning against the wall.

When she saw her husband enter the kitchen, Mrs. de Petri ran up to him and threw her arms around him. The Israelis let her hold him, then asked her to sit down. Captain de Petri told her to obey.

Ba'ar spoke. "We have come to your country, and your city, and your home, to save lives. For us to do this will require your cooperation, Captain de Petri. We will instruct you later what you are to do. You must follow those instructions to the letter. We have full knowledge of every detail of your police operation. We will know if you try to mislead us.

"Several of us will escort your wife and daughter somewhere. Rest assured it is a safe place, and be assured also there is no way you will be able to find it. Your family will be comfortably provided for. Remember, though, they will always be not only in our care, but also in our custody."

De Petri nodded his head slowly, as if this were routine information he was absorbing from one of his lieutenants. When the Israeli paused for breath, de Petri's head stopped bobbing.

"If you follow our instructions, your wife and daughter will be released, unharmed. But I caution you—if your cooperation is not absolute, and if your obedience is not total, we will be compelled to kill them. Do you understand?"

De Petri nodded silently. His wife muffled a cry and her eyes showed fear. She held her arms out to her husband. Gently, two of the Israelis held her back.

"Please, Mrs. de Petri," Ba'ar said, brandishing his gun. "It is difficult enough. Just do as we say. Will you do that?"

Holding her daughter's hand so tightly the knuckles turned white, she nodded assent.

"Your gags will be removed, then," Ba'ar said. "You will be escorted from the apartment. A vehicle is waiting directly outside. You are to enter the vehicle, and say nothing. Please do not shout or attempt to run. Captain de Petri, as you can see, is in a most vulnerable situation, and if you cause any disturbance we will be forced to shoot his eyes out."

Mrs. de Petri and her daughter left with four of the Israelis. After waiting ten minutes, Ba'ar removed the cuffs from the captain's hands. Ba'ar and the other remaining Israeli holstered their guns.

"I am a fairly good judge of people," Ba'ar said, "and I believe you are also. Therefore I know that you know that we mean our words, and you will obey. Do not forget—although our guns are no longer at your head, and will not be there during our activities together, our guns are at the heads of your wife and daughter. I am sure that you will not force us to use those guns.

"This is what you are to do. . . ."

As he had done for nearly twenty years, Captain de Petri left his apartment shortly after six the next morning. He walked to the subway, dropped a token into the turnstile, and waited for a train. He got off at Grand Central terminal and walked two blocks north and three blocks east to the gap in the buses surrounding the General Assembly building. Without a word, he passed the patrolman stationed there, not acknowledging his salute. He entered the mobile command room. He drank a cup of coffee and thought. He drank another cup. Then he picked up the walkie-talkie that connected with all of the vehicles within the cordoned-off area, and flicked the switch to "on."

"Everyone in to see me," he said, and turned the switch off.

The doors and tank turrets of the vehicles all opened, and the men filed into the command room. De Petri counted them, all present, and began.

"Men, we have received orders from Washington. Top-secret. The president of the United States has decided that this bullshit has to end. He wants us to take over the Hall."

There were a few whistles from the back of the room.

De Petri slammed his hand down on the table. "Quiet, damn it. We have no time for bullshit. Just listen up. A special operation has been designed in Washington for us to get the goddamn Arabs out of there and get back the UN. It's different from the contingency plans we've heard about before. Washington has secretly brought a bunch of Israeli commandoes into the country. No one else knows about it. They're guys who are specially trained for this kind of operation, they've smoked out plenty of Arabs before. They're going to put you through a crash rehearsal for us to take the building."

De Petri tried to speak with a sense of urgency minus panic. To demonstrate calmness, he reached into his desk drawer, pulled out a wooden cigar box, and withdrew a cigar. Slowly, he tore away the cellophane wrapper, crumpling it in his hand and letting it slip to the floor. He bit the end off the cigar and spat it out, then lit a match, and drew strongly until the tip glowed red. A dense puff of gray-white smoke enveloped his face and drifted to the ceiling. He jabbed the cigar in the direction of his listeners.

"Now there is one thing that is more important than anything else. Nobody, repeat, nobody, can know about this operation. You don't even talk about it with yourselves. Understood?"

He looked around. No one said anything.

"Okay. Now, you're to leave here in twos. You'll walk to the Hotel Tudor, go to the fifth floor, and there'll be civilian clothes waiting for you. Change, leave your uniforms in the room, and go back outside. You'll see an unmarked bus waiting in front of the hotel. It'll take you to the place where you'll be trained. On the way to the hotel, don't call or tell anyone. If word gets out it'll get to the Arabs inside the Hall, and all our asses'll be cooked. Got it?"

De Petri called out the first two names.

Within an hour, a standard New York City transit bus, on loan for emergency purposes and filled with 46 plain-clothed members of the NYPD Special Operations Division, was heading toward the George Washington Bridge. The driver was Israeli. He would not answer any of the policemen's questions, except to smile and indicate that the entire situation would soon be well in hand.

Four hours later, the bus stopped at a roadside diner along the Pennsylvania Turnpike. The men filed out and ate. When they reboarded they asked the driver when they would reach the training grounds. The Israeli said they'd get there, don't worry, but for security reasons they couldn't yet know where it would be. The bus continued west.

Hours before that stop, other men, wearing the police uniforms left behind in the fifth-floor rooms at the Tudor, had straggled in twos and threes back to the UN, past the buses, and into the tanks and carriers that surrounded the General Assembly building. Ba'ar entered the command room. Captain de Petri was seated, head in his hands, staring down at the desktop.

Ba'ar smiled at him. "You did very well, Captain," he said. "You have done a service for humanity. Now continue to do so and everything will turn out all right." He fingered the nametag on his uniform. "By the way, Captain, the uniform fits fine, but do I look like an O'Reilly?"

The New York City bus passed another tollbooth and entered the Ohio Turnpike.

Ba'ar pulled up a chair and sat across the desk from de Petri. "Now tell me everything you know about the inside of that building."

ℵ OCTOBER 20: ℵ
THE FOLLOWING DAY

THE WHITE HOUSE

Following the Eighth Plague and el-Wasi's warnings of harsh treatment to come for the ambassadors, the Emergency Group had held round-the-clock meetings. That the secret of the plagues had been kept intact was a testament to the scope of the demands that the group members placed on their staffs scattered throughout the bureaucracy in Washington and abroad. For no fewer than 480 people were now, directly or indirectly, participating nearly full time in the research effort to solve the riddle of the plagues. The questions they were asked to answer did not permit them time for gossip.

Moreover, no one outside the Emergency Group itself knew why the questions were being asked or what they added up to. Doubtless some guessed that somebody had clues concerning the nature of the future terror, but every major set of questions—to the Pentagon, the CIA, the Na-

tional Security Council, and the State Department staffs—
was first screened for form by a committee consisting of
Sykes, Williston, and Doolittle.

By late in the afternoon, a steady stream of memos and
documents was flowing in. By eight that evening, the entire
assemblage was groggy and giddiness was setting in. Pinckney asked if this was the way it had been when "Jerry Ford
planned the Mayaguez attack."

"I was abroad in those years," Williston said, straight-
faced. "But I was later officially informed that the administration worked this hard only when trying to figure out
the title for Mr. Ford's memoirs."

Nancy Dolby scribbled a few words onto her pad and
then waved it in the air. "I've got it," she announced.

Sykes was dubious. "What? You know where the next
plague will be?"

"No, I've figured out the title for Ford's memoirs." She
paused for effect and then said: "Portions of the Preceding
Presidency Were Prerecorded."

The thought struck the vice-president and Jones at the
same time: Nancy Dolby had uttered something frivolous;
there was something humorous about just that. They began
to laugh. Soon the entire table, save Tal, who didn't comprehend the joke, was caught in a convulsive wave of laughter. Now between gasps they were contemplating what the
jacket of the memoirs would look like. Pinckney's suggestion that it depict a presidential pipe shown with a bubble
gum bubble emerging from the end started a new wave of
hysteria, tears, and coughing.

Tal rapped on the table for order and reminded them to
return to the subject at hand: anticipating the nature of the
Ninth Plague—darkness. The concensus was that could only
mean a blackout sometime the following day. The question
was where. Sykes described the technical simplicity of cut-
ting off a city's power suddenly and surreptitiously.

Tal argued that el-Wasi's next Plague would not, however, be a blackout.

Each plague had inflicted severe human pain, suffering,
and inconvenience, and some had caused death. And the
order of destruction seemed constantly escalating; succeed-

ing plagues were worse than the previous ones, though obviously none could be quantified. How, then, would a blackout fit into this scheme? It wouldn't. It couldn't. He rejected the responses of several that he was being naive about the effects of blackouts in major urban areas. Just look at the widespread looting in New York after the July 1977 blackout, Dolby reminded. She had wanted to call the mayor all afternoon to advise him to discuss, as discreetly as possible, the need for Con Edison to increase its security at its control stations. Williston forbade her. She had persisted until Tal persuaded her that since New York City was already the main center of the terror and since el-Wasi was making his demands to the world through television, the last thing he could afford was to cut the power there if he did decide to cause a blackout, which Tal strongly doubted.

As the others scrutinized the reports to determine where such a blackout would occur, Tal and Dolby remained silent. Dolby scribbled disjointed words on her pad. Ignoring the debate around him, Tal concentrated on his own plans.

Dolby tried to keep from looking at him, but her own thoughts kept straying toward him. Somehow, never having met him outside these sterile quarters or the company of others at dinner, a personal word never having been exchanged between the two of them alone, she felt close to him. She jotted onto her pad, in block capital letters, "TAL," and drew a line next to the name. She tried to conjure up the appropriate word to jot down beside it but could think of none. She pretended to scan the faces in the room, to catch his face once more. His look was not at her, nor anyone; he was immersed in thought. She thought she noticed Doolittle watching her watch Tal, and she quickly turned back to her pad to the name she had written. She had no adjective. So next to his name she wrote the only word that fit him: "Tal," again.

Sykes rang for food. A cart loaded with sandwiches, soup, and more coffee was rolled in. Pinckney took the cart from the Marine sergeant and began pushing it toward the conference table. "Courtesy of the Brotherhood of Arab Unity," he said, "el-Wasi's catering service is branching out." The sight of the moving tray mesmerized the others, and Pinckney flushed when he saw he was the only person smiling. In truth the cart did resemble the one on which the ambassadors were brought their meager meals, and the reminder sobered those who were still giddy.

They ate without discussing business. A depression had set in. They stared at each other. The realization began to hit: There no longer seemed any real reason for being there in the bowels of the executive mansion at that hour, suffering fatigue of the imagination, but they were condemned to continue trying to solve an insoluble puzzle.

Tal could not rally any support for his proposition that the Ninth Plague would be other than a blackout. He soon gave up trying and let the others speak; instead, he read reports intended to enlighten the inquisitive members of the Plague Ten team. Who would an Islamic zealot consider fodder for terror based on the killing of the first-born? One report showed the times and locations of over one thousand meetings of Boy Scouts around the world during the next week. Somewhat fewer Girl Scout meetings were scheduled. Lists of orphanages, foundling hospitals, maternity wards and the like sat in thick clumps on the floor. None of it seemed plausible; certainly none of it would be preventable.

By 3 A.M. most had fallen asleep. Doolittle was turning pages but he had difficulty focusing on the words. Tal gave out at four. At six, when the Marine guards changed shifts, and when the incoming sergeant entered the room to tidy it up, he discovered assorted sleeping bodies on the sofa, in the one soft chair in the corner by the telephone, and slumped over the table. He backed up hurriedly and closed the door quietly. At 6:20, Pinckney moved in his sleep and fell off his chair. The thump awakened the room. Sykes looked at his watch, muttered to himself, then had the sergeant direct his groggy colleagues to sleeping quarters in the basement of the East Wing. He called for the next session to begin at ten sharp.

By 10:15 they were assembled and quiet; the room had been tidied; the coffee was fresh. The coffee stirring ritual consumed five more minutes and the vice-president asked

Sykes to offer a statement of progress; he knew the General could be counted on for summing up succinctly, whereas when the others had nothing to say they could talk forever. Two minutes into the General's statement, at 10:22, the telephone rang for Corbin Williston.

"Williston," he answered. "Yes. Where? Rome? How long ago? How bad? What else? All right, keep me posted the minute anything changes." He hung up. He looked around the table, staring directly at Tal. "You were wrong," he said.

"Blackout?"

"The entire city of Rome. Apparently deliberate."

"When?"

"Couple of minutes ago."

"What else do you know?"

"Nothing. It just happened. It's seven hours different there, so it's"—he turned his wrist up—"about 5:25 in Rome. Getting dark; rush hour traffic will be at its peak."

"A blackout won't affect it; Italian traffic is always screwed up," said Pinckney. No one smiled.

"Why?" Tal asked.

"Why what?"

"Why did they do it? It just doesn't make any sense."

"You said that all yesterday, but here it is tomorrow and here it is they've gone and done it."

"It doesn't fit."

"But it's darkness; that's what the Ninth Plague was, wasn't it?"

"Yes, but darkness during the day, not at night. At night it's already dark. And why only a blackout after everything else they've done?"

"Maybe they ran out of ideas."

"I don't think so. Why would they? There has to be some reason for it, something we're missing, some connection with the overall scheme. Mr. Vice-President?"

"Yes."

"May I offer my excuses? I must make a call." He stood up. Williston pointed to the phone in the back of the room. Tal shook his head. "No, it must be private. I will be back shortly."

He walked through the tunnel, took the stairs in the EOB to the ground floor, clipping to his jacket the security tag he had been issued when he first arrived in Washington. He walked down the long ornate corridor, observing the high doors bracketed with the names of, he assumed, important officials, none of whom he had ever heard of. He came to the main entrance, where he inquired of a guard for a public telephone. The guard, eyeing the red tag, pointed to a booth.

He deposited a dime and requested the overseas operator. He gave an Israeli number, placing a collect call from Dr. Ableman. As soon as the line was clear, he said: "This is Ableman. Connect me to Red Sea." Two minutes later he was talking to one of his agents in Rome.

"Troubles?" Tal asked in Hebrew.

"Indeed."

"Tell me, what activities are being planned for this evening?"

"Activities?"

"Opera, concerts, circuses, rallies, conventions, theaters, political caucuses, boy scouts, anything and everything."

"There are no political events scheduled that I have heard of. A new government is to be formed, but a new government is always being formed and there is no meeting tonight. The circus doesn't arrive for a month. Some theater. The usual stuff."

"What about the unusual?"

"Nothing."

"What else?"

"There have been two strikes in town; picket lines. Perhaps they will be called off, unless they can find their way in the darkness."

"Any open air concerts, charity performances, anything?"

"No. Not unless you include the Vatican."

"What's there?"

"It is the annual pilgrimage of Saint someone or other."

"Pilgrimage? Tonight?"

"All week. Priests have arrived from everywhere.

Scraggly lot if you ask me. The papers say several thousand. They have been meeting with the pope each evening."

"At what time?"

"Midnight."

"Listen closely. Something is going to happen in Rome tonight. Something very important, something that we have to prevent. I think I am beginning to see it now. I think the blackout is a cover, and the Tenth Plague will occur in your territory, probably within hours. They will try something outrageous. Prevent it. But take them alive if you can. Get answers. Use maximum persuasion if necessary, but get answers immediately. Call me when you have them."

"Where?"

"Jerusalem will know."

"I understand."

Tal fished the dime back out of his pocket. He made another collect call, this time to Dr. Betterman in New York. "Today would be convenient for surgery," he said.

"When?"

"Sometime in the early evening. You will hear from me."

Tal walked back quickly down the corridor, and, when he found the tunnel, ran all the way back to the meeting room in the White House. He paused at the door, then opened it and peered in without stepping inside. He signaled to the vice-president. "May I have a word with you?" he asked.

The vice-president pointed to himself. "Me?"

"Yes, sir. May we talk out here, please?"

The vice-president looked at the others, shrugged his shoulders, and left the room. "What is it?"

"I must see the president."

"What?"

"It is of the utmost importance. I think I understand the blackout in Rome."

"Tell me, man. Why so secretive?"

"I cannot, sir."

"Well, will you tell the president?"

"No, sir, not at this time."

"I can't ask the president to listen to a mystery."

"I am going to have to ask you both to take me at faith for the present."

"But you have been wrong for the past twenty-four hours about the blackout. I know you to be an honorable man, but I don't know how we can take anything on faith."

"Let me put it this way. Something is going to happen. Very soon. Something very dramatic. I want to put a proposition to the president that depends on my being correct. If I am not, then he will not be obligated in the slightest."

"What do you wish him to do?"

"I want him to appear on television this evening. Can such a thing be arranged?"

"Yes, of course."

"On an hour's notice?"

"That's all?"

"Maybe less."

"It can be done if necessary."

"It will be necessary, I assure you, if there is ever to be a solution to our problem at the United Nations."

"But why can't you tell me the specifics now, and why can't you tell the president?"

"Because I am risking something that the president might feel strongly about."

"Can't we share that risk?"

"No. I think that you would try to prevent the risk from being taken."

"And that would be wrong?"

"It would be disastrous. I do not wish to place you or the president or anyone inside that room in the position of having to take upon themselves the decision to alter the situation. I will bear the consequences."

"I rather imagine the world will bear them."

"Yes, you are right, sir, but they will bear them if the risk is not undertaken as well."

"I am afraid we are getting nowhere."

"I must see the president. For just five minutes. Just to get his agreement in advance, to tell him personally, and to seek his pledge of cooperation if I am correct."

"How will we know if you are?"

"It will be unmistakable. The situation is so dramatic

that there will be no doubt at all when it happens."

"When will it happen? Or when will we know?"

"Within a few hours."

"And what will you want the president to do or say on television?"

"That depends on what happens. I cannot say now. We will have to improvise."

"But you have an idea?"

"An idea, yes."

"You cannot say what?"

"No, sir. Again, I must beg your trust."

The vice-president looked very uncomfortable as he weighed the alternatives in his mind. Tal waited, never taking his eyes off the American's face.

Finally, the vice-president sighed. "Very well, I will do as you ask. We will go upstairs in a few minutes. As far as I know, the president is here now. I will inform him that we are coming to see him—both of us. Do you object to that?"

"No, sir. On the contrary, I think it would be useful for you to be there."

"And one other."

"Who?"

"Corbin Williston."

Tal hesitated. "Why?"

"I think it important that he consider himself a part of any conspiracy that you may be hatching. He is a capable ally but he can also be a vigorous opponent. Let's tip the balance."

"I see your point. Very well. I agree."

The vice-president opened the door. "Corbin, may we see you outside?"

FORT BRAGG, NORTH CAROLINA

Just before noon, Colonel McDougal received a shattering call from Sykes, who sounded tired and unsteady.

"It's tonight," he said hoarsely.

"What is?" McDougal asked.

"You are. It is. I assume you will get orders to go to New York tonight. I cannot talk more now. It's not secure."

"But General—"

The phone went dead. McDougal put his knuckles to his temples. He would have to think fast. He sat for two minutes, then stood up ramrod straight. He pushed a button on the intercom and when his aide answered, instructed him to get Sykes on the telephone. Fifteen minutes went by. He swore incessantly into the intercom; each time his aide replied that Sykes had still not been located. After thirty minutes, McDougal gave up. He took out a message pad and scribbled a one-line note: "Rate chances five percent or less," signed it, and took it personally to the communications center for classification and encryption to Sykes at the Pentagon.

Then he summoned the officers of K Detachment to the briefing room. They assembled within ten minutes. "Gentlemen," he said, "you'll show your stuff tonight. We are going to New York."

They gave him a standing ovation.

THE VATICAN

Zubair Kaab had been unable to nap. He sat, open-eyed, in a large armchair in his third-floor room in the Ausonia Pension in Rome, Italy. He rubbed the sleepiness from his eyes, rose, and parted the curtains. The night was pitch-black.

Kaab lit a candle and woke the other three men sleeping in cots in the room. Kaab was the first to speak.

"Hashim el-Wasi has placed his trust in us. We have succeeded so far. We must not fail him now." The others murmured their agreement.

Kaab walked to the closet and removed the two suitcases they had brought. He opened them, removed four parcels wrapped in brown paper tied with string, and handed one to each of the other men, keeping one for himself. Each opened his parcel and removed the articles of clothing piece by piece, grunting with satisfaction.

They helped each other strap Ingram 10s against their torsos. Then they dressed. By 10 P.M. Rome time the four Palestinians, fully clothed in priests' vestments, left the pension.

They followed the Corso Vittorio Emanuele, crossed a small bridge, and turned left at the Via Della Conciliazone. Ten minutes later, they reached the thick, high wall that surrounds the Vatican and separates it from Rome.

The Vatican City is a sovereign state, established in 1929 by treaty signed by the government of Mussolini and the Holy See. Entering the city requires no formalities: just a walk through any of the several gates in the wall surrounding the city.

Kaab led the three other men past the wall and into the vast Square of St. Peter's. Thousands of priests and pilgrims already thronged the immense sprawling square, cramming toward the front in anticipation of the pope's appearance.

The four Palestinians stood and watched from the rear of the Square. The pope would soon be speaking from the front, over three hundred yards away, from atop the triple flight of steps leading from the square to St. Peter's Basilica. Kaab began threading his way through the masses, toward the front, the three others following. Thousands of candles lit the Square.

At exactly midnight, the pope, resplendent in his purple robes, walked slowly out of St. Peter's. His left hand held the pastoral staff. His right arm waved, in grand sweeping gesture, to the applauding clergymen who by now had completely filled the Square.

The pope stood still, smiling, as the ovation and blessings in front of him swept across the Square. Then, arms stretched before him, he closed his eyes and began:

"Ave Maria, piena di grazia: il Signore e teco: tu sei benedetta fra le donne,"

The crowd fell silent.

"e benedetto il frutto del ventre tuo, Gesu. Santa Maria, Madre di Dio,"

The crowd strained to hear the pope's words. Silence. Before him, the pope saw a sea of men in black raiment straining their heads up toward him. He smiled again and raised out his arms.

"prega per noi peccatori, adesso e nell'ora della nostra morte. Cosi sia."

The mass of priests before him could scarcely see more than a figure facing them from atop the steps, gesturing, speaking. Then, suddenly, like interlopers racing across a stage, four priests began dashing up the stairs toward the pope, shouting *"Al hamdu lillah"*—Praise be to God. The pope's words stopped. He saw the faces of the four men coming closer. They did not look like priestly faces. Then he saw them pull the submachine guns from under their cassocks.

The pope froze, speechless, motionless. From ten feet away the four men turned their guns toward him.

The sound of machinegun fire clattered through the air. Kaab saw the pope's mouth fall open. He turned to his right and saw the bodies of his three comrades suddenly jerk forward. Then he saw them slump to the ground as their legs collapsed beneath them like rubber. He saw their vestments reddening. Then he saw seven athletic-looking young priests racing toward him, each carrying an uzi, shouting to each other in Hebrew.

Kaab began racing toward the church portico, the seven priests chasing behind him. Inside the portico, he ran toward the last door on the right and pulled.

The Porta Santa is officially opened only at the beginning of each Holy Year. On this day, it was locked. Kaab spun around, groping for the trigger of his gun. Suddenly he felt a sharp pain against the back of his head. His knees hit painfully against the marble floor. A body slammed against his back, and his chest thudded hard against the floor. His head followed, pinned to the floor. A weight of other bodies piled onto him. Then he felt nothing.

When Kaab awoke moments later, he was facing the ceiling, hands tied tightly under his back, legs tied tightly together. A group of men standing over him were holding candles. Though his head was turned toward the magnificent cherubs painted across the dome, he didn't notice them. It was understandable. The cassock-clad man sitting on his chest was introducing himself, in Arabic, as Simeon Levi of the Israeli Secret Service. Kaab did not respond. He could feel Levi's uzi pressed inside his mouth against his tonsils. Six other clergymen around him also had their uzis trained on him.

"Your friends are dead," Levi told him. "They were lucky. You will not be so lucky. You will not die until you first have eaten your testicles, and then your eyeballs. You will begin this meal in exactly five seconds. You can avoid it if you answer a few very simple questions. Do you want to answer them?"

Kaab saw a priest standing over him fondling the long blade of a hunting-knife. Gurgles came from Kaab's throat, and his lips pressed in attempted speech against the muzzle of Levi's uzi. Levi withdrew the muzzle to Kaab's lips.

"Does that mean yes?" Levi asked.

"Yes," said Kaab.

"What does el-Wasi have planned next?" Levi asked.

"I don't know."

Levi jammed the uzi back inside Kaab's throat. It broke off several of his teeth. Kaab tried to speak again.

Levi withdrew the weapon.

"I will tell you what I know. I don't know everything. Nobody does, except el-Wasi. I know only our assignment. We were to cause the blackout, and then assassinate the pope."

"What is to come next?"

"I don't know. I know something is to come next. I don't know what, or where, or which men will do it. El-Wasi kept such knowledge to himself. He did not want any of us to know too much in case something went wrong. Like this."

"How do you know that something else is scheduled to happen?"

"We had many men and many groups—too many for the small number of incidents that have so far occurred."

"Then someone, the next group, is waiting for a signal to proceed?"

Kaab did not respond. The gun was thrust to the back of his throat. He gagged violently, tears streaming down his sweaty face. He tried to nod his head, but it was pinned to the ground. "Unnnh," he finally managed to grunt from deep within.

The gun was removed. "That was yes?"

Kaab nodded.

"They are waiting for a signal?"

"Yes."

"And what is it?"

Kaab closed his eyes and spit out chips of his teeth, blood seeping out of his lips. Suddenly he felt an intense pain in the groin.

"The signal," Levi said.

"Yes."

"What is it?"

"The knowledge that my mission succeeded, that the pope is dead."

Within minutes, Simeon Levi was on the telephone with Avram Tal, and within an hour Zubair Kaab was on his way to Israel under heavy guard in an El Al jet.

THE WHITE HOUSE

At 5:19 P.M., following a talk with Levi in Rome, Tal made a one-minute call to New York from the EOB. When he returned to the White House, he, the vice-president, and Williston were summoned to the Oval Office.

Minutes before, Williston had heard from his Rome station of the attempt on the pope's life. It had surprised him enormously. Before the call it had not occurred to Williston—nor to anyone else in the Emergency Group, except Tal—that trouble would repeat itself in the Eternal City. He had also been jarred by a note that General Sykes had surreptitiously slipped him in the West Wing basement room: "K solution out." The news was unwelcome but hardly unexpected. Williston hurriedly placed a call to Langley and gave a terse message: "Option Bravo."

An attache brought them to the door of the Oval Office and knocked once on the door, departing as soon as the president bade them enter. "Corbin has told me the news," the president said, as he motioned the three to sit. "Is that the dramatic event which you predicted to me this morning—the attempted assassination of the pope?"

"I think there can be no question," Tal replied.

"I do not doubt that it is dramatic. But we have had a good deal of drama these past few weeks. I want to be sure it is *our* drama, you see, before I agree to your request, whatever it may be."

"Yes sir, Mr. President, I can appreciate that."

"First of all, it is curious, in a way—a way I am quite glad of, don't misunderstand me—but it is curious that this attempt failed. Unlike the others. Why?"

"Mr. President, there was one previous failure, as you know."

"Yes, the Sixth Plague." He had been well briefed.

"So it is not inevitable that the terrorists should succeed."

"But today someone seems to have anticipated the possibility—unlike the radioactive disposal truck. Who fended off the attackers? Not the Vatican security forces?"

"No, Mr. President."

"Then?"

Tal was silent.

"Your men?" the president prodded.

Tal did not respond. He stared unblinkingly into the president's eyes.

"I see," the president said, returning the stare. "You did not tell us because you trusted your men to avert this calamity—"

"Yes, sir."

"—and because you wanted the drama to be played out, for some reason."

"Yes, sir."

"To convince me?"

"Partly."

"And?"

"To convince el-Wasi, Mr. President. It is important that this attempt be known to the world; otherwise the telecast that I am asking you to make tonight would be useless."

"All right, we will come to that. But first tell me how you explain this Plague—how do you link the attempt on the pope's life to the Tenth Plague of Exodus?"

"Yes, sir. As you know, the Tenth Plague was—"

"The killing of the firstborn of the Egyptians."

"Yes, sir."

"What does that have to do with the pope?"

"Consider the pope as a representative, Mr. President."

"Of whom?"

"Of Christendom—of all Christianity. And what is Christianity?"

"Questions. I want answers."

"Yes, sir. I meant that rhetorically. I will answer it. Christianity is a religion that arose out of the Jewish experience—the first major religion to do so. If religions can be said to be born, then Christianity is surely the firstborn of the Jews, and Catholicism is the form it took. The pope is the symbol of Catholicism—so the pope is the logical intended victim of el-Wasi's Tenth Plague."

The president pondered Tal's analysis. Then, "Does this satisfy you?" he asked the other two.

"It is a closer connection than most of the others," the vice-president responded. Williston nodded in agreement.

"You seem right," the president said. "Let's assume you are. What do you propose for me to do?"

"Mr. President," Tal began, "we do not have a great deal of time. If we are to succeed, I myself must leave in minutes. What I ask of you is to buy us time, as much as we can get. That is why I wish you to appear on television. I want you to do so because I understand that the president can preempt regular programming."

"It is one of my very few powers," the president said dryly, "and only if I do it rarely. And I don't 'preempt.' The networks simply find me more commercially attractive than low comedy."

"Can you do it at six tonight?"

The president looked at his watch. "That's in thirty-three minutes," he said, and sat back to wait for an explanation.

"It is important the program begin promptly at six," Tal

said, "because it is crucial to preempt all regular newscasts, especially in the East. The news from Rome is still confused, I imagine, but the situation may begin to be reported accurately by then. We want to prevent that."

"Prevent the news from being reported accurately?"

"Prevent the news from being reported."

"That's all?"

"No."

"I didn't think so."

"No, sir. There's one more critical element. I would like you to announce that in view of the pope's assassination, the United States is now ready to begin negotiations with el-Wasi."

The president sat bolt upright in his chair. The vice-president instinctively stood.

"What?" they said almost in unison, the shock evident in both voices. Williston was silent, but his face betrayed the formation of a tiny smile.

"I know it sounds rather strange, Mr. President, but I assure you it is essential."

"But the pope is not dead."

"No, sir, he is not."

"So you are asking me to go on national television and tell not one but two lies to the American people. Lie number one, that the pope was killed. Lie number two, that we will negotiate. We have said repeatedly that we would not negotiate. We will not. How can I say that we will? Besides," he added, "these are not just any lies. These are lies that will easily be detected as false almost as soon as I speak them."

"Lies, Mr. President, if you wish to phrase it that way." Tal spoke impassively.

"Wish to?" the president said, heatedly. "I wish to do no such thing. You are asking me to break a sacred compact I made with the American people when they elected me to this office. This government does not conduct its business in an atmosphere of falsehoods. How can I do what you're asking?" He returned Tal's stare with a scowl.

"I appreciate the strength of your beliefs, Mr. President, and the wisdom of your policy. But these are not ordinary circumstances, and in such a broadcast rests our only hope of salvation."

"To deceive the American people on nationwide television—"

"Is also to deceive el-Wasi, Mr. President. It is the only way we can reach him. Our only direct link to him is television. He relies on television because he obviously believes television does not lie. But it can. If we aim his own weapon at him, this one time, we will use it to destroy this madness."

"Which happens how?"

"Mr. President, as long as el-Wasi believes his plot against the pope has succeeded he will do nothing with regard to any future Plague."

"You think there are more than ten?"

"Yes, sir. I am sure there are more planned. My agent in Rome has told me, and it makes sense. El-Wasi could not be confident that his strategy would succeed in a few weeks." Tal sat forward to emphasize the importance of his message. "If the object of the Tenth Plague had been accomplished, el-Wasi would merely wait for the next act of terror to take place, the pope's assassination being the signal for the eleventh team. But if el-Wasi learns that it has failed, he will of necessity give a signal himself to reactivate the chain of atrocities. What is critical for us, now, is to prevent him from giving that signal." He pounded a fist into the palm of his other hand.

"But how does having the president lying, telling the public that the pope has been assassinated, help?" the vice-president asked.

"Because when the president appears on television, that cancels out news programs that might report to the contrary. At least while the president is speaking. So we buy time."

"How much time do you need to buy?" the president asked.

"Until, say, eight tonight."

"Two hours? What can you hope to accomplish in two hours?"

Tal paused. A lie to the president of the United States

could be dangerous. But now not to lie could be even more dangerous.

"Mr. President," he said, "Israeli agents have taken one of el-Wasi's men in Rome. We expect to know within minutes the location of the next terrorist team. For fifteen days we have been deploying agents throughout the world. No likely place of attack is beyond two hours' reach. Obviously, if you can give us three hours we would prefer that."

"And with these two or three hours?"

"We will neutralize the next team. We will buy even more time—time enough to track down the team after that, and time enough to have your people, Mr. President, plan and execute a successful attack on el-Wasi."

"Is that a possibility?" the president asked, looking at Williston.

Williston looked from one to the other. Tal caught his breath, despite himself. Finally Williston said without expression: "Yes, sir, it is a possibility."

"I still don't like it," the president said. "To tell a public lie—that cuts against the deepest grain of my convictions. You had better be right, Colonel Tal. I regard your request not to be made by you personally but by your country. Your country had better be right."

"In a deceitful world, Mr. President, deceit is sometimes a necessary policy."

"I do not need lectures on integrity."

"I appreciate that, sir."

"How will I explain afterward? How does one undo such a palpable falsehood?"

"Mr. President, time is excruciatingly short. I must leave the undoing, as well as the doing, to you. In the long run you will have ample time and ample reasons to give. But now I must press you to give your word to me. The dramatic event I promised has occurred and the Tenth Plague has been avoided. I need you, we will need you, on television, in only thirty minutes."

The president stood up, face ashen. "Do what you have to do. For the love of Jesus, I hope you are right." He pushed a button, summoning an aide, who appeared within seconds and was instructed to arrange with the networks the programming of a special message from the White House of the utmost urgency, to be promptly at 6 P.M. and to be followed by a press conference.

Tal offered his hand to the president, who grasped it. "Thank you," Tal said. The president said nothing. Tal walked to the door. As he reached it, he heard a single word from the desk across the room: "Shalom." Tal walked out the door without looking back, Williston behind him. They walked down some steps and through a corridor.

"And now?" Williston asked. "What do you plan to do for the next, shall we say, three hours?"

"There is little time," Tal said earnestly. "I need your help."

"Of course."

"I need a helicopter. No questions asked."

"It is waiting outside."

"Here and now?" Tal could not hide the surprise in his voice.

Williston looked evenly at the Israeli, his face betraying no sign of emotion. "You are very shrewd," he said. "I would like to employ you myself. But you do make a tiny error in assuming we are everything you are not. We are not stupid. That cock-and-bull story you told the president—don't you think I know that you cannot seek out and destroy those elusive sabotage teams within two hours? And if you did you would not have bought much time at all. No, you are after bigger fish—in New York. No, no, do not interrupt me, I will say my piece and then you can go. Surgeons as skilled as Dr. Ableman and Dr. Betterman cannot arrive and operate in the United States without attracting our attention."

"You have known of these doctors—for how long?"

"Let's say a few days."

"And the president?"

"Does not need to know. Some things are better left unspoken in his room."

"Then?"

"You can go. Your secret is safe. I know nothing. The success is ours if you achieve it. If you don't the failure is yours."

Tal replied without breaking stride, "I agree to your terms."

"Good, but there is one more item."

"Yes?"

"I cannot leave the president dangling on that televised limb. You must give us a signal the instant it is done. And the president will be able to explain while he still controls air time."

"I agree. The signal?"

"Well—let us say, 'Maccabeus.'"

"You are thorough, Corbin, very thorough. Yes, 'Maccabeus.'"

Williston escorted him in silence outside. It had grown dark, and the silhouette of the helicopter was barely visible against the expanse of grass that fronted the office in which they had just been speaking. Tal clambered into the craft, and as the door swung shut looked down at the figure in a gray suit, already receding as the pilot began to climb. There was time for a salute, and Tal rendered it and watched the White House and then the rest of Washington fall away beneath him, the lighted white buildings shrinking into a toy city. The pilot looked at him. "New York, sir?"

"You have your instructions?"

"Yes, sir."

"We are to land—where?"

"Midtown, sir. Top of the Pan Am building."

"It is open to air traffic?"

"No, sir. Closed since that accident that cut a few people to ribbons a while ago. But they say you can climb down from a helicopter in less than ten seconds."

Tal sat back. "I have done that."

"Well, sir, I can land and leave as quickly. We will not need to ask their permission."

"Don't spare the fuel, Captain."

"No, sir," said the pilot, racing north.

ABC-TV STUDIO,
NEW YORK CITY

At 5:36 P.M., a Ford Econoline van pulled up on Sixty-sixth Street, just off Central Park West. Traffic was beginning its nightly rush-hour crawl. No time to circle for a parking space or garage. The van pulled alongside a hydrant and stopped abruptly. The driver slapped a large ABC-TV news sticker on the inside of the windshield and the three men who were crammed into the front seat jumped out and opened the rear doors. They pulled out a large dolly and let it clatter to the ground. Then they gingerly removed from the van several large slabs of wood, lightly wrapped in a burlap cloth, and a box, all of which they carefully placed on the dolly.

They told the guard in the lobby of the ABC building that they were delivering studio props. Seeing three men in dark blue ABC work overalls, he shrugged and pointed to an open book, on a table, instructing them that everyone entering the building after 5:30 had to sign. While one casually hunched over to sign the other two were already wheeling the dolly to the bank of elevators in the center of the lobby. The guard ceased to pay them any mind: He would see plenty of others before the night was over. He always did.

Seconds later, they stepped onto the ninth floor. The receptionist's chair was empty. The typewriter was covered. The men pulled the dolly into a corridor, and propped the slabs of wood against the wall. Then, without a word, they separated, and began trying doors down the different corridors leading off the reception area.

The first four doors Danny Nahteev tugged at were all locked. The next one was not even closed. He looked in. He could see the back of a seated man's head. His legs were propped up on a console. The man's head faced up in the direction of a bank of 40 television monitors on the far wall. Normally they would have displayed a variety of pictures, all images emanating from the various Channel

7 cameras, whether live, canned commercials, or taped network programs. By pushing a series of buttons, this man—the "switcher"—would determine which of the 40 images would actually be transmitted over the ABC antenna to the viewing public.

Nahteev looked at the screens. Tonight, with the exception of the top row, which showed the president on the network feed to the rest of the country, each of the others showed the same motionless picture, the same picture they had shown without interruption for two weeks: the delegates' entrance to the UN General Assembly building.

Nahteev tiptoed into the room. Carefully, quietly, he eased the door shut. The seated man did not stir. He was asleep.

With his right hand, Nahteev took a .38 caliber pistol from under his coat. He tiptoed noiselessly behind the seated figure. Then, in one motion, he cupped his left hand quickly and strongly over the seated man's mouth and shoved the muzzle of the .38 against the man's right ear. When he felt resistance, he slid the pinky and thumb of his left hand down to the man's neck. The man began to struggle but Nahteev applied increasing pressure until the man's resistance stopped.

Nahteev spoke quietly to him. "There is a gun against your head but I will not hurt you if you obey. Do you understand? Will you obey?" He could feel the seated man try to nod his head up and down.

"Good." Nahteev relaxed the pressure against the man's mouth. He reached the hand holding the gun toward his rear pocket and removed a small walkie-talkie. "Studio 9," he whispered into it. Within seconds, the other two Israelis had entered the room, pulling in the large wood slabs and the box on the dolly. The last to enter locked the door.

The seated man ventured to speak when he saw the other two men enter. "You fellows have the wrong room," he said. "There's nothing here. Look," he said, pointing to the monitors.

"A very dull picture," Nahteev said.

"Yes," said the man, "please, there is nothing here to take."

"You have us wrong, my friend," Nahteev answered. "We have come to give you something. You must do one tiny thing or two when I tell you to."

Nahteev nodded at the other two men. Wordlessly, they leaned the wooden slabs against a wall and opened the box, removing various tools, an assortment of wood, bolts, nails, and screws, a set of heavy hinges, and some shapeless soft cloth.

They stripped the muslin away, revealing large painted boards, and began assembling the prop. First a door frame took shape, then a few yards of a building facade around the door frame; the facade was painted with a stone facing. They bolted it into place. The entire set was hammered to the floor and supported from behind with several two-by-fours. The two men tested their creation by kicking it from behind. It did not budge. Then they tugged the largest and heaviest slab, the door, behind the set and affixed the long hinges to it. These they then attached, after some struggle, to the frame. When it stood on its own, one of the men picked up the cloth and unraveled it, revealing a shining doorknob. He inserted it into the pre-drilled hole and shut the door.

The ABC technician had watched the construction with some bewilderment. Finally, he understood. "My God," he said, "it's the UN door."

"Very good," said Nahteev, still holding the gun to the man's head. "Wheel it over here," he said to one of his men, gesturing across the room to where a TV camera stood.

"Now," said Nahteev to the technician, when that was done, "stand up very slowly and walk equally slowly to that camera. I want you to turn it on and focus it on our door." Nahteev kept looking over his shoulder at the monitors. "I don't see our door," he said, when it had been plugged in.

"Of course not," said the technician. "The picture from this camera is controlled from up there." He pointed to the keyboard.

"Well, let's go back up there and you put our door on the lower left screen—can you do that? But only on that screen. Let the picture go outside this room and you are dead. Understand?"

The man nodded, did as he was bidden. Shortly, the lower left screen showed what was obviously a stage set door. Nahteev waved the technician back to the camera. "Now focus it so none of the studio wall shows up." After five minutes of pulling and pushing by the technician, Nahteev had the picture he wanted: an exact replica of the picture on all the other screens.

"Will the real door please stand up," the technician muttered.

"I beg your pardon?"

"Just a joke."

"I don't want jokes. I don't want talking. I want absolute, unquestioning obedience." He pushed the gun against the man's temple.

The technician winced. "Yes, sir," he said.

"Okay," said Nahteev, "now we wait. Move back from the controls and you can sit down," he said to the technician. Nahteev removed the pistol from the man's head, but kept it loosely pointed at him from his perch near the monitors. The man pushed his chair out of arm's reach of the controls and sagged into it.

"Are you hungry?" Nahteev asked.

"No," the technician said.

"I am. I think since we will be here awhile we ought to have some food. May I use this phone?" He picked it up, dialed. While waiting for it to be answered, he looked at his watch. Pretty good: only two minutes, late, at 6:22 P.M.

"Dr. Betterman," he said into the phone, "my stomach is much better. I am in Studio 9. I wonder whether you might allow me something to eat?"

NEW YORK CITY

At 6:28 P.M., one of many crowded elevators in the Pan Am building opened on the first floor. First to exit was Avram Tal. He ran to a newsstand to ask directions to the nearest public phone but saw it halfway there, on his left, and raced to it. The row of eleven phone booths was totally occupied. Inside the last booth, a heavy-set man was fumbling in his pocket for a coin.

Tal banged frantically on the glass door. The fat man ignored him. Tal banged again. The fat man turned his back to the door and pressed the heel of one shoe against the door to keep it shut. Tal kicked the door hard. It gave only slightly. The fat man turned around. He was chewing on a big unlit cigar. Somewhere deep in his throat a loud and obscene word was forming and moving to his lips.

Before it got there the fat man saw the open nose of Tal's .38 flat against the glass door, pointing directly at the fat man's head. He swallowed his word and nearly the cigar. He opened the door and raised his hands over his head, trembling. Tal told him to put his hands down and get out of the booth. The fat man said he had no money. Tal replied that he wanted no money, only the phone.

Tal dropped in a dime and dialed. A telephone rang in a police van on First Avenue. "Grogan," said the answering voice. It sounded like someone else.

"Too many names, Dr. Betterman," Tal said.

"Ah, Dr. Ableman. You are in town?"

"Yes."

"You are just in time. The cameras are in place."

"And the operating room?"

"We are awaiting only the delivery of our supplies. Come see for yourself."

"Thank you, Dr. Betterman, I think I will."

Tal raced out of the Pan Am building onto Forty-fifth Street, past the fat man, who was scurrying around yelling for the police. Tal ran east and, at First Avenue, turned left. Though he had seen all the pictures, the reality of it nevertheless startled him. What seemed to be thousands of policemen lined the avenue. None looked familiar. He pushed through the crowd and fought his way to the line of buses. There, twirling his nightstick, was a wonderful sight: Uri Shir, now in a police uniform, on the periphery patrol.

"Pardon me, officer," Tal yelled. Shir looked around, started to grin, saw Tal's stern look and changed his expression into a frown.

"Yes, what is it?" Shir responded.

"A word with you, sir."

"All right, all right," said Shir, "clear the way." He jabbed at several people with his nightstick to let Tal pass.

"From the mayor's office," said Tal in a loud voice.

"Hooray, the mayor's come to save us," someone said.

They conferred briefly, Shir nodding his head vigorously all the while. "Over there," he said audibly, pointing inside the gate. "Let him pass," he yelled to the other policemen as Tal strode quickly onto the UN grounds.

The president stood before the podium on the stage of the White House briefing room. In the Johnson years the space had been a swimming pool, but Richard Nixon covered it over and decreed that the press would ask their questions from this basement room. Now the president spoke from the room because the setting did not demand the formal speech that would be required if he were to have addressed the nation from the Oval Office. It was also easier to set up the cameras in a hurry in a room whose chief purpose was to permit that. Moreover, to stage a two- or three-hour preemption of the networks would require more talking than the president alone could muster on a half-hour's notice. Let the reporters be part of this charade. And let them be locked in and locked out: those who came would have to stay, no running off to file stories prematurely; those who had news that the pope was still alive would not come in to ask embarrassing questions.

By 6:40 the president had finished his review of the Middle East situation and of the devastating effects around the world of the terrorists' actions. Governments on the verge of collapse. Municipal budgets at the breaking point. Riots.

Forty minutes of talk on thirty minutes' notice. Not bad, but not nearly long enough. Time now to drop the second bombshell. The announcement that the pope had died would be as nothing compared to what he was about to say. He paused, took a sip of water, looked around the room, drew a breath.

"I have taken this time to review the history of the conflict and of our responsibilities in order to set in perspective the announcement that, with much regret and a heavy heart, it is now my duty to make. I can assure you that never have I done as much soul-searching as I have done this afternoon in the wake of the news that the latest act of madness was the death this evening in the Vatican City of His Holiness the Pope. This dastardly act is the culmination of more than two weeks of steady outrages. They must come to an end. Despite my early pledge to make no deal with the Palestinians in the United Nations, I now state that the United States is willing to undertake negotiations directly with Hashim el-Wasi."

Every reporter in the crowded room bolted up. Hands were waving furiously. "Mr. President," some yelled out. A breach of protocol, the president thought ruefully; no questions and no interruptions until the president was finished. This was an unseemly display. But so, he thought to his disgust, was what he himself was doing.

But protocol would be maintained; the president would speak a few minutes more. "Please," he said, "I will answer questions, to the extent that they do not breach security, in a few moments. I do, however, have something more to say."

In the General Assembly Hall, el-Wasi raised his gun and fired a single round into the dome. "This is it," he crowed triumphantly into the microphone; "the president is making his concession speech. I want you all to hear this." He indicated to Zaid ibn Haritha, standing near the podium, to pull the television close to the microphone, in order to broadcast the speech throughout the Hall.

"We have won," ibn Haritha said exultantly.

"Perhaps, perhaps," el-Wasi replied. "It seems so, but we must have more than seeming. Let us listen carefully to what the president proposes. May Allah guide his hands."

* * *

At 7:10 there was a knock outside the door of Studio 9. "Who's there?" Nahteev demanded.

"Relax, Danny," said a voice, "we have brought you dinner."

"A moment." One of the Israelis drew his gun, advanced to the door and unlocked it. He stepped back three paces. "Open it slowly."

The door opened inward. Standing outside was a man in a white uniform on which the words "Delicious Caterers" were sewn in heavy red cloth. "Your food, sir," said the man with a bow and a wink. He tugged at an extra-large wheeled serving cart, with white tablecloth draped all across it, and pulled it in to the room. "Where do you want it?"

"Over there," Nahteev said, pointing to a spot equidistant between the false door and the camera. The caterer reached beneath the tablecloth and extracted a lump of folded clothing.

"For you," he said, tossing it across the room to a third man.

"Better get dressed, Shmuel," Nahteev said. Shmuel let the cloth unfold and began to dress himself in the white robe and headdress.

"Jesus Christ, I don't believe it."

The mayor waved his hand toward the four television sets in the spacious room at City Hall. "I don't believe it, but I see it. The miracle of television."

"I don't believe in miracles anymore," Newman said.

"Keep the faith, baby," the mayor muttered.

"Do you suppose the president will actually let them bomb out every last Israeli—I mean, for real?"

"No, I'm guessing his negotiations will amount to a large-scale emigration."

"You mean bring them all over here?"

"Perhaps."

"To New York?"

"Well—"

"That'd be something, now wouldn't it?" Newman was counting votes.

Colonel Arthur McDougal sat in his office at Fort Bragg, his only company the television set tuned to his commander-in-chief. When the president announced his intention to negotiate, McDougal blanched. The last shred of hope that somehow, someone had worked out a plan and would give K Detachment its five percent chance had now vanished. There would be no orders. There would be no summons. He had failed the president of the United States. It seemed obvious to McDougal that because K Detachment could come up with nothing better than a five percent plan, the president had had to capitulate. And whose fault was it? As commander of K Detachment, McDougal was to blame.

He opened his upper left desk drawer. Lying next to a stack of personal stationery was his service revolver. If it had been his own country standing at the brink there would have been only one course left to him. He would have shot himself. He reached into the drawer, but passed his hand over the gun and took out a sheet of paper which he slapped down on the desk. Shaking, he penned his resignation.

Uri Shir stood on the corner of Forty-sixth Street and First Avenue, contemplating the crowd. It was getting progressively more sullen as it listened to the president's address on the radio. But it hung on the speech, remaining, for the moment, quiet. Shir looked at his watch: 7:15. The night was cold. The agent disguised in this ludicrously stiff blue uniform could see his breath as he turned his head every few seconds to survey the streets and the people. Well, it was better than being dressed as a hotdog vendor.

He thought of his "friends," the bizarre assortment of crazies who drifted in his sector of the watch. The lady with the bright red bandana tied around her forehead and the great gray skirts hiding the tennis shoes. Over there, muttering to herself as usual about repentance. And the panhandler with the white New York Athletic Club cap was still offering his pens for sale. Several other regulars weaving in and out. It seemed, despite what Tal's appeareance in the flesh portended, an easy night. Harmless lizards.

A commotion. People clustered around a man at mid-block. The evening paper held aloft, someone running. What's this? "FOIL ATTEMPT ON POPE; PRESIDENT SPEAKS." There was a stir in the crowd. News travels fast in a country without censorship.

"Do you hear me? Do you hear me? Answer, answer." Shir heard the words as an insistent buzzing in the air. Strange words—why? He suddenly realized: he had caught the meaning without at first being conscious of the language. This was not English or Hebrew—but Arabic! It dawned on him at last. Arabic? Now he could see one of his crazies running along the perimeter of the police line. The bent-over man with the growth of beard, ragged pants and green shoes, and that ever-present radio. But what? Held not to his ear but his mouth. Why? "Pope lives, not dead. Confirm, do you hear me, respond, respond," the crazy shouted loudly in Arabic, oblivious of anyone around him, as he raced down the street in Shir's direction.

The buzzing turned into a terrible ringing and filled Shir's head. This was no crazy; not indigenous, anyway. El-Wasi's man, the seventh man, maintained, like Shir himself, as a perimeter patrol. Of course. This was el-Wasi's insurance policy against deceit; had been his insurance policy all along, for all the days that Shir had stood his watch.

The wide open desert closed in on the agent; he felt himself suddenly poured back down a funnel, dropped to a particular spot, insignificant no more. Too significant: all the world might hang on the meaning of this and his reaction to it.

The man was trying to communicate with el-Wasi—he must be desperate, breaking into a run in plain sight yelling in Arabic. The radio was a walkie-talkie! The man was running up the street because he had to get in range.

Without conscious thought, Shir reached for his pistol, yanked it from the holster, took aim, fired a single shot. The bullet pierced the man's head. He pitched headlong into the sewer grating on the corner.

The crowd nearby moved back as if one, curiosity over-come by fear. Shir jumped into the street, ran to the body, there joined by two of his fellows. "What happened?" one asked.

"Arab. El-Wasi's seventh man," Shir spat out. He pointed to the radio, lying on the ground near the body. "Walkie-talkie."

"Ah."

"Reinforcements," Shir called out. Four officers rushed over. There was a huddle, hurried explanations, pointing. Two men dragged the body inside the police perimeter. Shir walked slowly to the command wagon, his gun held lightly in his right hand. The numbness was beginning to spread within. He climbed into the wagon, holstered the gun. He had done his job that night. He sat down.

"Report," said Tal. Shir gave him the details. "Stay seated," Tal commanded, "you have earned your rest." Shir looked straight ahead, at a television set inside the van, focused on the front door of the UN delegates' entrance, several yards away. He did not see the picture.

Outside, a crowd strained against the ropes. Word spread. Action: a real killing. A body in the street. Traces of blood could be seen, pointed to. "What happened? What's going on?" people shouted. The policemen shrugged.

At 7:22, the police department truck that had for sev-enteen days been transporting food for those inside the General Assembly Hall rolled up to the gate at the First Avenue entrance to the delegates' driveway and stopped. Three men inside the van pushed open the rear door. Two hopped down and helped the third guide the large, mobile, multi-tiered food cart down a small ramp and onto the side-walk. A white linen tablecloth was draped over the top and hung down the sides.

Captain de Petri was on the sidewalk waiting for them. "I'll take it from here," he said, and quickly pushed the tray into the driveway. As he began pushing it toward the area just outside the delegates' entrance, Tal signalled to Mor-decai Ofir, who wore a patrolman's uniform with the name-tag "Grogan" on the left breast, and Ofir walked hurriedly to help de Petri push the cart, guiding it to the usual spot ten feet in front of the delegates' door.

El-Wasi turned for a moment from the television carrying the president's news conference to watch Channel 7 on his other set. Listening at the same time to the president's voice, he saw the policemen silently pushing the cart to the front of the delegates' entrance. He saw the two policemen leave the cart in place, then watched the two policemen walk off the TV screen. When el-Wasi saw the cart alone in front of the delegates' door, he turned back to the other TV to watch the president, and called out in Arabic to ibn Haritha, that it was okay to bring in the food.

In Studio 9 at the ABC building, Danny Nahteev stood calmly, watching the TV monitors and holding the muzzle of his gun level with the technician's ear. The two uniformed figures disappeared from the screens. When the cart stood alone in front of the delegates' door, Nahteev shouted at the caterer. "Tilt it slightly toward me," he commanded, eyeing the TV monitors as the caterer began to shift the cart slightly. Nahteev gave further directions until the picture on the lower left screen precisely matched that on the others. "Good," he said, "leave it right there."

Nahteev kept the gun trained at the switcher's head. Without turning he ordered: "Shmuel, go around behind the door." The man, dressed as an Arab complete with head-gear, walked briskly out of sight behind the lustrous brown door housed in the stage set.

Nahteev took a step back to the technician. He jabbed the barrel of his pistol against the back of the man's head.

"What's the matter?" the man asked, trembling.

"Do exactly what I say. Go over to your control panel, and transmit that picture"—he pointed to the lower left monitor—"to your home viewers. If you make a mistake or any noise, I will blow your head off."

The man took a few steps toward the console. He pushed two buttons. There was the briefest flicker on all but the top row of screens. Then the others all looked as placid as they had looked for the past fifteen days. And no different from the lower left screen. The technician nodded and said: "It's done."

Nahteev pointed to the lower left screen. "Can you put the real UN door on that one?" he asked, as if an afterthought.

"Sure," the man said.

"Then do it. It's the last thing you'll have to do tonight."

He pushed another button, then two more. Another flicker, this time on the lower left screen only.

"Now move back," Nahteev ordered. The man pushed his chair far away from the keyboard. They both looked at his handiwork. The top row continued to show the president's news conference, seen by all ABC viewers except those in New York. New Yorkers saw a door, the door shown on the remaining 35 screens. But only one was real and only those in Studio 9 knew it.

The questions were incessant, the questioners impertinent. "Mr. President," said the White House correspondent for the *New York Times,* "you have said repeatedly that you would not negotiate with Hashim el-Wasi. And Mr. el-Wasi has said repeatedly that he would not negotiate either, because the dismantling of Israel is a non-negotiable, final demand. What room is there for maneuver? Are you saying that you intend to give in to his demand? Are we not morally bankrupt if we do?"

The president wiped his forehead with a handkerchief, sweat from the bright lights having long since drenched his shirt. "I believe there is always room for negotiation. I have always insisted on the right of Israel to exist as a sovereign state. On the other hand, it goes without saying that the world as a whole has a right to exist free of terror. We must strike a balance."

"Mr. President—"

"Mr. President—"

"Mr. President, a follow-up question—" the *Times* correspondent shouted above the din.

Nancy Dolby had come close to tears after the president stunned the Emergency Group with his second announcement, but she composed herself quickly. She was at a loss. Several times she picked up her pencil to write something on her yellow pad, and each time let it fall without making a mark.

"Son of a bitch," Watkins said. "After all our work. Nothing. He never even consulted us."

"We didn't exactly come up with anything better," Dr. Jones replied.

"Just like the man in the coffee shop said," Dolby remarked.

"What?"

"A couple of weeks ago. Right after Chicago. He said he was sure that the president would give in sooner or later. Oil money. I can't believe it." She covered her face in her hands.

"Well now, folks," Sykes piped up, "don't be so goddamn naive."

"Naive?" Pinckney echoed.

"Right."

"What do you mean?" Jones asked.

"Hasn't it occurred to anyone that our ranks are rather thin tonight?"

"Sure, but I assume they're down there with the president."

"The vice-president and Kowalski, okay. But he doesn't need the Director of the CIA to conduct a press conference. So where is Williston? And where is Super Agent Tal? Tell me that. We haven't seen him for hours. Something's up."

"Do you really think so?"

"I have nothing else to believe in tonight."

Fifteen Israeli commandoes crouched behind the New York City police cars that circled the delegates' entrance. All held weapons trained at the door.

From inside the mobile command post, Tal watched through a window. Crumpled on the floor, in a heap, lay his clothes.

"How do I look, Captain de Petri?" he asked, smiling but not shifting his gaze from the window.

De Petri was now certain they had all gone crazy. First

the crack S.O.D. unit gets kidnapped and now the leader of this bunch of foreigners is standing in front of him, dressed in the white flowing robe and hat of a goddamn Arab. De Petri said nothing.

Tal kept staring out the window at the delegates' entrance.

The door moved, very slightly.

Zaid ibn Haritha peeked outside. Nobody there.

He opened the door a bit wider, saw the food cart in its customary position. He saw the crowds as usual, the police cars in the center of the street, the policemen lining the avenue.

He swung the door wide open.

At Studio 9, Nahteev saw, on the lower left screen, the door open. "Now, Shmuel, now," he yelled. The fake door inside the studio swung open, and a white-robed figure stepped out, displayed on millions of home screens, including el-Wasi's. Shmuel walked ten steps toward the multi-tiered food cart. He reached it, took it by the handle, and gently rolled it back toward the door, still open. When the cart was fully behind, shrouded in the darkness of the back of the studio, he shut the door. Thirty-four screens showed the same placid scene.

Zaid ibn Haritha began walking toward the cart. At his seventh step, several dozen bullets severed, for all practical purposes, his head from his body. Not much more than a red stump remained on the top of his neck after the bullets hit. The simultaneous rifle-fire had spat out suddenly and loud, a moment before the Arab would have reached the food cart. He never heard the noise and felt pain only momentarily. His body collapsed on the ground, exactly where he had taken his last step.

Most of the crowd behind the buses began retreating in panic at the renewed sound of shots. Several whose curiosity this time overcame their fear peered through the slight separations among the buses and glimpsed what seemed to be another Arab racing from inside the mobile command car toward a fallen body, with a dozen policemen who had just shot the first Arab running after him.

Tal glanced down at the robed body beside the cart. When he saw the gory stump he did not stop. He raced inside the delegates' door. Two others, right behind him, pulled the cart in alongside. In seconds, two dozen other commandoes, dressed in police uniforms, were inside the building as well. All carried uzis; one had a bazooka. The last to enter slammed the delegates' door shut behind him.

The mayor dialed Commissioner Andrews for confirmation that the police were prepared for the mob scene that the president's announcement would undoubtedly precipitate.

"Mr. Mayor," Andrews boasted, "this was one of the possibilities we had to consider. We're covered for it. You'll find it on the last page of the poop sheet I gave you when this crap first hit the fan."

The mayor hung up. Without turning from the television sets, he asked Manny Newman to fetch him the report on police deployment from the two stacks of papers on the credenza.

Tal led his men quickly up the staircase leading from the first floor to the second, nearest the door that, in turn, was nearest the staircase to the third floor that Tal had seen so many times on videotaped reruns of Harold Saperstein's frightened walk. One of Tal's commandoes, having removed all the food, dragged the cart up the steps to the second-floor landing.

Tal strapped two uzis firmly onto the top of the cart. The submachine guns were fastened securely but Tal allowed flexibility for rotation. When the guns were in place, Tal again covered the top of the cart with the white tablecloth. He pushed the cart to the door—the door they had labeled "six o'clock"—the door that he was betting his life would not be wired.

He paused in front and pulled down the kaffiyeh as low as it would fit on his head. For one last time he touched the transmitter on his chest, concealed beneath the robe. It felt comfortable. He looked back at his men. They were huddled against the side wall, out of view from the inside of the Hall when the door would open.

Tal touched the doorknob lightly. Then he carefully cradled it in his hand. As naturally as thinking of his own name, he said to himself: Sh'mah Yisrael Adonai Elohainu Adonai Echod." Hear O Israel the Lord Our God the Lord is One. Then he turned the knob, slowly, very slowly, and began to push the door open.

"Mr. President," demanded a man from the *Dallas Times Herald*, "why can't we storm the UN? For the love of God, does it make sense to destroy an entire nation and shatter the integrity of the United States' international commitments?"

"I think I have already answered that question," the president responded calmly, somehow beyond emotion. "We have studied the logistics thoroughly. Expert military analysts have explored the possibilities inch-by-inch, and have concluded, and I concur, that the terrorists are in earnest when they say they would blow the building up, themselves included, at the first sign of an invasion. But beyond that, of course, is the fact that we are all hostages, in a sense; not of Mr. el-Wasi alone, but of his terrorist teams. We do not know where they are; we cannot cut them off; we cannot, therefore, strike down the one man who might be persuaded to call them off."

Captain de Petri stood immobile for several seconds in the mobile command center after Tal had raced outside. He turned toward the heap of clothing on the floor, shook his head, and sat. Fidgety, he rose almost as quickly and walked past the television to the front door. He looked toward the delegates' entrance. One of the Israeli commandoes, still in police uniform, was searching the headless body.

Captain de Petri didn't care. He wondered whether his wife and daughter were comfortable, or harmed, or alive. Or whether, by some miracle, they were already home. He picked up the telephone.

"Not yet, Captain," an accented voice ordered from outside. De Petri looked up and saw a by now familiar uniformed man standing there. "We told you they won't be harmed if you and they behave. We meant it. You have all behaved admirably. This will soon be over."

The captain replaced the phone in its cradle. He sat. Then he stood again. There was nothing to do.

The TV was tuned to the president's news conference. De Petri switched channels; still the president. He rotated the dial again, to Channel 7. He saw the delegates' entrance on the screen. The scene was placid. There was no body laying on the ground and no one searching the body. Just a door. De Petri turned from the television and peered out the command vehicle. Again he saw the body on the ground and the uniformed man searching it. He jerked his head back to the television and saw the entrance on the screen, with nothing else there.

Captain de Petri blinked hard several times. Then he looked outside again and saw the body being searched and then looked again at the TV screen. He shut his eyes and squeezed them tight. It had been a rough few weeks. Maybe he should get some real good sleep.

Ten blocks south of the building in which Danny Nahteev controlled the Channel 7 airwaves, several news executives of the CBS network stood around a similar control room. This was a special night. Even the president of the network had wandered in.

"How long do you think he'll keep talking?" one man asked in disgust, toting up 27 minutes of advertising already lost forever to the network's coffers.

"God knows."

"He doesn't even tell God."

Silence.

"Laugh, that's a joke."

"Shut the hell up, Henry."

"Okay, fellas, quiet down," the news division president said. He was entitled: It was his budget that was paying for the programming.

The phone rang. The news division head took the call. "Make it quick," he said. "I really can't talk—what? When? Are you sure? Who else confirms? Yes? Seen him with his own eyes? Jesus. I can't believe it. Yes, yes. Well, I don't know. You have footage? Christ, yes we can, if we have to. Look, phone in the copy to the news desk and we'll have everyone standing by." He slammed the phone down. The others were all staring at him.

"You aren't going to believe this."

"We're waiting."

"The pope is alive."

"What the hell are you talking about?"

"That was Anderson in Los Angeles. L.A., for God's sake. He says its all over the wires. Hadn't we heard? The pope came out about 45 minutes after the attack and continued with the Mass, like nothing ever happened. Our own guy in Rome saw him with his own eyes."

"So what's that all about?" someone asked, pointing to the president on the screen.

"Beats me. Something's funny. He's been on for over 90 minutes, making major policy based on facts that he should have known were false before he went on. Listen, the CIA may be bad, but not that bad. They do have access to wire services."

"And television."

"Yeah, except no one's been on television stating the facts—just that garbage, whatever it's about."

"The AP is apparently making mincemeat of that jerk there—and of us, too, I suppose. They're saying it's the worst foreign policy blunder in American history."

"It's a story."

"Christ, yes."

"Why don't we go on? I heard you say we have footage. What a great piece of broadcasting that would be."

"Takes too long to set up the video."

"Then cut in for 90 seconds, bring our viewers up to date? They won't miss much of that bilge anyway." The man who made the suggestion looked at the news division president.

"I'm agreeable. It's news, God knows. Good news. Hot news." But he looked to the network president. They all did. He was staring at the screens.

"Nancy, it's for you." Pinckney handed her the phone.

"Hello?" she said quizzically, wondering who would be calling her now, there, and for what earthly reason.

"Listen, sweetheart, this city is crazy enough without us having to worry that we've let a klepto into the administration, stealing confidential documents and doing God-knows-what with them."

She recognized the voice on the first word. "Why, Manny, what *do* you mean?"

"Cut the shit, we both know you swiped that police report. We need it immediately. Where is it?"

"Manny darling, I don't know what you *could* be talking about."

"The report, Nancy. That goddamn police report could be disastrous if it falls into the wrong hands."

Now she understood. The police report. Tal's absence. But if the connection was what she thought, why the president's concession?

"If that report's not back here by midnight, Nancy," Newman continued, "don't bother ever returning to this city. You'll be through."

Dolby answered in her most intimate voice. "If that report doesn't become unnecessary by midnight, there won't be a city worth returning to. That report never did the city any good lying around close to you. But if you find another copy, will you do me a personal favor? Stick it up your rectum."

El-Wasi looked up from the TV and saw the back of the white-robed figure enter the Hall through the rear door, pulling the food cart in behind him. He saw the figure turn the cart around toward the front of the Hall.

Tal began pushing the cart slowly, holding it from the rear. His hands, beneath the white cloth on top of the cart, were tightened into fists around the barrels of the uzis, fingers against the gunlocks. He steered the cart toward the center aisle in the rear by pushing against the hidden barrels. Tal kept his head tilted slightly down, but his eyes searched the room. As he reached the center aisle at the rear, he whispered, barely moving his lips, "five thirty-five." Then he whispered, "delegates seated."

A man at the control board in the CBS studio swiveled his chair around. "Mr. Cronkite wants to know when we're going to give him the signal. He's ready."

"We're not," the network president said at last.

"But they'll cream us tomorrow if we don't report the news. Jesus, first time television was ever beaten so badly by the wires. It's already in the early headlines."

"I'm sorry," the network president said softly, "but no one has ever cut in on the President of the United States and I don't intend to start a new tradition. We won't cut in. Time enough to ask these questions when he's finished."

"He'll be finished, all right."

"Maybe so."

"Two o'clock." The Israeli commandoes outside the rear door of the Hall strained to hear the receiver. Mordecai Ofir, holding the receiver, gestured with his head. He tip-toed several steps to the rear door where Tal had entered. He put the walkie-talkie gently on the floor and placed his left hand on the doorknob. His right hand held his gun. Twenty-eight others huddled in close behind him.

El-Wasi stayed seated at the podium, staring at the television. The president was saying that he did not want to discuss the repatriation of the Jews, that the "problem of resettlement" was purely hypothetical "at the present time." El-Wasi turned to his left and called out "Bekr" to an Arab seated at the far front corner. Bekr began walking toward el-Wasi. "Look at this," el-Wasi said. "I want you to see his expression when he talks about this hypothetical problem." They were both smiling.

Tal approached the area where the delegates sat. He

whispered "ten o'clock." He saw Bekr come alongside el-Wasi at the podium. Tal continued toward the rostrum.

All the commandoes outside the Hall gripped the triggers of their uzis.

The cart was now within twenty feet of the rostrum. El-Wasi suddenly looked up from the screen, fully aware for the first time of the close approach. "Where are you going, you idiot?" he called out in Arabic.

Under the linen on the cart, Tal tightened the index fingers of both hands around the triggers of the guns. He quickened his pace toward the rostrum.

"Have you gone crazy?" el-Wasi shouted over the microphone. "Leave the cart back there like always. What the hell are you doing?"

Tal took three more quick steps.

El-Wasi reached for his submachine gun and began to shout: "Something's wrong—"

Tal pressed the triggers. An uzi emits 10 rounds per second. By the end of the first second, the contorted figures of el-Wasi and Bekr had been blown back from the podium, ripped apart by the force of the slugs. Their bodies had flown upward like scarecrows and now lay motionless, together, blood pouring freely onto the floor. Instantly, without waiting to see where they fell, Tal dove for the floor.

At the first sound of gunfire, Mordecai Ofir hurtled through the rear door of the Hall and in the same motion opened fire blindly at the five-thirty-five position. He had not even seen his target before two of his bullets, a fraction of a second apart, ripped through the Arab's ascending aorta and left pulmonary aorta, killing him instantly. —

The man at ten o'clock was confused. Here was Zaid ibn Haritha pulling the cart in too close. What for? Why would Zaid kill el-Wasi and Bekr? From what was Zaid taking cover? Instinctively the man pivoted around, gun outstretched and pointing in the direction of the cart, when he heard a hail of gunfire from the rear. Again he pivoted, and this time he saw real enemies: a dozen men, more, rushing in from the back, firing. He dove for the floor. Thoughts flashed: Bekr and el-Wasi were dead or dying; he would be overpowered soon. He could not hold out against a platoon. Zaid had fallen or was taking cover; traitor and coward. He saw his compatriot in the rear of the Hall plummet to the ground. Only one other left. He had to get to the button. El-Wasi had made that point paramount above all others. If invaded, blow up the Hall. Whoever is left, blow up the Hall. There are to be no survivors. It was very simple, really; the button closed a switch that would detonate the explosives. The entire Hall would collapse—a rubble of bodies and stones. "Musaab, the button," he shouted in Arabic. "I am going to set it off. Cover me." Crouching, and clutching his gun in one hand, he rushed toward the stage.

From under the cart, Tal felt for the straps on his lower left leg. He ripped the robe and yanked a small pistol from the holster. Now he peered around the side of the cart, using it as a shield. He stretched out his right arm, holding it steady against the upper railing of the cart. He pressed the trigger. The Arab screamed and sagged but kept moving. Tal fired again. The bullet lodged inside the Arab's brain.

Musaab Umair began to fire at the cart. Tal hit the floor. The shooting ceased. Two seconds went by. Tal looked up, saw Umair wrestling with something in his hand. It looked like a grenade.

Instinctively, Tal leaped to his feet. He fired once, struck Umair in the stomach. Umair howled in pain and his hands flew open, dropping the grenade at his feet. He doubled over in agony. Tal turned to the left slightly and fired at an oblique angle into Umair's side. He did not wait to see whether the bullet had struck, but dove again for the floor, behind the cart to shield himself against the blast.

Umair fell on top of the grenade. It exploded two seconds later, tearing his body to shreds, knocking out a portion of the west wall, and sending debris flying into a few seats in the nearby rows of delegates. The force of the blast slammed into the cart, sending it skidding backwards. Tal went limp and let the cart carry him until it stopped, wedging against the lower metal support of a delegate's chair. He felt a sharp pain through his legs. He held his breath and waited.

The firing ceased. Less than half a minute after the invasion began, the room was silent, a tableau that would remain forever frozen in Tal's mind. The delegates huddled on the floor, hands and arms bent over their heads, motionless.

The mute bodies of eight men were beyond all seeing and notions of discomfort: Hashim el-Wasi and Bekr in conjoint heaps at the center of the stage. The five thirty-five body, bleeding at the rear of the Hall. Musaab Umair in countless bits, not all of which would be recovered. The ten o'clock man with a bullet in his head, lying three feet from the button he sought. And three unlucky delegates, who had been crouching too close to the epicenter of the grenade's blast.

Tal poked his head up to survey the room. He saw nothing moving, and so sat up. His legs throbbed. Waving to his men at the rear of the Hall, he plucked a walkie-talkie from his belt and depressed the transmit button.

"Shir?"

"Thank God, Avram," came the static-filled reply.

Tal stood up, gritting his teeth against the pain, and waited for one of his men, now running from the back, to deliver a bullhorn with which to address the delegates. Those who did not comprehend lay huddled on the floor.

The private telephone rang in a small alcove off the press briefing room in the White House. Williston picked it up. A voice said: "Maccabeus has restored the Temple." The phone went dead. Williston scribbled excitedly on a plain piece of paper, signed and ripped it from his notepad, and called an aide to deliver it immediately to the president. The folded note was carried across the stage in full view of a television audience estimated at over 150 million, and placed in the shaking hands of the chief executive.

In New York, the crowd outside the UN heard the president stop in mid-sentence. Those with acute hearing could make out the muttered exclamation: "This is what I've been waiting for." They could not see, of course, what most of the rest of the nation saw: his face breaking into a grin of ostentatious dimensions. "My fellow citizens," he said, "the charade is over. The siege is at an end."

אOCTOBER 21:א
ONE DAY LATER

CARIBE HILTON HOTEL,
SAN JUAN, PUERTO RICO

Now Khalid Awwam understood. He sipped his piña colada, put the glass back down on the bar of the patio terrace in the Caribe Hilton in San Juan, Puerto Rico. He read the articles under large headlines in the *Daily News* for the fifth time, and looked into space. His eyes focused again outside the terrace, onto the sun-drenched swimming pool. It was filled with bathers. To his left he saw the crowded beach. Not as crowded as at Christmas, when it would be insufferable, but busy enough. For Americans with money, any time was the right time for sun.

Khalid Awwam finally understood the full implications of his assignment. He looked down at the suitcase near his leg. It held no clothing. Inside instead were two Ingram 10s, ammunition, and fifteen hand grenades.

Now that the plagues had become the common property of the newspapers, he comprehended his projected role.

Hashim el-Wasi obviously had meant not only to revisit the plagues upon the world, but to recycle them again if one cycle had not been enough to accomplish his goal. Awwam's team was to inaugurate the second round of plagues. In less than half an hour, if he chose, the waters would be red again. All he had to do was place three calls—one to Room 27 of the Doctor's Cave Beach Hotel in Montego Bay, Jamaica; one to Room 14 of the Meridien in Pointe de Bout, Martinique; and the third to Room 532 of the Frenchman's Reef Hotel in St. Thomas, Virgin Islands. Members of his team were registered in these rooms and armed as he was armed.

This time the red would be blood and the waters would be the pools and beaches of a wide cross-section of Caribbean resorts. "I will smite with the rod that is in mine hand upon the waters which are in the river, and they shall be turned to blood."

If he decided to go through with it. If he called his men at the other hotels and instructed them to turn the waters red, a great many people would die. So would tourism in the Caribbean, and the economy in the Caribbean, and governments there, and the way of life as it is known throughout the Caribbean. And the second round of plagues, broader and wider than the first, as a concentric circle is to the center, would have begun. For if Awwam instructed his group to proceed, the recycled second plague commando team would act upon that signal, and do whatever it was they were to do. It would be a scourge, and the entire series of worldwide scourges would be reactivated until—until what? Awwam did not know. Only el-Wasi had known what would come next.

The thought of further action was glorious. But it lacked a center. The fact was, Awwam did not have a grand plan; only el-Wasi had one, and that had now dissolved. A better scheme might now be devised, with a new center, one that would hold.

And Khalid Awwam could be at that center! And at the center of the Palestine that would follow if the scheme succeeded where el-Wasi's had failed. Patience. Patience and some imagination, a new design.

Awwam turned again to the Caribe Hilton pool. He counted, individually, sixteen people, mainly children, in the water. On the beach twenty yards away, dozens more.

Outside a fenced area, where the sea beat steadily against the same rocks it had been buffeting for thousands of years, fifty yards beyond the pool, a waiting speedboat idled, manned by one of four pilots all idling at this very moment throughout the Caribbean. Before the local police could act, Awwam and his colleagues would have transferred to a seaplane, marked as Prinair, the inter-island line. They would rendezvous in Santo Domingo.

Yet perhaps it would be best to wait until he had designed a new master plan. His own. To stamp himself el-Wasi's successor, the new head of the Palestinian liberation movement. Perhaps he should only act in furtherance of his own design. Surely he was clever enough to construct one. Why waste his efforts on another man's project?

Yet it would be a shame to waste this opportunity, here, now, after all the planning and preparation. Awwam touched the suitcase at his side. He tugged up at the handle and felt the full weight of the weaponry inside. How these people would be surprised! How the world would be surprised, the world that was so smugly congratulating itself on the still-inexplicable disaster in the General Assembly Hall. The taste would be sweet.

He reached inside his trouser pocket, felt the coins he had carried with him for several days. It was time to call his colleagues. They would be expecting his call, soon, either to cancel or confirm the planned event. He must not now seem weak or indecisive.

If he went forward, he would trigger a cataclysmic chain of events—but to what end? And with whom could he bargain? Who would listen to him? But if he took the time to devise a new master plan—a year or two or three?— would the commando teams still be available?

He looked at his watch: 12:38 P.M. Time enough. Give it a little more thought.

Awwam ordered another drink.

More Bestsellers from Berkley
The books you've been hearing about and want to read

___**THE AMERICANS**   04681-8—$2.95
  Alistair Cooke

___**THE THIRD TIME AROUND**   04732-6 —$2.75
  George Burns

___**DUNE**   04687-7—$2.75
  Frank Herbert

___**FAT IS A FEMINIST ISSUE**   04380-0—$2.50
  Susie Orbach

___**THE LAST CONVERTIBLE**   04034-8—$2.50
  Anton Myrer

___**LEAH'S JOURNEY**   04690-7—$2.75
  Gloria Goldreich

___**SHALLOWS OF NIGHT**   04453-X — $2.50
  Eric Van Lustbader

___**MAYDAY**   04729-6 —$2.95
  Thomas H. Block

___**WIZARD**   04828-4 — $2.50
  John Varley

___**THE SECOND DEADLY SIN**   04806-3—$2.95
  Lawrence Sanders

___**THE SUNSET WARRIOR**   04452-1—$2.50
  Eric Van Lustbader

___**WE ARE THE EARTHQUAKE GENERATION**   04991-4—$2.75
  Jeffrey Goodman

Available at your local bookstore or return this form to:

85F

Berkley Book Mailing Service
P.O. Box 690
Rockville Centre, NY 11570

Please send me the above titles. I am enclosing $_____
(Please add 75¢ per copy to cover postage and handling). Send check or money
order—no cash or C.O.D.'s. Allow six weeks for delivery.

NAME_____

ADDRESS_____

CITY_____ STATE/ZIP_____